THE HERMETIC INSCRIPTION

TWO SOULS ENTANGLE IN SHADOWS, UNCOVERING SECRETS THAT DESTROY WORLDS.

STEPHEN SHUBRAI

The Hermetic Inscription
© STEPHEN SHUBRAI, 2025

All rights reserved. No part of this book may be reproduced, distributed, or transmitted in any form or by any means, including photocopying, recording, or other electronic or mechanical methods, without the prior written permission of the publisher, except in the case of brief quotations embodied in critical reviews and certain other noncommercial uses permitted by copyright law.

This is a work of fiction. Names, characters, places, and incidents either are products of the author's imagination or are used fictitiously. Any resemblance to actual persons, living or dead, or actual events is purely coincidental.

Published by Stephen Shubrai

Cover Design by CORNELIA SWART

ISBN:

First Edition: March, 2025

For permissions, inquiries, or media requests, contact:
Instagram: Stxphxn_0901_

CONTENT WARNING

This book contains themes and imagery that may be unsettling or triggering for some readers. While it is a work of fiction, it delves into dark, esoteric, and psychological themes that may not be suitable for all audiences.

Trigger Warnings

Occult Symbolism & Mysticism – Includes references to alchemy, ancient rituals, and forbidden knowledge.
Psychological Horror & Existential Dread – Themes of madness, obsession, and the unknown are explored.
Unreliable Reality & Distorted Perception – Characters may experience hallucinations, cryptic visions, and shifting realities.
Dark Academic & Gothic Elements – Themes of lost knowledge, hidden texts, and secrecy.
Moral Ambiguity & Ethical Dilemmas – Characters may be forced to make difficult choices regarding power and truth.
Mild Violence & Death Themes – References to historical tragedies, forgotten scholars, and the consequences of forbidden wisdom.
This book is intended for mature readers who enjoy mystery, dark fantasy, and philosophical intrigue. Reader discretion is advised.

*To the restless souls who find solace in the unknown,
To the seekers of truth who brave the shadows,
And to the dreamers who see beyond the veil of the ordinary,
This is for you.
May your courage never waver,
Your curiosity never fades,
And your heart remains steadfast in the pursuit of the extraordinary.*

Shadows Beneath the Canvas

The clock on the wall ticked with an unrelenting cadence, its steady rhythm slicing through the muffled hum of the room, marking each fleeting second as the evening sank deeper into the embrace of night. The year was 1947, and New York City, a sprawling monument to ambition and excess, thrummed with a vitality that seemed almost too perfect, too immaculate, as if designed to mask the simmering undercurrents of secrecy and danger that coursed beneath its surface.

From the glittering marquees of Broadway to the smoky, dimly lit corners of Harlem's jazz clubs, the city pulsated with life, an unending symphony of laughter, music, and the click of heels against rain-slicked sidewalks. Opulent galas unfolded behind gilded doors, where the elite sipped champagne and exchanged sly smiles, their conversations laced with veiled intentions. Beneath this dazzling facade, however, was a darker narrative—a shadowy underbelly where every whispered word carried the weight of betrayal and every glance was steeped in unspoken truths.

The city seemed alive, a restless giant whose heart beat to the rhythm of its ceaseless energy, yet its soul was fractured. Down narrow alleyways and in dimly lit speakeasies, deals were struck and lives were bartered away. In the labyrinth of its streets, ambition collided with desperation, creating a fragile dance of survival. It was a place where trust was a rare commodity, and where even the brightest lights could not extinguish the growing darkness that crept, inch by inch, into every corner.

Dea Turner lingered in the softly illuminated corridor of the prestigious Van Buren Art Gallery, her gloved fingers delicately gripping an invitation as fragile as it was opulent. The card was a masterpiece in itself, adorned with intricate filigree and embossed in gold, a subtle proclamation of exclusivity that bespoke privilege and influence. Dea possessed neither, but tonight she was determined to inhabit their world, if only as a shadow among luminaries.

Her auburn curls, usually unruly, had been meticulously tamed and pinned beneath the sophisticated sweep of a wide-brimmed hat. The hat's shadow veiled her amber eyes, adding an enigmatic allure to her appearance. Her dress, a sleek sheath of obsidian silk, skimmed her figure with an elegance she wished matched her wavering composure. Every step she took felt rehearsed, every glance measured, yet her heart beat with the urgency of an interloper hoping her charade would hold under scrutiny.

"Miss Turner," a voice intoned behind her, rich and smooth yet laced with an undercurrent that sent a shiver through the still air. She turned swiftly, her emerald eyes locking with those of a man whose mere presence seemed to drain the light from the corridor, leaving it cloaked in an almost palpable shadow.

Prex Donovan stood before her, a figure carved with precision and intent. His tailored suit, immaculate and impossibly expensive, clung to him as though the fabric itself dared not falter. Yet, it wasn't the craftsmanship of his attire that demanded attention, it was his eyes. Storm-gray and unyielding, they held a depth that whispered of danger, a tempest restrained behind a thin veneer of civility.

He extended a hand, his movements unhurried, deliberate. The faintest smirk played at the corners of his mouth, a subtle curve that was neither warm nor inviting but spoke of control, a man who found amusement not in kindness but in conquest.

"Mr. Donovan," she replied, her voice composed, though the rhythm of her heartbeat betrayed her calm façade. For a brief moment, she hesitated before slipping her hand into his, his touch radiating a disarming warmth that stood in stark contrast to the enigmatic chill surrounding him.

"You're not quite the unassuming gallery clerk I was introduced to last week," he observed, his tone rich with a curiosity that bordered on suspicion.

Dea's lips curved into a poised smile, the kind perfected over years of masking truths. *"And you're hardly the typical art aficionado."*

He laughed softly, the sound resonating with a low, almost predatory undertone. *"Touché,"* he replied, his gaze sharp as if cataloging every nuance of her response.

Before she could utter a reply, the muted murmur of conversation swelled into a chorus of laughter and animated chatter as the doors to the main gallery swung open. The unveiling of the much-anticipated masterpiece, The Veil of Elysium, was imminent, and anticipation charged the air like an unspoken promise. The crowd - a dynamic blend of Manhattan's high society, seasoned art connoisseurs, and critics poised for their moment of judgment - surged forward in a unified tide, sweeping them effortlessly into the grandeur of the hall. Velvet ropes and gilded accents framed the room, where the aura of expectation hung as heavy and vibrant as the glinting chandeliers above.

The room was a symphony of opulence, a canvas painted with wealth and artistry. Gilded ceilings soared above, their intricate patterns shimmering like woven gold under the gentle caress of light spilling from ornate crystal chandeliers. These luminaries, cascading prisms of refracted brilliance, cast an amber glow that bathed the assembled guests in a soft, almost ethereal radiance.

Every corner of the grand hall spoke of meticulous craftsmanship: *the polished marble floors, veined with emerald and onyx, reflected the grandeur above, while tapestries of the finest silk adorned the walls,* their scenes of mythical grandeur whispering tales of distant lands and forgotten legends.

At the heart of this lavish spectacle, beneath a crimson velvet curtain heavy with anticipation, stood the object of the evening's intrigue - a painting that had captivated not only the city's imagination but also its collective heartbeat. Speculation had swirled like an unstoppable tempest: some whispered that the artist had imbued the canvas with forbidden secrets, veiling truths so profound they could reshape destinies. Others murmured of a curse, a shadowy blight waiting to unfurl upon those who dared look too long or too deeply.

The air was electric, charged with curiosity and trepidation, as eyes darted toward the concealed masterpiece. Among the murmuring crowd, voices rose and fell, their cadences weaving a tapestry of awe, skepticism, and barely concealed dread. This was not merely an unveiling; it was a moment on the precipice of revelation, poised to transform the ordinary into legend.

Dea's sharp gaze flitted across the room, meticulously cataloging each face, each gesture, as though assembling a puzzle in her mind. The gallery buzzed with muted conversations, a symphony of murmurs layered over the soft clink of champagne glasses. But Dea wasn't here for the art. She barely spared a glance at the canvases that lined the walls, their vibrant hues and intricate brushstrokes dissolving into the periphery of her focus.

Her purpose was singular: answers. Answers to the cryptic message she had stumbled upon in the gallery's archives, hidden between mundane records, as though it had been waiting for her to uncover it. Answers about the man now standing so close beside her that she could feel the faint warmth radiating from him, a presence as disarming as it was unsettling.

His sharp suit and easy smile might have lulled a less discerning observer, but Dea was no stranger to masks. Every glance he cast her way, every carefully measured word, seemed to carry double meanings she couldn't yet decipher. Comfort and threat. Ally and adversary. He embodied contradictions that set her instincts on edge, her pulse thrumming in a rhythm of caution and curiosity.

She forced herself to breathe evenly, her outward demeanor calm, even as her thoughts spiraled with questions. What did he know about the message? Why was he here now, in this moment? And most importantly, was he the key to unlocking the truth - or the gatekeeper determined to keep it buried?

"Do you believe in fate, Miss Turner?" Prex's voice was barely more than a whisper, delicate and fleeting, yet it carried an undertone of something profound. The rising curtain, heavy with velvet and promise, seemed to echo the tension in the air as the moment drew nearer.

Miss Turner turned her gaze to him, her expression a careful enigma, as if guarding the weight of her thoughts. *"Fate,"* she said after a pause, her tone measured and laced with quiet defiance, *"is just a coincidence draped in the illusion of purpose, an idea adorned to make sense of the chaos."*

His smirk grew sharper, a fleeting shadow of amusement dancing on his lips, but he remained silent. Instead, his eyes, dark and unreadable, shifted with deliberate precision to the painting unveiled before them. As the crimson curtain slid away, pooling at the base of the gilded frame, it revealed the masterpiece—*The Veil of Elysium.*

A collective gasp rippled through the gathered crowd, a wave of astonishment that seemed to resonate in the stillness of the gallery. The painting was a symphony of light and shadow, its ethereal hues and intricate details capturing a world that teetered between the tangible and the divine. Soft whispers of wonder and disbelief flickered across the room like fragile flames, yet no voice rose above the reverent hush.

For a moment, even Dea found herself caught in its spell, her breath stilled as though the canvas had stolen it away. The depiction was otherworldly - a shrouded figure stood at the edge of an endless meadow, veiled in a diaphanous mist that shimmered with iridescent hues. The interplay of colors, neither fully of dawn nor dusk, seemed to hold secrets of a realm just beyond mortal comprehension.

The silence pressed on her ears, almost deafening, as her

thoughts wrestled with the image. It was not just a painting; it was an invocation, a challenge to perceive something more profound, something intangible. She felt her pulse quicken, and yet, the room seemed to slow, as if time itself bent in reverence to the vision before them.

The painting was hauntingly beautiful, almost unsettling in its depth and emotion. A solitary woman stood at the edge of a shadowy, dense forest, her silhouette a delicate contrast to the inky blackness that enveloped her. The trees behind her loomed like silent sentinels, their twisted forms casting long, distorted shadows. Her face was obscured by a veil, not of cloth, but of something far more ethereal, as though the fabric of the veil itself were a living thing. It seemed to undulate with a faint, otherworldly light, as though it were breathing, shifting in a rhythm that was both mesmerizing and unnerving. The light, pale and ghostly, flickered across the veil, hinting at the shape of her features beneath it - an ethereal, half-formed face, as if the woman was neither fully present nor entirely absent, existing somewhere between the realm of the living and the unseen.

But it wasn't the woman herself or the forest that held Dea's gaze. It was the hidden script, the faint trace of something written into the shadows of the painting. At first, it was barely perceptible - just a whisper of ink, a shadow within the shadow. But Dea knew what to look for, had always known. It was a secret, a message for those with eyes sharp enough to find it. The letters were delicate, barely visible against the dark backdrop, as though the ink had been applied with an artist's careful, deliberate hand, its presence meant only for those who sought it out. The script seemed to pulse with a quiet urgency, as if the words carried a weight beyond their physical form, their meaning something elusive yet pressing, waiting to be uncovered.

There was a sense of profound mystery in the hidden writing, as though it belonged to another world, a message from a time long past - or perhaps one that had yet to come. Dea's heart quickened as she deciphered the letters, the ancient, fragile symbols evoking a sense of lost knowledge, like a forgotten language that spoke directly to her soul. Each word she uncovered seemed to shift, to change, as if the meaning of the message was alive, transforming with every glance. It was a puzzle, a riddle suspended in time, one that demanded more than mere attention; it required understanding, a communion of mind and spirit to unlock the secrets that lay beneath the surface of the painting's haunting beauty.

"What do you see?" Prex's voice was a low murmur, a sound that seemed to vibrate in the air between them. His eyes, dark and intent, were fixed on her, searching, probing for something only he seemed to understand.

Dea swallowed, her heart rate quickening, as if the words themselves could unlock some hidden door inside her. Her gaze flicked over the abstract painting before her, the splashes of color and shadow forming a chaotic dance that stirred something deep within her - a sense of intrigue, perhaps even trepidation. She felt his eyes still on her, waiting for an answer, the weight of his unspoken expectations pressing down on her.

She took a steadying breath, trying to keep her voice from betraying the rapid thumping of her pulse. *"I see a mystery,"* she said, her words measured, deliberate. *"An enigma, woven into every stroke of the brush, each layer of color hiding a deeper truth, a secret yet to be uncovered."*

The room around them seemed to quiet, the applause of the opening art show fading into the background as Dea's words lingered in the air. Prex's expression shifted slightly, a subtle, knowing smile tugging at the corner of his lips. It was a smile that didn't quite reach his eyes, those dark depths that seemed to hold far more than any casual observer could ever comprehend. He leaned in just slightly, lowering his voice so that it only reached her ears. *"Then let's solve it,"* he murmured, the promise in his tone carrying a hint of something dangerous, something thrilling.

For a moment, Dea was paralyzed. The challenge in his voice was undeniable, and she could almost hear the unspoken invitation to dive into a world she wasn't sure she was ready for.

She had known Prex Donovan for years, but this was different. There was an intensity in him now, something sharp, something that made her question whether she truly understood the man standing beside her.

The applause around them swelled, as if the world had resumed its pace, but Dea's mind raced. She had just crossed a threshold. The mystery of the painting was no longer a simple question of art - it was a puzzle, a labyrinth of secrets that only someone with Prex's cold, calculating mind could hope to unravel. But what if the game he was inviting her to play was one where the stakes were far higher than she was willing to risk?

And Prex Donovan? He wasn't just a companion in this, he was either the key to unlocking everything or the architect of her undoing. A man of secrets, hidden motives, and a mind as sharp as a blade, he could be both her greatest ally and her most formidable adversary.

As the noise of the gallery filled her ears once more, Dea realized that she had just stepped into something far deeper than she had ever anticipated. A game, a riddle, a danger that could either bind her to Prex in ways she could neither anticipate nor escape - or tear her apart entirely.

The question now was simple: Could she solve it, or was she already a pawn in a game that had been set in motion long before she had even known the rules?

Echoes of the Abyss

The city streets lay slick with the remnants of a recent downpour, their surfaces glistening in the dim, wavering glow of scattered streetlamps. The wet cobblestones reflected the fleeting flashes of passing headlights, like mirrors to the chaos that had once filled these roads but was now swept away by the storm. Prex Donovan's footsteps echoed in the otherwise quiet night, the rhythmic beat of his boots a solitary soundtrack to the silence that stretched between him and Dea.

They walked side by side, a muted harmony born from years of unspoken understanding. The air smelled of fresh rain and lingering diesel, a familiar, urban perfume that clung to everything it touched. A soft mist still clung to the edges of their coats, the dampness seeping into the fabric, unnoticed by both of them. The world around them seemed to have paused, holding its breath, as if waiting for something neither of them were ready to face.

In the distance, the sound of a saxophone floated on the breeze, its melancholy notes drifting from a nearby jazz club, where the evening crowd had thinned out in the wake of the storm. The music's slow, mournful cadence cut through the stillness, underscoring the strange intimacy of the moment. It was as though the city itself was exhaling, its pulse slowed by the rain, offering these two figures the space to carry the weight of their shared secrets.

The streets had emptied, leaving the pair in the rare quiet of a city that had briefly surrendered to the weather's will. No chatter, no hurried footsteps, no laughter or cries. Just the rhythm of rain-soaked soles against stone, the subtle hum of a saxophone weaving through the night, and the distance between Prex and Dea that, though unbroken, seemed impossible to bridge. It was a space filled with everything unsaid, everything that neither of them dared to reveal, each one lost in the thoughts they could never share.

Dea wrapped her coat tighter around her slender frame, the fabric pulling against the wind that whipped through the narrow alleyway. Her thoughts were a tumult of confusion, twisting and writhing like the wild raindrops that clung to her lashes, each drop as fleeting and fragile as the answers she sought. The cryptic message hidden within the layers of The Veil of Elysium replayed in her mind, each word a fragment of something she couldn't quite grasp. The sentences tangled in her consciousness, their meaning elusive, slipping away like smoke with every attempt to hold on. She could feel the weight of the words pressing down on her chest, tightening with the knowledge that the puzzle was far from solved.

She stole a glance at Prex, who walked a few paces ahead of her. His silhouette was almost indistinguishable in the dim light, his face concealed beneath the shadow of his fedora, his features unreadable. He was a man of infinite enigmas, an observer of the world who moved through it like a ghost. It was impossible to tell whether he was an ally or a lurking adversary. Dea had learned not to trust appearances, and yet, something about him felt undeniably familiar, as if their paths were meant to cross.

The silence between them thickened, pressing in on her. The rhythm of their footsteps echoed in the alley, punctuated only by the occasional gust of wind that carried the scent of wet pavement and distant fires. Her mind buzzed, but it was the heaviness in the air that made her pause, as though the city itself held its breath in anticipation.

"*You're quiet,*" Prex's voice sliced through the silence, low and almost swallowed by the night. It was a sound both distant and immediate, as though it came from a faraway place yet was directed solely at her.

Dea didn't look at him at first, her focus still lost in the labyrinth of her thoughts. "*Thinking,*" she replied curtly, her words edged with a slight tension she couldn't suppress. She didn't have the luxury of time, nor did she have the inclination to indulge in small talk. Not when the answers she needed hung just beyond her reach.

"*About the painting?*" Prex's question came with a hint of curiosity, but there was something else beneath it.

Something almost too knowing.

Dea hesitated, her eyes flickering toward the shadows around them before she gave a brief, reluctant nod. The memory of the painting was still fresh, its colors seeping into her mind like a stain that couldn't be washed away. "*The words...*" she trailed off, her voice catching slightly as the weight of the puzzle pressed against her chest. "*They felt deliberate, like a warning, or a threat. I can't tell which.*"

Prex stopped abruptly, his pace slowing to a near halt. Dea was just a step behind when he turned, his dark eyes locking onto hers with a sudden, unsettling intensity. The sharpness of his gaze sent a tremor down her spine, and for a moment, she felt as though she were standing in front of an abyss—*one that had the power to consume her whole.*

"*Warnings are only useful if you know what they're about,*" he said, his voice dropping lower, like the whisper of a secret only meant for her ears. His words were precise, calculated, each syllable a thread woven into the air between them. "*Do you?*"

Dea felt the weight of his question settle over her, heavy and foreboding. She met his eyes, searching for any hint of his true intentions, but his face remained an unreadable mask. She couldn't let herself falter, not now. "*Not yet,*" she admitted, her voice steady, though it was laced with the undercurrent of frustration. *"But I intend to find out. No matter the cost."*

A ghost of a smile, fleeting and almost imperceptible, tugged at the corners of Prex's lips. It was a smile that didn't reach his eyes, one that seemed more like a cryptic gesture than anything resembling warmth. *"Good,"* he murmured, his tone laced with something she couldn't quite place. *"Because you're not the only one looking for answers."*

Dea held his gaze for a beat longer, trying to decipher the meaning behind his words. Was he telling her that they were on the same side, or was this just another game he was playing? She couldn't tell, but she knew one thing for certain: the road ahead was darker than she had imagined, and she wasn't walking it alone.

With a deliberate turn, Prex started walking again, his pace steady and unwavering. Dea followed, her thoughts still a swirl of uncertainty, but her resolve firm. Whatever dangers lay ahead, she would face them head-on, for there was nothing more dangerous than the unknown - especially when it held the power to unravel everything she had ever believed.

Before Dea could even process the words forming on her tongue, a shift of movement caught her attention, casting a flicker of uncertainty through the night. Her gaze sharpened instinctively, the darkness around them thickening as a shadow materialized from the depths of the alley ahead.

Prex's reaction was almost imperceptible, a smooth, calculated motion that belied his years of experience. His fingers twitched, gliding subtly toward the pocket of his jacket, where she knew all too well he kept a concealed weapon - a habit born of necessity in their world. Dea's heartbeat quickened, a pulse of adrenaline surging through her veins as she stood close enough to sense the tension in his every fiber. The streetlights above flickered briefly, casting jagged rays of light that made the figure in the alley seem almost otherworldly.

From the darkness, a man stepped forward, his figure draped in the heavy folds of a trench coat, its fabric rustling faintly as he moved. The brim of his hat hung low, shadowing his face and obscuring his features, save for the faint glint of something dangerous that seemed to linger around him.

"Donovan," the man's voice rasped, each word carrying the weight of years spent in shadows. It was gravelly, roughened by time and whatever life he had lived in the dark corners of the world. *"You're late."*

Prex's lip curled slightly, a dry and almost amused quirk that barely touched his steely composure. His posture remained deceptively casual, but Dea knew better than to think him unprepared. There was a sharpness in the way he held himself, the subtle tension coiled in his frame. His hand, though relaxed in position, never fully relinquished its place near his concealed weapon.

"Traffic," Prex replied, his voice steady, devoid of any emotion beyond the barest trace of irritation. It was a simple word, yet it carried a thousand unsaid things - things Dea was sure only he could understand.

She watched as the man in the trench coat's hand shifted, reaching inside his coat with the deliberate precision of one accustomed to secrecy. In the next instant, he produced a small, weathered envelope - its edges worn, its surface faded by time, a testament to the delicate nature of the contents within. The man passed it over without a second thought, his gaze flickering only momentarily to Dea. The brief exchange of eyes was enough for her to feel the weight of his silent judgment. His eyes, dark and unyielding, lingered on her as if considering whether her presence was an affront to the fragile balance of this exchange.

"She shouldn't be here," he said, the words coming out like an old curse, the warning lingering between them like smoke.

Prex's gaze didn't shift from the envelope, but his voice- low and certain-cut through the tension without hesitation. *"She's with me,"* he said, his tone final, a quiet declaration of ownership over the situation. There was no room for negotiation in his words, no space for anyone to challenge what he'd said. Not now, not here.

The man's eyes narrowed, but he offered no further protest, his reluctance swallowed by the undeniable certainty that hung in the air like a stillborn storm. Prex's hand finally withdrew from his pocket, the envelope now securely in his grasp as he turned slightly, a silent invitation for Dea to follow him.

For a moment, there was nothing but the distant hum of the city's undercurrent, the quiet sound of Dea's own breath as it steadied. She felt the sharp weight of the moment, the delicate balance of trust and danger that hummed between them like a wire ready to snap.

The man, cloaked in shadows, offered no word of warning before he disappeared, his figure melting into the darkness with an eerie swiftness that seemed almost unnatural. Dea's heart pounded as she turned back to Prex, who remained silent, his posture tense, eyes distant as if already processing the storm of thoughts racing through his mind.

He handed her the envelope without a word, his hand brushing hers for the briefest moment-an almost imperceptible gesture, but one that sent a ripple of unease through her. Dea's fingers trembled slightly as she took the envelope, the edges slick from the dampness in the air. She could almost feel the weight of the message inside pressing against her palm, a tangible manifestation of the uncertainty that hung in the air.

Her pulse quickened as she pulled the photograph from the envelope. It was a strange image, one that seemed to shimmer beneath the dim glow of the streetlamp overhead. The photograph itself was worn, the edges curling ever so slightly, as though it had been handled many times before. The image depicted The Veil of Elysium- that haunting masterpiece, the one that had captivated her since childhood. Yet, there was something disturbingly off about it now.

The woman who had once been a mere blur of mystery, her face obscured beneath an intricately woven veil, was no longer hidden. Her veil had been lifted, revealing a face that was both foreign and achingly familiar. Dea's breath caught in her throat as her gaze fixed upon the face- her own.

It was her. But not her. It was the mirror image of her, yet distorted in a way that made her question her own existence. The eyes in the photograph were hers- those same stormy, storm-tossed eyes- but they gleamed with a certain knowingness, a sense of sorrow that she hadn't seen in her own reflection. A life lived through a different lens, perhaps. Or was it? Dea's stomach churned, her mind struggling to grasp the reality of what she was seeing.

The photograph felt like a trap, a snare tightening around her chest. The image before her was a riddle wrapped in an enigma, an echo of something she could not yet comprehend. A cold shiver ran down her spine as she whispered, barely more than a breath, *"What does this mean?"*

Prex didn't answer immediately. He didn't need to. The hardness in his expression, the grim set of his jaw, said it all. He took the photograph from her hands with a gentleness that belied the tension in his movements. His eyes flickered over the image once more, his brows furrowing. A fleeting moment of vulnerability crossed his face- one that Dea hadn't seen before. Then, with a practiced motion, he slipped the photograph back into the envelope and sealed it.

"It means we're running out of time," he said finally, his voice low and filled with a quiet urgency that resonated deep within Dea's bones. The words hung in the air like a curse, a prophecy whose full meaning they had yet to uncover.

She could feel the weight of his words like an anchor, pulling her under, dragging her deeper into the tide of mystery that had begun to overtake them both. Her thoughts raced as the rain began to fall again, a soft but steady rhythm that beat against the cobblestone streets. It was as though the rain itself mourned the secrets they were no longer able to keep at bay.

The world around them seemed to close in, the city streets blurring into a hazy mist as Dea's gaze drifted to the shadows where the man had vanished. They had no answers. No way of knowing where to go from here. The questions piled upon her, each one heavier than the last, but the answer remained elusive, slipping through her fingers like the rainwater that pooled at her feet.

Prex's eyes met hers once more, the unspoken burden between them growing thicker with every passing moment. The photograph had opened a door that neither of them could close. The storm was coming, and they were both caught in its eye, trapped in a puzzle that was far more intricate- and far more dangerous- than they could have ever imagined.

Whispers in the Fog

The Hudson River unfurled before them, a dark, liquid ribbon shimmering faintly under the ethereal glow of the moon. Its surface mirrored the fractured light in uneven ripples, broken intermittently by the gentle swell of the current. The faint, rhythmic lapping of the waves against the wooden pylons of Pier 17 was the only audible sound, a soft undercurrent to the oppressive quiet that hung between Prex and Dea.

They stood side by side, yet the chasm of unspoken words and unresolved emotions widened between them with each passing moment. The icy tendrils of the night crept through their heavy coats, a bitter reminder of winter's encroaching grip. Dea pulled her scarf tighter around her neck, her breath escaping in fragile wisps that disappeared into the night. Prex remained still, his hands buried deep in his pockets, his gaze fixed somewhere beyond the horizon, as though searching for answers in the darkness.

A dense fog rolled in from the water, swallowing the distant skyline and cloaking the docks in a ghostly pallor. Its embrace was both suffocating and intimate, muffling the world around them until it felt as though they were the only two souls left in existence. The sharp tang of brine mingled with the faint metallic scent of the river, a scent both familiar and strangely foreign in the heavy air.

Prex finally broke the stillness, shifting his weight as if to speak, but the words faltered on his tongue. Dea turned her face slightly, her profile outlined by the dim, silvery light. Her expression was unreadable, her eyes shadowed yet shimmering with something he couldn't quite decipher- resolve, perhaps, or a fragile hope she dared not voice.

Between them, the silence grew louder, weighted with everything they hadn't said. The river seemed to carry their unspoken thoughts away, dispersing them into its depths, leaving only the fragile remnants of what once was- or what might still be.

Dea's fingers quivered as they traced the edges of the photograph, her breath hitching as if the air itself had grown too heavy to draw. Her eyes were riveted to the image, unable to tear themselves away, her mind a whirlpool of thoughts that refused to settle. The woman in the painting stared back at her with an almost eerie familiarity- every curve of her face, the tilt of her head, the depth in her gaze- a mirror crafted with unnerving precision. It wasn't just a resemblance; it was her.

"This... this can't be real," she whispered, her voice thin and uncertain, as though even saying it aloud might unravel the fragile fabric of reality. She spoke more to the phantom of her disbelief than to Prex, who loomed nearby, his presence both grounding and unsettling.

Prex leaned against the doorframe, his arms crossed, the soft leather of his jacket creaking with the movement. His usual detached calm had been replaced by a subtle tension that rippled beneath his stoic exterior. He'd been watching her intently ever since they'd left the gallery, his dark eyes scanning her every reaction like a predator measuring the distance to its prey. Now, his voice, deep and deliberate, broke the silence like a fissure in stone.

"It's real enough," he said, each word heavy with meaning, his tone betraying the unease he rarely allowed to surface. *"The real question is, why?"*

Dea's grip on the photograph tightened, the edges digging into her palms as if the sharpness of the paper could anchor her to something tangible. Her mind raced through the possibilities, each more implausible than the last. Was it a trick, some cruel illusion designed to unearth her deepest vulnerabilities? Or was it something more- something tethered to the strange, unspoken truths she had spent her life avoiding?

"How could someone... paint me? And not just me, but... but this me," she said, her voice cracking under the weight of her confusion. *"The details are too exact. The scar above my eyebrow, the way my hair falls when I don't pin it back- it's impossible."*

Prex pushed himself off the doorframe and took a step closer, his boots heavy against the wooden floor. He regarded her with an intensity that seemed to bore straight through her, his expression a mixture of curiosity and something far darker.

"Impossible doesn't mean what you think it does," he replied, his voice low, almost conspiratorial. *"Not in the world we're dealing with. You need to think bigger, Dea. Who painted it? How did they know? And most importantly..."*

He paused, his gaze locking onto hers with a gravity that made her stomach churn.

"What are they trying to tell you?"

Dea turned toward him, her emerald eyes piercing despite the dull haze that clung to her like an unwelcome fog. There was no mistaking the sharpness in her gaze, a blade honed by anger and desperation. *"You dragged me into this,"* she said, her voice taut with controlled fury. *"Don't act like you don't have answers."*

Prex's jaw tightened, his lips thinning into a resolute line. He held her gaze for a moment too long, as if weighing the cost of truth against the solace of ignorance. *"Answers?"* he murmured, his voice low and measured. *"Perhaps. But not the ones you're hoping to find."*

Her expression faltered for the briefest of moments, a flicker of uncertainty breaking through her mask of defiance. Before she could muster a retort, the silence around them fractured- a faint rustling, like the whisper of dry leaves carried on an unseen wind, emerged from the shadows.

Prex moved instinctively, his hand ghosting toward the worn leather holster strapped to his side. The revolver within seemed to hum with latent promise, its weight a familiar reassurance against his palm. His posture stiffened, muscles coiling as his gaze swept the darkness with the precision of a predator.

Dea froze, her breath catching audibly in her throat. The sound was subtle at first, almost imperceptible, but it grew louder with each passing second, a crescendo of unease that seemed to thrum in the very air around them.

"What is it?" she whispered, her voice barely audible, as though speaking any louder might summon whatever lurked beyond the veil of shadows.

Prex didn't answer immediately. His eyes remained fixed on the obscured edges of their surroundings, scanning for movement, for any hint of what lay hidden. The rustling intensified, carrying with it an uncanny cadence that set her nerves on edge.

"Stay close," he muttered finally, the words clipped and brimming with unspoken urgency.

Dea obeyed, though the space between them felt as fragile as a thread stretched taut. The atmosphere thickened, heavy with the weight of anticipation, as they stood together on the precipice of the unknown.

"Stay behind me," Prex commanded, his voice low but unyielding, a quiet authority that brooked no argument. The air around them was thick with tension, every sound muffled by the oppressive weight of the encroaching fog. It clung to the earth like a living thing, swirling in restless eddies that whispered secrets only the brave or foolish would dare to hear.

As if in response to his words, the mist began to part, unraveling like a curtain drawn back by unseen hands. From its shrouded depths emerged a lone figure, cloaked in black from head to toe. The man's silhouette was sharp against the ghostly haze, his every movement precise, calculated, and exuding an aura of quiet menace. A scarf obscured the lower half of his face, leaving only his eyes visible- cold, piercing, and unyielding like tempered steel.

Each step he took was measured, the sound of his boots faint but deliberate, as though he had all the time in the world to close the distance. The air seemed to grow colder with his approach, and though he carried no visible weapon, an undeniable weight of danger clung to him like a second skin.

Prex shifted his stance subtly, positioning himself as a shield between the stranger and those he sought to protect. His hand hovered near his side, fingers flexing instinctively as though preparing to draw a blade- or perhaps simply to act with the swiftness born of necessity.

"Who are you?" he called, his tone steady despite the sharp edge of vigilance. The fog seemed to hold its breath, waiting, as the stranger halted just a few paces away.

For a long moment, silence reigned, broken only by the faint rustle of the fog creeping around their feet. Then, the man in black tilted his head ever so slightly, his steel-gray eyes narrowing as if weighing Prex's worth- or his resolve.

"Donovan," the man sneered, his voice dripping with disdain, each syllable a deliberate challenge. *"Still chasing phantoms, I see."*

Prex didn't so much as blink. His gaze remained steady, unwavering. *"And you're still skulking in the shadows, Mercer. Some things truly are immutable."*

The man- Mercer- allowed a wry chuckle to escape his lips, the sound brittle as dried leaves crushed underfoot. *"Ah, but this time, you've stumbled onto something far beyond your depth. That painting you've so foolishly unearthed... it's not mere decoration. It's a map."*

Dea's breath caught audibly, her wide eyes betraying both curiosity and trepidation. *"A map? A map to what?"* she asked, her voice edged with a fragile hope for an innocuous answer.

Mercer's cold gaze shifted to her, his expression a labyrinth of emotions she couldn't decipher. When he finally spoke, his words carried the weight of foreboding. *"To something people would spill oceans of blood for. Something they already have."*

Prex moved instinctively, stepping in front of Dea as if his very presence could shield her from the implications of Mercer's words. His stance was resolute, his tone unyielding. *"If you've come to threaten us, you're wasting your breath."*

Mercer's head tilted ever so slightly, a predator appraising his prey. Then, slowly, he shook his head. *"No threat, Donovan. A warning. Turn back. Take the girl and vanish before it's too late."*

Prex's jaw clenched, his eyes narrowing into icy slits. *"That's not going to happen."*

The tension between them became a tangible force, crackling like the air before a thunderstorm. The fog seemed almost alive, swirling and coiling around them as if it too felt the weight of their standoff. Finally, Mercer exhaled, a long, resigned breath, and the sharp lines of his face softened just enough to betray a sliver of disappointment.

"Very well," he said, his voice quieter now, tinged with an ominous finality. *"Have it your way. But remember this moment when you find yourselves drowning in regret."*

Without another word, Mercer stepped back into the mist, his form dissolving into the shadows as though the fog had claimed him. In mere heartbeats, he was gone, leaving only an uneasy stillness in his wake.

Dea's voice quivered as she broke the silence, her words barely more than a whisper. *"A map? What does he mean?"*

Prex's expression hardened further, his gaze fixed on the swirling haze where Mercer had disappeared. *"It means,"* he said, each word deliberate and heavy, *"that we've stumbled into something far more dangerous than we thought."*

Dea's hands trembled as she clutched the photograph closer, her knuckles pale against the worn edges of the image. The Veil of Elysium, once an enigma that beckoned with the allure of curiosity, had transformed into something far more sinister. Its secrets were no longer a tantalizing puzzle- they were a threat. And that threat was closing in, fast and merciless.

The Cipher of Shadows

The train hurtled through the inky night, its iron wheels forging a relentless rhythm that reverberated like a heartbeat through the confined space. Outside the frost-clouded window, the landscape dissolved into an endless blur of shadow and light, as if the world itself were fleeing alongside the locomotive. Inside their private compartment, Prex and Dea sat in silence, an invisible yet palpable tension coiling between them.
The dim overhead lamp emitted a faint amber glow, soft yet insufficient to fully banish the encroaching darkness that pooled in the corners of the room. Long shadows sprawled across the wooden panels, their shapes shifting subtly with the train's undulating motion. Between them, on the narrow, timeworn table, lay the photograph.
Its edges were frayed, the corners softened by time and handling. Yet the image itself was arrestingly vivid, its details etched with a clarity that defied its age. The photograph seemed to hum with an energy of its own, commanding attention as though it harbored truths waiting to be unearthed.
Prex leaned back, his posture deceptively relaxed, though his fingers tapped a faint, erratic rhythm against the armrest. His eyes, dark and brooding, were locked on the photograph, as if he

were willing it to surrender its secrets. Dea, seated across from him, sat motionless, her hands folded tightly in her lap. The light caught the delicate curve of her profile, highlighting the subtle tension in her jaw and the faint furrow in her brow.

Dea's fingers brushed over the brittle edge of the photograph, her touch lingering as if it might yield answers. Her eyes traced the faded ink scrawled across the back, the letters uneven and jagged, as though written in haste or desperation. Her mind churned with possibilities, each one more unsettling than the last. *"A map to what, though?"* she murmured, her voice barely more than a breath. *"Treasure? Secrets? Or something far worse?"*

Across the dimly lit room, Prex leaned back in his chair with a deliberate nonchalance that didn't quite mask his unease. The wide brim of his weathered hat dipped forward, casting shadows over his sharp features. Only the faint gleam of his eyes betrayed his vigilance. *"If Mercer's got his claws in this,"* he said at last, his voice low and rough,

"it's not gold we're talking about. The bastard doesn't stick his neck out for shiny trinkets. No, this is bigger- his kind of big. Power. The kind that makes men like him forget how fragile they really are."

"Power?" Dea echoed, her voice laced with skepticism, though her pulse quickened. She turned the photograph over again, as if it might reveal some hidden truth under her scrutiny. *"What kind of power could a painting hold? It's just pigment on canvas, isn't it?"*

Prex didn't answer right away. Instead, he reached into the pocket of his weather-beaten jacket, drawing out a crumpled cigarette. His movements were slow, deliberate, as if buying time. With a practiced flick of his tarnished lighter, a flame flared to life, casting fleeting light across his face. For a moment, the tension etched into his features was stark- creases born of years of tangled schemes and dangerous gambits. He took a drag, the ember glowing bright, before exhaling a curl of smoke that spiraled lazily toward the ceiling.

"Some paintings tell stories," he said finally, his tone heavy

with something close to reverence. *"Others? They keep secrets. And if Mercer's chasing this one, you can bet your life it's not just a pretty picture. Whatever it's hiding, it's the kind of thing that could tilt the scales, of power, of fate, maybe even of reality itself."*
The silence that followed felt thick and oppressive, broken only by the distant hum of the city outside. Dea's grip on the photograph tightened, her mind racing through the implications of Prex's words. If Mercer's pursuit of the painting was truly about power, then the stakes were higher than she could have imagined. But what kind of power could lie within the worn edges of a forgotten piece of art?
And more importantly, what price would they pay to uncover it?
"The kind that makes people disappear," Prex said at last, his voice low and even, punctuated by the slow exhalation of a thin, pale stream of smoke that coiled upward like a phantom escaping into the dim light.
Dea's stomach clenched with an almost audible twist, her thoughts immediately snapping to Mercer's warning. His words, sharp and deliberate, echoed in her memory, carrying a gravity that had been impossible to dismiss. It wasn't just what he'd said but how he'd said it- as if he'd already seen what she was now only beginning to comprehend.
"You've dealt with him before," she said, her voice steady, though she felt the weight of the question pressing against her chest. It wasn't really a question. It was a conclusion she wished wasn't true.
Prex nodded, the motion slow, deliberate, as if each fraction of movement was heavy with recollection. His gaze was distant, fixed not on her but somewhere behind her, or perhaps beyond, in the recesses of a memory he clearly did not want to revisit.
"Once," he admitted, the word hanging in the air like the smoke still dissipating around them.
"It didn't end well. For anyone."
He paused, his jaw tightening as his eyes flickered with something unspoken- regret? Fear? Or perhaps both, tangled together

in a way he could no longer distinguish.

Dea didn't press him further, though her mind raced with questions she wasn't sure she wanted answers to. The weight of his words was enough. This wasn't the kind of man you crossed and walked away unchanged- or at all.

The train jolted with a subtle but deliberate force, the vibration traveling through the floor and up into Dea's core. Her fingers reflexively clutched the edge of the small wooden table, the varnished surface cool beneath her palm. The cabin swayed rhythmically, the steady clatter of wheels against tracks punctuating the silence between them. Beyond the fogged window, the outside world was smothered in darkness, a void where shapes blurred into fleeting silhouettes. It was as though the train was tunneling not just through space but through inevitability, speeding toward a future neither could predict nor avoid.

"Do you think he's right?" Dea's voice broke the stillness, barely louder than the whisper of the wind that ghosted through the thin seals of the train. There was an edge to her tone, fragile but laced with determination. *"That we should just... walk away?"*

Prex shifted slightly in his seat, his shoulders squaring as he leaned forward. The overhead light cast shadows along the sharp planes of his face, softening only around his eyes- intense pools of emotion that pinned her in place. He studied her for a moment, the silence stretching until it felt as if the train itself held its breath.

"Do you?" he asked finally, his voice low but steady, like the undercurrent of a river before it meets the falls.

Dea opened her mouth, then hesitated. The words lodged in her throat as she turned her gaze to the swirling void beyond the window. How could she put into words the pull she felt, the magnetic need to see it through, even as dread coiled tightly in her chest? Finally, she drew a deep breath and shook her head, the movement small but resolute.

"No," she said, her voice firmer this time. *"I need to know. Even if it's dangerous. Even if it changes everything."*

A shadow of a smile flickered across Prex's lips, fleeting and subtle, yet enough to send a ripple of heat through her. He leaned back, his posture loosening but his gaze remaining as sharp as ever.

"Good," he said, his tone carrying a weight of finality. *"Because walking away was never really an option. Not for us."*

The train plunged deeper into the night, the world outside receding further into obscurity. Yet, within the dim confines of the cabin, something unspoken solidified between them- a fragile but unbreakable pact, forged in the heart of uncertainty.

Before she could respond, a sharp knock resonated through the compartment door, shattering the fragile silence that had enveloped them. Both froze, their breaths suspended as if the air itself had been drained from the room. Time seemed to elongate, each second stretching into an eternity fraught with unspoken tension.

Prex was the first to move. His hand, calloused and steady, slipped beneath the worn fabric of his coat to grip the cold steel of his revolver. The weapon, a reassuring weight against his palm, seemed to ground him as he rose from his seat. His movements were deliberate, a predator in his element, each step carefully measured to avoid the creak of the aged floorboards.

"Who's there?" he called out, his voice carrying an edge of authority, unwavering despite the tension crackling in the air.

"Conductor," came the reply, muffled by the door but discernible. The tone was clipped, urgent, yet tinged with an undercurrent of unease.

Prex's eyes flicked toward Dea, her figure still as stone. She met his gaze and gave a single, resolute nod, her expression unreadable but her intent clear. Reassured, he turned back to the door and eased it open, the hinges protesting faintly in the hushed corridor.

Through the narrow gap, the dim light of the hallway revealed a man clad in the familiar uniform of a conductor. His face, illuminated by the flickering glow of the gas lamps, was pale and taut, a mask of tension poorly concealing whatever storm brewed behind his eyes. Beads of sweat glistened on his brow, and his hands, though clasped tightly around his clipboard, trembled ever so slightly.

"Forgive me for disturbing you, sir," the conductor's voice was barely above a whisper, his tone tinged with a nervous urgency. *"There's been an incident in the dining car."*

Prex's expression hardened, his calm demeanor faltering for only a moment. His fingers tightened around the edge of the door, the subtle creak of the wood echoing in the tense silence. *"What kind of incident?"* he asked, his voice steady but carrying an undercurrent of suspicion.

The conductor shifted uneasily on his feet, glancing over his shoulder as if expecting something- or someone- to appear. He lowered his voice even further, as if the words themselves might be dangerous. *"A man was found unconscious. No one knows how he got there. But..."* He paused, casting a furtive glance in both directions. *"There's a symbol. It's been carved into his arm."*

Prex's brow furrowed, his pulse quickening at the mention of the symbol. His mind immediately began to race, considering the possibilities. *"A symbol,"* he repeated, more to himself than to the conductor. *"What kind of symbol?"*

The conductor hesitated, clearly reluctant to describe it, but his obligation to the task was stronger than his fear. *"It's... unusual. We've never seen anything like it. The kind of thing that looks deliberate, like a warning."*

Prex's gaze narrowed, his curiosity now sharp as a blade. *"You thought I might want to see it."*

The conductor nodded, the tension in his shoulders evident. *"Yes, sir. We thought it best to involve you. After all, you're the one who... has experience with such matters."*

Prex didn't respond immediately. The mention of his *"experience"* was enough to remind him of the darker aspects of his past. But that was a story for another time. His focus remained on the task at hand. Someone had gone to great lengths to make sure he was brought into this. The question was why.

"We'll be right there," Prex muttered, his voice low and edged with urgency, as he swiftly shut the door behind him, cutting off

the conductor's protests before they could even fully form.

Dea was already on her feet, her movements sharp with a mix of instinct and fear. Her wide eyes flicked toward him, brimming with a nervous energy that she couldn't quite suppress. *"A symbol?"* she repeated, her voice a breathless whisper as though speaking the word aloud might bring the weight of it crashing down on them both. *"Do you think it's connected?"*

Prex gave a grim, almost imperceptible nod. His hand, steady despite the tension in the air, slid the revolver smoothly into its holster. The metallic click echoed in the silence between them, a sound that felt too loud for the quiet, haunted stillness of the train. *"If it's not,"* he said, his voice tight, *"we've got bigger problems than we thought."*

Without waiting for her response, he moved, his pace measured but swift, his body coiled with purpose. Dea followed close behind, her footsteps hesitant but driven by the same sense of impending danger. The corridor ahead seemed to stretch on forever, its narrow walls humming with the low, constant thrum of the train's engine, a mechanical heartbeat that only served to amplify the growing unease between them. The sound felt like it was vibrating through her bones, making every second feel longer, more drawn out.

The dining car lay just ahead, its entrance slightly ajar, the faint flicker of dim, yellowed light spilling into the hallway like a half-forgotten memory. The door swung open with a soft groan as Prex nudged it with his shoulder, stepping inside with caution that belied the speed at which his senses were already on alert.

The scene that greeted them made Dea's breath catch in her throat, a sharp, involuntary gasp that she quickly stifled. The dining car, usually a place of calm, was anything but. Tables were overturned, chairs scattered haphazardly across the floor. The once-gleaming windows were now smeared with something dark and sticky, casting warped reflections in the dim light. The air smelled faintly of iron, and for a moment, it seemed to press down on her chest, as though the car itself had become a tomb, holding its secrets in tight, suffocating silence.

Dea's heart raced as her eyes swept over the carnage, her mind struggling to process the chaos that had unfolded in such a short time. But it was the symbol- scrawled across one of the walls in what looked like a hastily spilled, dark ink- that drew her attention most. It was jagged and unfamiliar, its form disturbingly precise amidst the disorder. Her breath caught again, and she could feel a chill creeping over her skin, like the weight of something ancient and ominous settling around them both.

"Prex," she whispered, her voice barely more than a thread of sound, *"this... this is worse than we thought."*

A man lay sprawled across one of the weathered tables, his limbs splayed awkwardly as though he had collapsed with no will to rise again. His face was deathly pale, the sickly hue of his skin making him appear almost ghostlike. His chest rose and fell with each shallow breath, the rise so slight it was nearly imperceptible. Sweat glistened on his forehead, his eyes half-lidded in an unconscious stupor, or perhaps something worse. His sleeve had been carelessly pushed up, revealing a crude symbol crudely etched into his forearm- a circle bisected by a jagged line. The symbol was imperfect, its edges uneven, as if carved by something sharp and impatient. Blood oozed from the wound, slow and steady, staining the pristine white of the tablecloth beneath him. It pooled in dark crimson splotches, an unnerving contrast to the otherwise clean, sterile surroundings.

Prex stood motionless, his eyes tracing the symbol with a sharp intensity, his lips pressed into a thin, tight line. His jaw tightened as if the very sight of it caused him physical discomfort. His gaze remained fixed, his mind calculating, working furiously to unravel the significance of what he was seeing. As his boots clicked softly against the cold stone floor, he stepped closer, casting a long shadow across the unconscious figure before him.

"That's not just a symbol," Prex muttered, his voice low but filled with an undercurrent of something dangerous. *"It's a message."*

Dea, standing a few steps behind him, felt the weight of his words settle heavily in the air. She swallowed hard, her throat dry with apprehension. Her eyes darted between the man on the table and Prex, who seemed far too calm in the face of such a chilling discovery. She felt a shiver crawl down her spine, the kind that told her something far more sinister was at play. *"What does it mean?"* she asked, her voice barely a whisper, though she was certain it wouldn't matter if they whispered or shouted. This felt like something that could not be escaped by simple sounds. Prex's gaze shifted to her, his eyes cold and unwavering. He took a slow step back, distancing himself from the figure on the table, though his focus never wavered from the symbol. *"It means we're being watched,"* he said, his voice almost detached, as though he had long ago learned to detach himself from the more human responses of fear or surprise. There was something deeply unsettling in his calmness- a certainty that whatever danger loomed was no longer a question of if, but when.

Dea's pulse quickened, and the chill that had settled in her bones deepened. There was no escape from it now. Whatever was happening, whatever had led to this moment, was already in motion. They were already too late to stop it.

Shadows in the Mist

The air outside the train was heavy with a dense mist that clung to everything it touched, transforming the world into a dreamlike blur. Prex and Dea stepped onto the platform, their feet sinking slightly into the cool, damp stone beneath them. The station, though quaint, felt like it had been abandoned by time itself. The walls, weathered and worn, stood in quiet testament to years of neglect, as if the place had surrendered to the oppressive silence that surrounded it.
A single, flickering lamp stood at the far end of the platform, casting long, wavering shadows that danced unnaturally across the cobblestones. The light, weak and uncertain, seemed to struggle against the weight of the fog, its glow barely piercing through the thick haze. The shadows, stretching like thin, elongated fingers, seemed to reach toward the travelers as if trying to pull them into the mystery that shrouded the station.
Above them, the train's engine emitted a low, guttural hiss, the sound almost resembling a breath taken by something ancient and mechanical. It was a sound that lingered in the air, vibrating through the mist, carrying with it an odd sense of unease. The train, an imposing shadow itself, rested on the tracks like a slumbering beast, its presence felt more than seen, as if it were wait-

ing for something- or someone- to awaken it from its stillness.

The platform seemed suspended in time, an outpost between worlds, where even the passing of seconds felt like an eternity. The air was thick with the scent of rain-soaked earth and damp wood, each breath a heavy pull that filled the lungs with a damp chill. It was as though the world had held its breath, waiting for something to break the silence that enveloped the station in a near-physical presence.

Dea pulled her coat tighter around her shoulders, the fabric rustling as it shielded her from the biting cold that crept into the night. Her breath formed small clouds in the air, her wide eyes darting uneasily across the dimly lit train car, searching for any sign of movement. The steady hum of the train had given way to an unsettling silence that seemed to stretch endlessly in every direction. She clenched her hands tightly together, her fingers trembling despite the warmth of her coat.

"Why would they stop the train here?" she murmured, her voice barely audible, as though speaking too loudly might awaken some unseen presence. She glanced out the window again, but the endless stretch of darkness beyond offered no comfort.

Prex stood a few paces away, his posture tense, every muscle in his body alert. His hand hovered near the revolver holstered at his hip, as though instinctively preparing for danger, even though he had seen nothing that warranted such caution. He scanned the surroundings with sharp eyes, his gaze lingering on every shadow, every creak of metal.

"They didn't stop it," he replied lowly, his voice tinged with a grim certainty. *"Someone else did."*

The words hung in the air, thick with an ominous undertone. Dea's breath caught in her throat as she turned to look at him, her pulse quickening. The realization settled over her like a heavy cloak. They weren't alone in this.

The incident that had brought them to this point still gnawed at her mind. The conductor, once a reassuring figure in their travels, had all but disappeared after guiding them into the dining car. She remembered his hurried, almost anxious demeanor, but had thought little of it at the time. Now, the absence of answers made the silence unbearable. What had happened to him? Where had he gone? And why had he left them so abruptly?

More troubling still was the unconscious man- now moved to a private compartment, his condition deteriorating by the hour. Dea had seen the blood on his clothes and the odd, almost ritualistic symbol carved into his arm. A strange, twisting design that seemed to burn itself into her memory, its meaning obscure yet somehow undeniably unsettling. It lingered in her thoughts, like a haunting refrain that repeated with every passing minute. A warning, perhaps. A message, yet to be deciphered.

The air in the car seemed to grow heavier, thick with unspoken fears. Dea's gaze shifted again to the dark corridor outside, where shadows seemed to move of their own accord. She felt a chill that wasn't just from the cold- a coldness that seeped into her very bones.

"Do you think..." she began, but her words faltered, as if the fear inside her was too vast to name.

Prex turned his sharp eyes to her. *"I don't know,"* he admitted, his voice a rough whisper. *"But someone doesn't want us to know what's happening. We need to be ready for anything."*

A soft, almost imperceptible rustling sound, like the whisper of leaves stirred by a hidden breeze, drew their attention to the far end of the platform. Prex paused, his senses sharpening, his gaze narrowing as the mist swirled in thick, ghostly tendrils around them. His hand, steady and practiced, gestured subtly to Dea, signaling her to remain behind. There was no need for words; the air itself seemed to demand silence, a tacit understanding between them that danger might be near.

With a practiced grace, Prex began moving forward, his steps measured and deliberate, each one landing with a soft thud that barely disturbed the thick fog. He navigated the fog with the careful precision of someone who knew its secrets, letting it swirl around him like a cloak. As he neared the source of the disturbance, the mist parted just enough to reveal the outline of a figure.

The figure was hunched over a battered suitcase, its edges worn and scuffed from time and travel. The suitcase's locks were broken, hanging uselessly from the corners as if they had given up any attempt at containment. Its contents- papers, old books, tattered clothing- spilled out haphazardly in a chaotic mess across the cold stone of the platform. The items fluttered lightly in the breeze that had begun to stir, some of them drifting further away like forgotten memories, caught in the eerie stillness of the night. The figure itself remained motionless, almost too still, as if waiting for something- or someone. The faint outline of a hood or cloak shrouded its face, leaving only the subtle curve of a shoulder and the trembling motion of its hands as it sorted through the disarray. It was a sight that, for a moment, felt like a dream, both too strange and too real to fully comprehend.

"Hey!" Prex shouted, his voice sharp, cutting through the thick silence like a blade.

The figure ahead froze, then, with a sudden, jerky motion, bolted into the darkened recesses of the alley. Prex's instincts kicked in immediately. His boots struck the slick cobblestones in a rhythmic drumbeat as he surged forward, a shadow himself, chasing the fleeting silhouette with fierce determination. The night air felt heavy against his chest, but the adrenaline kept him moving, each step a beat of urgency.

Dea lingered for a moment at the edge of the alley, her breath quick and shallow, her heart hammering against her ribcage like a frantic prisoner trying to escape. A mix of fear and anticipation gripped her, but she knew she couldn't stay behind. Her legs moved almost of their own accord, following Prex into the unknown, her footsteps echoing softly against the wet stone.

The chase led them swiftly to an area that felt abandoned by time itself: a derelict warehouse crouched at the edge of the city, just beyond the train station. Its dilapidated structure loomed like a forgotten monument to decay. The windows were shattered, some of them barely clinging to their frames as if protesting their inevitable collapse. The building's weathered walls were streaked with layers of graffiti, each layer more cryptic than the last. The messages seemed less like rebellious art and more like desperate warnings- symbols and words that twisted and merged, offering no clarity, only a sense of foreboding.

Prex's hand gripped the door handle, his fingers brushing over the rusted metal. He pushed with caution, the hinges groaning loudly in protest, their screech almost deafening in the stillness of the night. It was a sound that seemed to rip the air, making the space feel even more alien. The door opened slowly, revealing an interior swallowed by shadows.

Inside, the atmosphere was thick and damp, as though the building had absorbed the years of neglect. The air smelled of rust and decay, a sharp metallic tang that clung to the back of the throat. The flickering glow of a distant light cast long, uneven shadows across the floor, flickering like a dying heartbeat, leading them deeper into the cavernous space. Their footsteps, slow and deliberate now, echoed eerily in the vast emptiness, the sound disorienting and amplified by the warehouse's hollowed-out interior.

The figure, elusive as a wisp of smoke, had vanished, swallowed by the darkness. Prex's eyes narrowed, scanning the shadows, but there was no sign of movement. Only the faintest trace of hurried footsteps reverberated through the vast expanse of the warehouse, a distant rhythm that beckoned them onward. It was a sound filled with tension, a hint that the chase was far from over.

"Prex," Dea whispered, her fingers gripping his arm tightly, her voice barely a breath. *"This doesn't feel right."*

He didn't need to look at her to know the fear in her eyes, the way her body was tense with unease. His own heart thudded harder, an unsettling rhythm in his chest. *"It's not,"* he murmured, his voice low and strained. *"Stay close."*

The words were a warning, but also a plea. He could feel the weight of the shadows around them, the air thick with a tension he couldn't shake. They moved through the narrow, dimly lit alley, the walls closing in as they rounded a corner into a room that felt far too still, too quiet. It was a place untouched by time, yet imbued with an unmistakable sense of dread.

At the center of the room, an old, makeshift table stood. Its surface was cluttered with yellowed papers, stained maps, and photographs that seemed to pulse with an eerie energy. A faint smell of dust and mildew lingered in the air. A lantern sat in the middle of the chaos, its flame flickering weakly, casting long, distorted shadows that crawled across the walls like silent specters. The soft glow illuminated the room in an unnatural way, as if the very light was struggling to stay alive.

Prex stepped forward, his boots creaking on the wooden floor, the only sound in the otherwise silent room. His eyes scanned the table, noting the disarray, the urgency in the scattered papers, as though someone had left in haste. His fingers brushed over a few of the maps - crisp edges curled with age - and he felt the weight of the moment press down upon him. The symbols on the maps were unfamiliar, and his stomach churned with a growing sense of dread.

Then his gaze fell upon the photographs. His hand trembled as he picked one up, a strange compulsion pulling him to it. The image was grainy, a black-and-white blur that hinted at something far too familiar. His breath hitched in his throat as he studied the photograph more closely. The figures in the picture were shadowy, indistinct, but one face was unmistakable. His own.

A cold shiver ran down his spine, his fingers tightening around the photo as though it were a lifeline, or perhaps a threat. It felt like time itself had stopped, the world shrinking to the moment in his hands. The light from the lantern flickered once more, casting a fleeting shadow across his face, making the photograph look even more haunting. A strange, inexplicable pull tugged at him, an unsettling sensation that whispered in the back of his mind: This is not coincidence.

"Prex?" Dea's voice broke through the fog in his mind, her tone sharp with concern. She stood just behind him, her own eyes scanning the room warily. *"What is it?"*

He didn't answer immediately, his gaze fixed on the image, the weight of the truth crashing over him like a storm. His pulse quickened as the realization hit him: this was no random place, no accident. Whoever had been here was watching them, was waiting. And they had known all along.

It was a picture of them, taken merely hours ago on the train.

Dea inhaled sharply, her breath catching in her throat as she stumbled back in disbelief. Her hand instinctively flew to her mouth, as if to stifle the incredulity rising within her. *"How... is that even possible?"* she whispered, her voice trembling, eyes fixed on the image in her hand.

Prex, however, didn't answer her. His gaze was firmly fixed on the large map pinned to the wall behind the table, the kind of map one would find in the dark corners of a mystery, waiting to be deciphered. The map was littered with red circles, each marking a different location, and beside each circle was a date. Some of the dates were weeks old, others were more recent, and yet, one in particular caught his attention. It was placed around their current location- right here, right now- and the date was today, the very same day they had set foot on this train.

His brow furrowed as the cold weight of realization settled in, his fingers inching closer to the map, brushing over the locations as if he were reading an invisible thread connecting them all. Each circle, each date, felt more like a warning than a clue, a haunting reminder that nothing in this place, in this situation, was as it seemed. Dea's voice broke the silence once more, but Prex didn't turn. He simply stared at the map, his mind racing as the pieces began to shift, settling into a picture far darker than they had anticipated.

"Dea," he murmured, his voice low and distant. *"Something's not right. This... this isn't just coincidence."*

Dea's gaze darted from him to the map, and her pulse quickened. Every instinct she had screamed at her to turn back, to stop digging, to forget they'd ever boarded this cursed train. But they had already crossed the line, hadn't they? There was no going back now.

"They knew we'd be here," Prex muttered under his breath, his voice heavy with the weight of realization. His eyes darted around the dimly lit room, seeking any sign of an escape or a

trap, but the walls seemed to close in on them. *"This whole thing was a setup... A carefully orchestrated trap."*

Before anyone could respond, the sharp, echoing sound of a floorboard creaking behind them made their bodies tense, muscles stiffening like coils ready to snap. In unison, they turned, the hairs on their necks standing on end.

A figure emerged from the shadows, stepping silently into the dim glow of the single flickering bulb above them. The figure's silhouette was imposing, draped in a long, flowing cloak, with a hood that obscured any discernible features. All that could be made out was the glint of cold metal in their hand- a knife, the blade honed to perfection, catching the faintest shimmer of light as if eager to taste blood.

"You shouldn't have come," the figure's voice rang out, low and unsettling, warped by some strange distortion as though it were not entirely their own. It echoed in the silence, sending a chill crawling down their spines. *"Now you've made your choice... Now you can't leave."*

The words hung in the air like an omen, heavy with malice. There was no doubt in their minds now that they were trapped, that every movement they had made since stepping into this forsaken place had been calculated, deliberate.

The knife gleamed in the shadowed light, its edge sharper than their every instinct. The air felt thick, oppressive, as if the room itself held its breath in anticipation. Prex's hand instinctively reached for his weapon, but he knew it was too late. The figure had already taken control of the situation. No one could escape now.

Prex's hand was steady as he drew his revolver, the cold metal pressing firmly against his palm. His finger rested lightly on the trigger, but his eyes were sharp, scanning the shadows that stretched across the dimly lit warehouse. He could feel his pulse quicken as the silence grew thick around him, the only sound the faint hum of distant machinery.

"Who are you?" His voice was low, deliberate, but the tension in his throat betrayed the urgency behind the question. *"What*

do you want?"

The figure in the shadows remained motionless for a moment, their presence a mere whisper against the cacophony of Prex's heartbeat. Then, without warning, they lunged. A flash of silver gleamed in the air as the knife, like a dancer in the night, slashed toward him with deadly precision.

Prex's instincts kicked in before his mind had fully processed the movement. He pulled the trigger in one fluid motion, the revolver kicking back in his grip with a deafening crack. The sharp report echoed off the walls, the sound reverberating through the cavernous space, bouncing off the steel beams and metal crates. The figure was struck, stumbling backward with a sharp gasp, the impact of the bullet sending them reeling. A crimson stain bloomed across their shoulder as they clutched at the wound, their breath ragged. Yet, despite the pain, they were swift- like a shadow slipping through the cracks in the world.

Before Prex could take a second shot, the figure disappeared into the depths of the warehouse, melting back into the obscurity from which they had emerged. The faint rustling of fabric, the scraping of boots on concrete, was the only trace they left behind, leaving Prex standing alone in the lingering silence, his heart still pounding, the revolver trembling in his hand.

"Dea, run!" Prex's voice rang out through the night, raw with urgency. His hand shot out, seizing hers with a frantic grip, and he yanked her toward the exit, the cold metal doors of the warehouse groaning as they pushed through.

The air outside was damp and thick with mist, the world around them a blur of grey and shadow. The fog curled around their ankles like fingers of the unknown, but they dared not slow their pace. Behind them, the oppressive gloom of the warehouse seemed to shudder with life- dark figures slithering like specters, moving in erratic, jerky motions. The sound of distant shouting reached their ears, mingling with the harsh, rhythmic pounding of boots on the concrete floor as their pursuers closed in.

The alleyways blurred as they sprinted, each footstep echoing off the damp walls, mingling with the oppressive cacophony of their breaths. Prex's hand tightened around Dea's, his knuckles white with exertion, and he dared not look back- he could feel the weight of danger pressing closer with each passing second. The train, their only hope of escape, seemed an eternity away.

Suddenly, the faint clatter of the train's wheels reached their ears, a sound both foreign and familiar- familiar in its promise of freedom, foreign in its fragility. As they neared the tracks, a rush of adrenaline surged through Prex, propelling him forward with renewed speed. Dea's breath hitched as she followed, the distant scream of a voice calling her name almost lost in the wind.

They reached the platform just as the train groaned to a halt, its iron sides steaming in the chill night. Prex's pulse raced, but there was no time to celebrate. With one last burst of strength, he hurled the compartment door open, pulling Dea inside and slamming it shut with a violent clang. His fingers fumbled for the lock, his heart hammering in his chest as though it might burst. The metallic snick of the lock was the only sound that followed the cacophony of their breaths- ragged, frantic, and filled with the lingering taste of fear.

Leaning against the door, Prex's chest rose and fell in frantic, uneven rhythms. His hands shook, the sweat on his brow cold against the night's chill, as he tried to steady his racing heart. His mind raced, but there was nothing but silence in the train's compartment now- save for the occasional scrape of metal against the tracks and the deepening rush of their breath.

They were safe, for the moment. But both knew- this was just the beginning.

Dea collapsed into the seat beside Prex, her breath shallow, and her face drained of color. The events that had unfolded were too surreal, too frightening. Her fingers gripped the armrest as she tried to steady her racing thoughts.

"Who were they?" she asked again, her voice cracking with a mixture of fear and confusion. *"Why were they following us?"*

Prex didn't immediately respond. His gaze was fixed out the window, the dim light of the evening casting long shadows across his face. His mind churned with possibilities, each darker than the last. The silence stretched between them, thick and oppressive. Finally, after what felt like an eternity, he spoke, his voice low and edged with uncertainty. *"I don't know,"* he muttered, almost as if speaking the words aloud would make them more real, more dangerous. *"But what just happened... it's not just about Mercer anymore. We've stumbled onto something much larger. Something we don't fully understand."*

Dea's heart skipped a beat as the weight of his words sank in. She could feel the blood rush to her head as a million questions filled her mind, but one pushed through louder than the rest. *"Bigger?"* she repeated, her brow furrowing in disbelief. *"How much bigger, Prex? What are we talking about here?"*

Prex turned to face her then, his eyes hard as stone, his jaw clenched. There was a haunted look in his eyes, something that sent an icy chill down her spine. *"Big enough,"* he said, his voice now almost a whisper, *"that we might not make it out alive."*

The words hung between them like a death sentence, each syllable laden with the gravity of the situation. The air seemed to grow colder, denser, as if the very world around them was holding its breath.

Echoes of the Forgotten

FLASHBACK

The rain cascaded in relentless torrents, drenching the narrow cobblestone streets of a quaint European village nestled deep in the rolling hills. The year was 1892, and the world outside seemed cloaked in an almost cinematic gloom, as if nature itself mourned in the symphony of falling rain. The air was heavy with the mingling scents of damp earth, aged wood, and the acrid tang of smoke spiraling from chimneys that punctuated the thatched rooftops of modest cottages. The occasional flicker of candlelight in the windows hinted at lives quietly enduring the storm. Within one such dwelling, in a shadowy corner of a dimly lit study, a lone figure was hunched over a timeworn desk. The man's appearance was a portrait of weariness—his hollowed cheeks and sallow complexion betrayed sleepless nights and an unrelenting burden of thought. His pale, bony fingers clutched a quill, the nib gliding with urgency across the yellowed parchment, leaving behind dark, slanted lines of ink that bled faintly at the edges. The desk bore the marks of years of use: scratches and ink stains that told silent tales of a writer's toil.

A single oil lamp cast a warm yet insufficient glow, its flame sputtering as if sharing the man's quiet despair. Shadows danced on the peeling wallpaper, creating ghostly figures that seemed to leer at the writer's vulnerability. Pausing his feverish scribbling, the man glanced toward the ornate clock perched on the mantelpiece. Its intricate hands pointed squarely to midnight, the chime long since silenced by the storm's cacophony. Time, however, felt meaningless in this moment—a cruel observer to the man's solitude.

With a trembling hand, he dipped the quill into the inkwell, its ebony surface reflecting the wavering light of the lamp. A faint tremor coursed through his fingers as he resumed writing, his movements deliberate yet fraught with emotion. Each stroke of the quill seemed to wrest a fragment of his soul onto the page. The letter he crafted was not intended for any living recipient, yet it brimmed with an intimacy that suggested it was meant for everyone—and no one at all.

The words poured forth, imbued with an aching sincerity. They spoke of regrets left to fester, of dreams abandoned, and of love unspoken. The sentences ebbed and flowed like the tides, some lines sharp and cutting, others languid and mournful. The walls of the room seemed to close in, the weight of his thoughts pressing heavily against the confined space, leaving an almost palpable tension in the air.

Outside, the storm raged on, a relentless force mirroring the tempest within the man's mind. Yet in the quiet confines of the study, time stood still, and the universe shrank to the solitary figure and the fragile parchment before him. This letter, a testament to his existence, carried a gravity that defied the anonymity of its addressee. With each word, the man seemed to drain himself of something precious yet burdensome, leaving behind only the hollow echo of his resolve.

And so, the quill continued its unrelenting journey across the page, weaving a tapestry of sorrow and truth, destined to endure long after the rain had ceased and the village had returned to its quiet routine.

Dearest reader,

If you are reading this, then the secrets I have uncovered have not been lost to time. But beware: knowledge comes at a cost, and the price of this truth is steep. What I have seen cannot be unseen. What I have done cannot be undone.

The artifact must remain hidden. Should it fall into the wrong hands, it will bring ruin beyond imagination. Trust no one.

The man's hand froze mid-sentence as a faint yet unmistakable sound rippled through the silence of the house—a floorboard groaning under the weight of an unexpected presence. His heart skipped a beat, the once-pleasant solitude now tainted with a creeping sense of dread. Slowly, he laid the quill down on the aged wooden desk, its feathered tip trembling as if mirroring his unease. His hand moved instinctively toward the drawer where a revolver lay concealed, its cold metal weight offering a fleeting sense of security.

His breathing grew shallow, each inhalation sharp and deliberate as his ears strained to detect further movement. The soft creak was followed by an eerie silence, amplifying the tension in the dimly lit room. The amber glow of a flickering oil lamp cast elongated shadows on the walls, dancing to an invisible rhythm of menace. The man's gaze flickered toward the doorway, his mind racing with possibilities—was this a common thief, or something far more sinister?

Then it came—a shadow. Dark and amorphous at first, it stretched across the hallway, growing larger with every agonizing second. The figure's deliberate steps reverberated like a drumbeat of inevitability. The man rose from his chair, his hand gripping the revolver with white-knuckled intensity. Every muscle in his body was taut, a spring ready to uncoil.

The door slammed open with a force that sent papers flying from the desk. A figure cloaked in black filled the doorway, their face obscured by the darkness of their hood. Instinct took over. The man squeezed the trigger, the deafening crack of the gunshot momentarily shattering the stillness. But his aim faltered, the bullet veering off-course and embedding itself into the wooden frame of the door.

The intruder remained unfazed, stepping forward with a menacing calm that sent chills racing down the man's spine. The room, once a haven of quiet contemplation, now felt like a cage closing in. The man's pulse pounded in his ears as he took a step back, the revolver trembling in his grasp. His mind screamed at him to act, to shoot again, but the figure seemed almost otherworldly, moving with a purpose that rendered his frantic thoughts meaningless.

The intruder moved with an almost unnatural swiftness, a blur of motion that left the man no time to react. In a heartbeat, the weapon he had so confidently brandished was wrenched from his grasp and sent clattering to the floor. Before he could muster even a shout, he was pinned firmly against the cold, unforgiving wall. His breath hitched as the cloaked figure loomed over him, their shadow swallowing him whole like an encroaching storm.

The letter he had clutched so tightly moments ago slipped from his trembling fingers and drifted to the ground, its significance momentarily eclipsed by the sheer terror of the moment. The air in the dimly lit room grew heavy, thick with an ominous tension that seemed to vibrate with the power of the figure's presence.

"Where is it?" The intruder's voice cut through the silence, low and menacing, each word sharp as a blade. It wasn't a question—it was a demand, as if denial were not an option.

The man's head shook vehemently, his face pale and slick with a sheen of sweat. His eyes darted wildly, searching for a way out, an escape that didn't exist.

"You'll never find it," he choked out, his voice trembling with defiance laced with fear. *"It's beyond your reach."*

The figure's grip tightened like a vice, and the man let out a strangled gasp, his defiance crumbling under the weight of the pressure.

"You underestimate me," the intruder hissed, their tone laced with an almost predatory certainty. It was not the boast of someone unsure of their strength—it was the warning of someone who had never failed.

Without another word, the intruder delivered a precise, calculated strike, rendering the man unconscious in a single, fluid motion. His body crumpled to the floor, lifeless save for the faint rise and fall of his chest. The room fell silent again, save for the faint rustle of the letter lying forgotten on the ground.

The figure's piercing gaze swept across the room, taking in every detail with an almost mechanical efficiency. Their eyes finally landed on the fallen letter, and they strode toward it with deliberate purpose. Kneeling, they retrieved it, the faint crackle of paper breaking the heavy quiet. For a moment, they were still, their face obscured by the shadows of the hood, betraying no emotion as they read the words inked upon the parchment.

Whatever secrets the letter contained, they evoked no outward reaction. The figure stood, tucking the letter into the folds of their cloak as if securing a treasure of immeasurable value. Then, without a sound, they vanished into the night, their departure as swift and silent as their arrival, leaving only the unconscious man and the lingering chill of fear in their wake.

The study was a chaotic mess, its usual order dismantled in the frenzied moments leading up to this eerie stillness. Books and papers lay scattered across the wooden floor, some pages torn and crumpled, others damp from the droplets of rain that had found their way in through a cracked window. The faint smell of wet paper mingled with the rich aroma of aged leather and spilled ink. Shadows danced on the walls, cast by the flickering light of a solitary candle struggling against the encroaching darkness. Outside, the steady patter of rain against the tall windows provided a rhythmic backdrop, broken only by the occasional rumble of distant thunder.

On the plush armchair near the fireplace, the man stirred, his head lolling to one side as he groaned in pain. A thin streak of blood trickled down his temple, matting his dark hair. His eyelids fluttered open, and for a moment, his vision swam, the dimly lit room a blur of shadows and shapes. He winced, bringing a trembling hand to his head, where a dull ache throbbed mercilessly.

As clarity returned, so did the sinking realization of what had transpired. His hand instinctively darted to the desk where he had last seen the letter, the one thing that mattered most—the one thing that could change everything. His fingers fumbled across the smooth surface, brushing aside a toppled inkwell and scattered quills. The letter was gone.

A cold wave of panic surged through him, cutting through the fog of his disorientation. His breathing quickened, the sound sharp and ragged in the quiet room. He pushed himself up, his movements sluggish and unsteady, his muscles protesting with every effort. His gaze swept the study, scanning the chaos for any sign of the envelope's distinct wax seal. But it was nowhere to be found.

Someone had been here. Someone had taken it.

The thought tightened his chest, and a thousand questions erupted in his mind. Who had breached the sanctity of his study? How had they known about the letter? And, most chillingly, what would they do with the information it contained?

The rain outside grew heavier, the rhythmic patter turning into a relentless drumming against the windowpanes. He staggered toward the door, his bare feet crunching on shards of broken glass. Every nerve in his body screamed at him to move, to act, to retrieve what was lost. But where would he begin? His sanctuary, once a place of contemplation and refuge, now felt like a trap closing in around him.

He staggered toward his desk, each step a fight against the weight of his own turmoil. His trembling hands fumbled as he pulled open a hidden compartment beneath the cluttered surface, revealing an ornate box shrouded in shadows. The box was no larger than a jewelry case, yet its presence seemed to fill the room, commanding attention with an almost malevolent allure. Its surface was a labyrinth of intricate carvings—symbols that appeared to shift and writhe as though alive, their meanings just beyond comprehension. The faint glint of the dim light reflected off the etchings, giving them an otherworldly sheen.

He lifted the box with a reverence laced with dread, cradling it as though it were both a sacred relic and a curse. His breathing was shallow, his chest rising and falling in uneven spurts, as though the weight of the artifact was suffocating him. Fear flashed in his eyes, but it was not the fear of the unknown—it was the fear of what he already knew. A lifetime of secrets pressed down on him, the burden of knowledge threatening to crush his resolve.

"They can't have it," he whispered, his voice barely audible over the drumming of the rain against the window. His words hung in the air like an oath, laced with desperation and a hint of defiance. *"Not now. Not ever."*

He clutched the box tighter, its sharp corners digging into his skin, a reminder of the danger he carried. Without another glance at the life he was abandoning, he turned and fled into the night. The storm outside greeted him with ferocity, rain lashing against his face and the howling wind tearing at his clothes. He pulled his coat tighter around the box, shielding it from the elements as if it were a fragile ember that could be extinguished by a single drop.

The streets were empty, eerily devoid of life, as though the storm had chased everyone into hiding. He moved swiftly, his steps splashing through puddles that mirrored the lightning streaking across the sky. Each clap of thunder seemed to echo his pounding heartbeat, a reminder of the relentless pursuit he knew was inevitable. Shadows stretched and twisted in the flickering streetlights, and he couldn't shake the feeling of unseen eyes watching his every move.

He knew he had no choice—there was no going back. The artifact's power was too great, its potential for destruction too immense. It was a Pandora's box in every sense, and in the wrong hands, it could usher in a chaos the world was unprepared to face. The thought sent a shiver down his spine, but he forced himself to focus on the path ahead. Every step was a commitment to the heavy burden he bore, every breath a reminder of the sacrifice he had to make.

The secrets he carried would haunt him for the rest of his days, a shadow that would cling to him no matter where he went. But that was a price he was willing to pay. He whispered a silent prayer to the stormy skies above, hoping against hope that he

could outrun the forces that would stop at nothing to claim what was in his possession.
Somewhere in the distance, a faint light glimmered, a beacon of the unknown future awaiting him. Clutching the box with renewed determination, he pressed on, knowing that his journey had only just begun.

PRESENT

Prex stared intently at the weathered photograph in his trembling hands, his mind a whirlwind of thoughts and fragmented realizations. The image held a strange, almost hypnotic pull, drawing his gaze back to the symbol etched deeply into the unconscious man's arm. The mark, jagged and intricate, bore an unsettling resemblance to the ancient carvings they had painstakingly documented from the enigmatic box described in the brittle pages of the journal they had unearthed just days before.

A chill ran down his spine as the weight of the discovery settled over him like a shroud. This wasn't a coincidence; the resemblance was too precise, too deliberate. His pulse quickened as dread crept in, its icy grip tightening around his thoughts. The journal had hinted at relics tied to forgotten epochs, whispers of malevolent forces that had lingered in the shadows of human history. Now, those cryptic musings seemed alarmingly close to the truth.

"What's wrong?" Dea's voice broke through the suffocating silence, her sharp eyes narrowing as they locked onto his. She had seen the way his expression shifted—the flicker of fear, the tightening of his jaw. *"Prex, what is it? You look like you've seen a ghost."*

He tore his gaze from the photograph and met hers, the conflict in his mind clear in the crease of his brow.

"It's not a ghost," he muttered, his voice low and strained. *"But it might be worse."*

Dea's frown deepened as she stepped closer, peering over his shoulder at the photograph. *"That mark..."* she began, her voice

trailing off as realization dawned. *"It's just like the one—"*
"Yes," Prex interrupted, his tone curt but laced with unease. *"The same symbol as the carvings on the box. The one the journal called 'the seal.'"*
Dea's eyes widened, and she glanced back at the photograph, her fingers instinctively brushing against her pendant as if seeking comfort. *"You don't think..."* she hesitated, *"you don't think this is connected to what the journal warned about, do you?"*
Prex exhaled sharply, his grip on the photograph tightening. *"I think we're dealing with something far older—and far more dangerous—than we realized,"* he admitted. His voice carried the weight of reluctant certainty. *"The journal hinted at a power sealed away for a reason. If this mark is what I think it is, someone—or something—has started to unearth what should have remained buried."*
The room seemed to grow colder as his words hung in the air, heavy with implication. The dim light cast long, flickering shadows on the walls, as if the very space around them reacted to the gravity of their revelation. Dea's hand dropped from her pendant, her knuckles white as she clenched her fists.
"What do we do now?" she asked, her voice steady despite the growing storm of fear in her chest.
Prex turned his attention back to the photograph, his mind already racing through the possibilities. They needed answers—quickly. But deep down, he feared that every step forward would only lead them closer to the danger lurking in the dark.
Dea's eyes narrowed, her gaze piercing through the dimly lit room. Her voice, sharp yet laced with unease, cut through the silence like a blade. *"What do you mean, Prex?"*
Prex shifted uncomfortably, his usually confident demeanor faltering under the weight of unspoken truths. He glanced toward the rain-speckled window, as though searching for answers in the rhythmic cascade of droplets. Finally, he exhaled deeply, his voice carrying a somber note that seemed to echo in the confines of the room. *"I mean, this... everything we're caught up in, it didn't begin with us. And it's naive to think it'll end with us,*

either."

The words hung heavily in the air, charged with a sense of inevitability that made Dea's chest tighten. The pattering rain outside intensified, a mournful symphony accompanying their conversation. It felt as though the heavens themselves were mourning the revelation—a truth too large and complex to comprehend fully. Dea's jaw tightened, and she crossed her arms over her chest as though shielding herself from the invisible weight of Prex's words. *"You're saying we're just... pieces in some endless game? That no matter what we do, it's all already decided?"*

Prex turned to face her, his expression a mixture of regret and determination. *"Not decided, Dea. Not entirely. But influenced. There are forces at play—forces older and more relentless than either of us can imagine. What we're dealing with... it's just the latest ripple in a sea of conflict that stretches back far beyond our lifetimes."*

Dea took a step closer, her voice dropping to a whisper, as though the shadows in the room might be listening. *"Then what's the point? Why fight if we're just another chapter in some endless story?"*

Prex's lips curled into a faint, bittersweet smile. *"Because every chapter matters. Every choice we make ripples outward, just like those before us. Maybe we can't rewrite the entire story, but we can still shape the part that's ours to tell."*

The room fell silent again, save for the persistent drumming of rain against the windowpane. Outside, the darkness seemed to press closer, a living entity eager to envelop them. The unease in their hearts grew, mirroring the storm raging beyond the fragile walls of their sanctuary.

As the weight of Prex's revelation settled over them, Dea couldn't shake the feeling that they were standing on the edge of something vast and unknowable. Their journey, already fraught with danger and uncertainty, now carried the added burden of history—and the ever-present shadows of those who had come before them.

Together, they braced themselves for the next step, unaware of just how close those shadows had drawn, their malevolent presence lurking unseen but ever closer, waiting for the perfect moment to strike.

The Web Unravels

The soft light of the morning sun forced its way through the thick, heavy curtains of their modestly rented room, spilling fragmented patterns onto the timeworn wooden floor. The interplay of light and shadow created a mosaic of quiet chaos, a contrast to the stillness that enveloped the space. Prex sat hunched over the small, scratched desk that had seen better days, his attention consumed by the map sprawled before him. Its once-crisp edges were frayed and curling with age, and faint smudges of ink bore testament to the many hands it had passed through. Each marked path and cryptic symbol seemed to whisper secrets, beckoning him to decode their meaning.

Dea stood a few feet away, her tall frame leaning casually against the window frame. The pale light danced across her features, softening the hard lines of determination etched on her face. Her arms were crossed loosely over her chest, a posture that belied the sharpness of her gaze. She peered through the gap in the curtains, watching the world outside stir to life. The street below bustled with activity as vendors set up their stalls, their voices mingling with the hum of early risers and the rhythmic clatter of horse-drawn carts. Children darted through the narrow alleyways, their laughter slicing through the morning air like a melody of innocence amid the adult urgency.

For a moment, Dea let her gaze linger on a flower seller carefully arranging her wares—bright marigolds and crimson roses that seemed to glow even under the subdued sunlight. A sigh escaped her lips, barely audible but heavy with unspoken thoughts.

"You've been staring at that map for hours," she finally said, her voice cutting through the quiet. It was neither harsh nor soft, carrying a tone of familiarity.

Prex didn't look up immediately. His brow furrowed in concentration as his fingers traced the faded ink lines, his lips moving silently as though rehearsing an incantation. Finally, he exhaled deeply and leaned back in the creaky wooden chair, rubbing his temple.

"Every path leads somewhere," he murmured, almost to himself, his voice a mix of frustration and curiosity. *"But it's the ones that end abruptly that worry me."*

Dea turned her attention back to him, the faintest flicker of concern crossing her face. *"Not every dead end is a trap,"* she replied. *"Some are just... ends."*

Prex glanced at her, his lips twitching into a faint, almost imperceptible smile. *"And some are where the real journey begins,"* he countered, his tone light but his eyes serious.

Their shared silence stretched, not uncomfortable but weighted with an understanding that words could not convey. Beyond the walls of their rented sanctuary, the world seemed to move with its own rhythm, but inside, it felt as though time itself had paused, waiting for them to make their move.

"What are we looking at?" Dea asked, her voice edged with both curiosity and apprehension.

Prex leaned over the weathered map spread across the table, his finger tracing a line before stopping on a small town encircled in red ink. His hand lingered, almost hesitant, as though touching the name itself might invoke whatever secrets it held. *"Here,"* he said, his tone heavy with implication. *"This is it. Ashford. According to the journal, this is where the artifact was last seen."*

Dea's brow furrowed as she stared at the map, the name offering no sense of familiarity. *"Ashford,"* she repeated, testing the name like it might unlock a memory. *"Never heard of it."*

"Most people haven't," Prex replied, a faint bitterness lacing his words. *"It's a forgotten place now, practically wiped off the map. But back in the 1890s, it was a booming mining town. Rich in resources, bustling with life... until it wasn't."*

Dea tilted her head, the weight of his words settling uneasily. *"What happened?"*

Prex's jaw tightened, his lips pressing into a thin line before he answered. *"The journal talks about... disappearances. Strange ones. People vanishing without a trace, leaving behind homes and possessions as if they planned to return but never did. It wasn't just the missing, though."* He paused, his gaze distant as though the echoes of the past were whispering to him too. *"There were reports of whispers in the mines. Faint, disembodied voices calling out to the workers. Shadows that moved when no one was there. At first, people dismissed it as exhaustion, hallucinations from working too hard. But then the miners began to disappear too."*

Dea shivered involuntarily, her arms crossing over her chest. *"And the artifact?"*

"It's said to have been hidden there," Prex continued, his voice lowering as though the walls themselves might overhear. *"The journal's author believed the artifact was no ordinary object. Whatever it is, it holds power. Power that doesn't want to be disturbed."*

"You're saying it's... alive?" she asked, her voice barely above a whisper.

"Not alive," Prex corrected, *"but aware. The journal hints that the artifact is more than just an object—it's connected to something ancient, something that exists beyond our understanding. And it's this connection that caused the disappearances. Anyone who got too close either vanished or fled, driven mad by the whispers and the shadows."*

Dea's eyes widened, her mind racing with the implications. *"If it's so dangerous, why are we even considering going after it?"*

"Because," Prex said, his gaze locking onto hers, *"if it's as powerful as the journal suggests, we can't leave it buried for someone else to find. It's only a matter of time before someone more reckless—or more dangerous—comes looking."*

Dea looked back at the map, her heart pounding. The red circle around Ashford now seemed to pulse with ominous intent, as though the town itself was daring them to uncover its secrets.

Dea felt an involuntary shiver run down her spine, her breath hitching as she absorbed the weight of Prex's words. *"And you really believe it's still there?"* she asked, her voice a mix of apprehension and disbelief.

Prex leaned back in his chair, the faint creak of the wood filling the silence as his eyes locked with hers. There was a calm intensity in his gaze, one that made her feel both reassured and uneasy at the same time. *"I don't just believe it, Dea. I think it's our best lead—maybe the only one we've got left."*

Before Dea could respond, a sharp knock at the door shattered the moment. Prex shot to his feet, his movements swift and fluid, a hand instinctively hovering near the holster at his side. The sudden tension in the room was palpable, and Dea felt her pulse quicken as she instinctively moved to the side, seeking the shadowed safety of the corner.

"Who is it?" Prex called out, his voice steady but laced with a low edge of warning.

There was a brief pause, followed by a muffled reply.

"Delivery."

Prex exchanged a quick glance with Dea, his brows knitting together in suspicion. She gave a small nod, her silent agreement that he should proceed with caution. Slowly, he unlatched the door and opened it just enough to see who was on the other side. Standing in the dimly lit hallway was a young boy, no older than ten, clutching a small, nondescript package wrapped in plain brown paper. His wide, curious eyes darted nervously to Prex, as though unsure of what to expect from the imposing figure towering above him.

"This was left for you downstairs," the boy said, his voice timid

yet steady as he held out the package with both hands. Without waiting for a response—or a tip—he turned on his heel and bolted down the hall, his hurried footsteps echoing faintly as he disappeared from view.

Prex closed the door with a soft click, his expression unreadable as he turned back toward the table. He placed the package down carefully, almost reverently, as though it were some fragile artifact that could break with the slightest mishandling.

Dea stepped closer, her earlier apprehension giving way to a gnawing curiosity that she couldn't suppress. Her eyes flicked to the package and back to Prex, her mind racing with questions. *"What do you think it is?"*

Prex didn't answer right away. Instead, he studied the package with the kind of scrutiny one might reserve for a riddle that needed solving. *"Could be nothing,"* he murmured finally, though the tension in his voice betrayed his own doubts. *"But if it's something..."*

He let the sentence trail off, leaving the weight of those unspoken possibilities to hang in the air. Dea felt her heart pounding in her chest, the anticipation almost unbearable as she watched him reach for the edge of the paper.

"Do you think it's from Mercer?" she asked, her voice laced with uncertainty, her fingers nervously tracing the edge of the worn-out map that lay spread across the table before them.

Prex's lips thinned into a tight line as he examined the unmarked parcel that had arrived under strange circumstances. His eyes flicked toward her for a brief moment, before he turned his gaze back to the mysterious bundle, his expression hardening. He reached into his coat pocket, fingers brushing against the cold steel of his knife, before drawing it out with swift precision. The blade gleamed momentarily under the dim light as he cut through the twine that held the package shut, his movements quick but deliberate.

As the twine fell away, the package opened to reveal a single sheet of paper, folded meticulously with sharp creases that suggested it had been in transit for longer than either of them cared to admit. Prex unfolded it slowly, the crisp sound of the paper breaking the heavy silence that had settled over the room. He scanned the words written on the page, his brow furrowing in concentration as his mind tried to process the cryptic message before him.

"Ashford is a trap. Turn back while you still can."

Dea's breath caught in her throat, her heart skipping a beat as the weight of the words hit her. Her fingers trembled slightly, and she instinctively reached out toward Prex, though she wasn't entirely sure why. The message was clear, yet its implications were far from simple.

"Do you think it's a warning?" Dea asked, her voice barely a whisper as the question hung in the air between them, thick with the tension that always seemed to accompany the unknown.

Prex's gaze remained fixed on the paper in his hands for a moment longer, his expression unreadable, betraying no sign of doubt or hesitation. The shadows under his eyes deepened, and he exhaled sharply, a sound that was almost imperceptible. Then, he straightened up, his jaw tightening with renewed purpose.

"Or a challenge," he replied, his voice low and gravelly, tinged with an edge of defiance. The words seemed to stir something within him, something that wasn't so much fear but rather a quiet, determined resolve.

Without another word, Prex let the paper slip from his fingers, watching it drift lazily to the floor like a leaf in the wind. His attention had already shifted back to the map, his mind refocusing on their next steps. The room seemed to shrink around them as he bent over the map once again, his fingers tracing a line on the parchment with the same care and precision he'd used to open the package.

Dea, still standing in the periphery, picked up the note, her thoughts racing as she weighed the possibilities. Her fingers gripped the paper tightly, the crinkling of the edges a sound that seemed to reverberate through her chest. She couldn't shake the feeling that this wasn't just a warning—it was a provocation. A test of their mettle. And they had no choice but to answer it.

With the paper in her hands, Dea turned her gaze toward Prex, her mind spinning with doubts and questions. But there was something in his demeanor, something unspoken in the way he carried himself, that kept her from voicing her fears. She could see it in his eyes—he wasn't backing down. Not now. Not ever. The path ahead was treacherous, but neither of them had ever been ones to retreat. And whatever Ashford was—trap or challenge—they were already too far in to turn back now.

"Prex," she whispered, her voice trembling with a mix of fear and uncertainty. *"What if they're right? What if this path we're taking is too dangerous, too fraught with risks we can't foresee?"*

Prex's gaze hardened as he turned to face her, his features set in an unyielding mask. His eyes, usually soft and full of warmth, now gleamed with a cold determination. *"It is dangerous, Dea,"* he said, his tone low but firm, as though the truth of the matter was inescapable. *"But that doesn't mean we turn back. We've come too far for that. We knew the risks when we set out on this journey."*

Dea swallowed hard, the weight of his words pressing down on her chest like a boulder. She had known, deep down, that this mission would not be without peril, but hearing it spoken aloud, with such finality, made it feel all the more real. Her fingers tightened around the strap of her bag as she tried to steady her breathing. She had been afraid of this moment—the moment when doubt crept in, when the fear of failure or worse, of the unknown, threatened to undo her resolve.

But Prex was right. They had crossed too many lines, taken too many risks to turn back now. The journey to Ashford, to whatever answers—or more likely, questions—lay ahead, was one they had no choice but to continue. The town was out there, a looming presence on the horizon, its silhouette barely visible against the backdrop of the morning sun. It stood like a shadow, its very existence shrouded in mystery, as though the earth itself had hidden its secrets beneath layers of time.

Dea took a deep breath and nodded, feeling the silent weight of resolve settle over her. *"You're right,"* she said quietly, more to herself than to him. *"We have to go. We have to find the truth."*

With a shared glance, they gathered their belongings—what little they had left—and stepped outside the room. The air was crisp, carrying with it the promise of a new day, but also the lingering scent of danger, of uncertainty. They both knew that Ashford would not give up its secrets easily, that whatever awaited them there would not be simple, nor would it be kind. Yet, despite the fear gnawing at her insides, Dea felt a spark of determination flare within her. There was no turning back. There was only the road ahead, leading them into the heart of the unknown.

The town of Ashford stood before them now, its outline more defined as they walked toward it, like a specter waiting patiently for its moment to reveal itself. Its streets were silent, almost too silent, as though the very air around it held its breath in anticipation. What lay buried in its past, what it had hidden from the world, would soon be uncovered. But at what cost? Only time would tell.

Shadows in Ashford

The journey to Ashford seemed interminable, the road stretching out like an endless ribbon, weaving through a landscape that appeared to have been forgotten by time itself. The trees lining the path were twisted and gnarled, their limbs extending toward the sky like the skeletal hands of long-dead giants, reaching for something—or perhaps someone. Their bare branches rustled in the wind, sending a shiver of unease down Prex's spine. Each tree seemed more alive in its desolation than the town they were heading toward, a silent testament to nature's dominance over the human world.

As the miles passed, the chill in the air deepened, creeping beneath their clothes and settling like an icy weight in their bones. The once-mild breeze had turned biting, lashing at their faces with a sharp, unforgiving cold. Prex's fingers curled tightly around the steering wheel, his knuckles white against the dark leather, as if he could somehow ward off the creeping sense of dread that had begun to invade his mind. He tried to focus on the road ahead, but the sight of the horizon, which had remained largely empty for miles, now seemed to mock him. It was as though the world was closing in, pressing them toward an inevitable, unknown fate.

Beside him, Dea sat with her eyes fixed on the view outside, though her gaze seemed faraway, unfocused, lost in a turbulent sea of thoughts. Her mind was a whirlwind of apprehension, curiosity, and a deep, gnawing uncertainty. Ashford, once a thriving town brimming with life, now stood at the edge of her thoughts as an enigma. What had happened here? Why had it fallen silent? The questions plagued her as much as the oppressive atmosphere outside, and though she longed to speak, she found her words caught somewhere deep within her.

The car crested a final hill, and there, nestled in the valley below, the town of Ashford came into view. It was not the picturesque village one might expect, nor was it the decaying ruin of a forgotten settlement. No, Ashford was something in between—an eerie husk, an echo of a once-thriving community. The buildings were weathered, their facades crumbling in places, the roofs sagging under years of neglect. Each structure seemed to lean in on the other, as though seeking the comfort of proximity in their shared isolation. The streets, once alive with the hustle and bustle of daily life, were now eerily empty, save for the occasional flicker of movement in the shadows—perhaps a cat, perhaps something else.

Dea's breath caught in her throat as her eyes swept over the town. There were no lights, no sign of movement—no life at all. The town seemed abandoned, left to be slowly reclaimed by the wilderness that encroached upon it. The windows were dark, their glass cracked or missing entirely, leaving empty sockets that seemed to stare back at her like hollow eyes. The buildings loomed over the streets like silent sentinels, guarding the secrets that lay hidden within.

The only sound that dared to break the silence was the mournful whisper of the wind, which wound its way through the narrow, empty alleyways, carrying with it the scent of decay and forgotten memories. It was a sound that seemed to echo from the very bones of Ashford itself, a whisper from the past that refused to die. The air was thick with the weight of that silence, as though the town itself was holding its breath, waiting for something—or someone—to disturb its eerie calm.

Prex slowed the car as they neared the outskirts of the town, his mind racing with thoughts of what they might find. What had happened to Ashford? And more importantly, what had drawn them here to this forsaken place?

"This place gives me the creeps," Dea muttered under her breath, her voice barely audible against the howling wind. She wrapped her coat tighter around her, the fabric swishing as she did, but it did little to ward off the chill that seemed to emanate from every corner of the desolate town.

Prex's lips pressed into a thin line, his eyes narrowing as they scanned the abandoned buildings ahead. His hand instinctively brushed the cold metal of the revolver holstered at his side, a gesture born from years of habit rather than actual fear. Still, the heavy silence in the air made his skin prickle with unease. He nodded without a word, his gaze sharp, like a hawk's as it searched for any signs of movement. *"Stay close,"* he said in a low, gravelly voice. *"We don't know what we're walking into."*

The old car came to a screeching halt, the tires skimming the dirt road before grinding to a standstill. The pair stared at the ruin that lay before them: a forgotten town that time had swallowed whole. The remnants of a once-bustling general store stood just ahead, its cracked windows and faded sign barely clinging to the building's skeleton. The sign swayed in the breeze, creaking ominously with each gust, like some spectral warning, a reminder of the place's decay.

Dea's eyes followed the rusted swing of the sign, her heart skipping a beat. The sound, so sharp and discordant in the otherwise eerie silence, echoed in her ears as if the very air around them was whispering secrets she wasn't ready to hear. A chill ran down her spine, and she fought the urge to tug Prex's arm and retreat. But something deep within her, something far darker than fear, kept her rooted to the spot.

Prex stepped out of the car first, his boots crunching on the gravel as he moved with deliberate purpose, his stance wide and wary. The harsh light from the car's headlights cast long shadows over his face, highlighting the tension in his jaw and the way his hand remained near his revolver, ready for anything. He didn't trust this place. Not for a second.

Dea reluctantly followed, her steps faltering as she kept her head down and her eyes darting from one shadow to another, her breath coming in shallow bursts. Every rustle of wind, every creak of the distant buildings, seemed amplified in the quiet. The darkness felt alive, and Dea's pulse quickened with each step she took.

"Where do we start?" she asked in a voice barely above a whisper, barely trusting herself to break the suffocating silence. Her words hung in the air for a moment before vanishing into the oppressive atmosphere that seemed to cling to everything in this forgotten place.

Prex didn't respond immediately, his eyes studying the surroundings with an intensity that seemed almost supernatural. He scanned every corner, every abandoned storefront, every darkened alley, as if expecting someone—or something—to jump out at any moment. Finally, he spoke, his voice calm, yet edged with something unreadable. *"We start where we find answers."*

The words hung in the air between them like an unspoken challenge. Dea swallowed hard, trying to steady her racing heart. They had no idea what they were about to uncover, but the weight of it pressed on her chest, and the sharp sting of uncertainty lingered in her mind. What lay ahead was a mystery, and it was a mystery they had no choice but to solve.

Prex unfurled the brittle, timeworn map with a careful, almost reverent gesture, his fingers skimming the faded, nearly illegible lines. He traced the path with slow precision, as if hoping the worn ink would suddenly come to life and reveal its secrets. *"The journal makes mention of a mine,"* he said, his voice low and purposeful, *"situated on the outskirts of this forsaken town. That's where the artifact is said to have been hidden."*

Dea's gaze shifted to the horizon, her eyes narrowing as they locked onto the jagged silhouette of a mountain, its peaks clawing at the heavens. The mountains seemed to loom over them, an ever-present, imposing figure in the distance. *"A mine. Naturally,"* she muttered under her breath, the words dripping with reluctant resignation. She could almost feel the weight of the mountain's ancient, unmoving presence pressing down on them. It was as though the very land itself held its breath, waiting.

The two of them continued on, their footsteps cautious, measured—each sound amplified in the haunting stillness of the empty town. The air felt thick with the weight of years gone by, of memories locked away in the crumbling buildings that surrounded them. Every creak of old wood, every rustle of windswept leaves, seemed to cut through the silence like a whispering ghost, making their nerves twitch with unease.

As they rounded a corner, the ruins of a dilapidated church came into view, its once-sturdy structure now standing in a mournful state of decay. The remnants of a steeple jutted up crookedly against the sky, a sad mockery of its former grandeur. Dea's eyes lingered on the church's entrance, drawn to the shattered stained-glass window above the arched doorway. Though most of the glass had long since crumbled away, the shards that remained still caught the light, shimmering with a faint, eerie glow.

In the dimming light of the day, Dea's gaze honed in on one fragment of the window that stood out from the rest. The fragmented pieces of glass depicted an enigmatic figure, standing tall with an outstretched arm. The figure held a circular object in their hand—its meaning lost to time—and within the circle, a jagged line cut across it, splitting the shape into two. It was a symbol that was strangely familiar to Dea. Her breath caught in her throat as she realized that it mirrored the very same mark that had been carved into the arm of the man they had encountered on the train. A shiver ran down her spine as she thought of the implications.

"The same symbol," Dea whispered, her voice barely audible as if speaking the words aloud might give them more power than they deserved. Her fingers instinctively went to the small pendant around her neck, the metal cool against her skin, as though it offered some form of comfort in the face of the growing mys-

tery that seemed to swirl around them.

"Prex," she called softly, her voice cutting through the stillness of the evening air. She gestured toward the window with a finger, pointing out something only she could see, something that had caught her attention.

He turned slowly, his sharp eyes narrowing as he followed the direction of her gaze. His expression was unreadable at first, but then a subtle tension flickered across his face as he took in the sight. The area before them seemed quiet, almost forgotten, but there was no mistaking the feeling in the air. *"Looks like we're in the right place,"* he murmured, his tone grave, but laced with a sense of purpose.

Without another word, they began walking, the gravel crunching beneath their boots as they made their way toward the edge of town. The once-thriving heart of the mining district was now eerily silent. The streets that led them there had become more desolate with each passing step, their edges overtaken by the wilderness, a reflection of the years that had worn down both nature and man-made structures alike.

The air grew thicker with the scent of damp earth as they neared the entrance. The path leading to it was scarcely visible, swallowed by an overgrowth of weeds and tangled vines. A heavy mist clung to the ground, curling around their ankles like fingers grasping for something long lost. The trees nearby stood like silent sentinels, their gnarled branches stretching out, reaching for the sky with an eerie quietness.

They finally arrived at the entrance of the mine, a once-imposing structure now reduced to little more than a decaying relic of the past. The wooden beams that framed the mouth of the mine had long since been consumed by rot and neglect, sagging under the weight of time. The stone walls, now cracked and crumbling in places, seemed to breathe a sigh of despair. It was as if the mine itself had given up, retreating into the earth, hidden from the world.

Above the entrance, hanging crookedly on rusted chains, was a faded sign. The metal was warped from years of exposure to the elements, the letters barely legible, as though the words had been etched in a forgotten language. Only fragments could still be made out: Ashford Mining Co. The name seemed to echo through the silence, a shadow of its former glory.

Prex took a moment to stand still, his gaze fixed on the sign. The weight of history seemed to press against him, a quiet reminder of what had once been—and what had been lost. Slowly, he turned to her, his voice low. *"Ready?"*

She nodded, her expression unreadable, but there was something in her eyes—something that told him she was not merely ready; *she was waiting for something far more than the obvious. They both knew that whatever lay beyond the decaying entrance of the Ashford Mining Company would not be easy to face. But it was a path they had chosen, and it was one they would now walk together.*

"This is it," Prex muttered, his voice barely above a whisper, thick with a sense of finality.

Dea's gaze remained fixed on the looming entrance ahead, her brow furrowed in uncertainty as the darkness beyond seemed to swallow the light. She hesitated, the weight of the decision pressing on her chest. *"Do we have a plan?"* she asked, her voice betraying a tinge of apprehension, the quiet murmurs of the world around them amplifying the tension.

Prex turned toward her, his eyes gleaming with an intensity that matched the gravity of the moment. *"Stay close, stay quiet, and for the love of the gods, don't touch anything unless we absolutely have to,"* he instructed, his tone firm but edged with a quiet urgency.

He drew a small match from his pouch and struck it with a practiced flick of his thumb. The flame sputtered to life, casting a pale orange glow across the narrow tunnel entrance. The light flickered, dancing across the jagged walls as they stepped forward. Dea could feel the heat from the lantern's flame, but it did little to chase away the cold that settled in her bones. The air was heavy, thick with the weight of centuries, and the scent of old stone, damp earth, and something ancient lingered in her nostrils. It was the smell of a place forgotten, untouched by time but not by decay.

The tunnel yawned before them, its walls a maze of crumbling stone and exposed roots that crept like fingers along the edges. The air tasted stale, as if the passage had not known fresh breath for generations. Every step seemed to echo louder than the last, their movements distorting the silence in unnatural ways.

The ground beneath their boots was uneven, the earth soft in some places, hard and cracked in others. The wooden supports that lined the walls creaked under the weight of time, groaning as if protesting their intrusion. It was clear that the tunnel was old—older than anything Dea had ever encountered. She could almost hear the whispers of its past, a history too long buried to be unearthed without consequence.

Prex led the way, the lantern's light casting long, trembling shadows along the walls. Dea followed closely, her every sense heightened, alert to any sound that might betray danger lurking in the dark. The further they descended, the colder it grew, and the closer she came to the feeling that something—something that had waited patiently for centuries—was watching them.

As they moved deeper, the tunnel twisted and bent, as if the very earth was trying to thwart their progress. The walls seemed to close in on them, and Dea's breathing became shallow, her thoughts lost in the eerie stillness. There was no turning back now. Whatever lay ahead would reveal itself in time. And she wasn't sure whether she was ready to face it.

As they ventured deeper into the cavernous tunnel, the faint sound of water dripping echoed eerily off the jagged stone walls. Each droplet splashed onto the cold, hard earth below, creating a rhythmic pattern that reverberated throughout the damp air. Dea's grip tightened instinctively around the flashlight, her fingers tingling as her pulse quickened with every cautious step. The beam of light flickered slightly, casting fleeting shadows that danced and warped across the uneven stone floor. The further they walked, the more the walls seemed to close in, the oppressive darkness pressing against them like a living, breathing entity. The air was thick with moisture, carrying the scent of wet earth and decay, making every inhale feel like a struggle.

Suddenly, Prex halted, raising a hand in a silent command. His body tensed, every muscle locked in place, as his sharp eyes scanned the area ahead with the intensity of a predator sensing danger.

"Wait," he murmured, his voice barely above a whisper, as though the sound itself might disturb the stillness around them.

Dea froze in place, her heart pounding in her chest, breath caught in her throat. She instinctively tightened her grip on the flashlight, its weak beam now trembling in her hand. *"What is it?"* she asked, her voice strained with both fear and curiosity.

Prex's eyes flickered downward, and his finger pointed to the ground. There, in the dust-covered earth, were the unmistakable imprints of footprints. They were fresh—disturbed just moments ago, their edges still sharp and clearly visible in the otherwise untouched surface. The marks seemed to lead deeper into the tunnel, disappearing into the thickening shadows beyond.

A cold shiver ran down Dea's spine. *"Someone's been here recently,"* she said, her voice barely audible. Her mind raced, images of danger flashing before her eyes. *Who else could be down here?*

Prex squatted down, examining the tracks more closely, his face hardening. *"We're not alone,"* he said, his tone dark and grave, his voice a hushed whisper that seemed to carry the weight of a thousand unspoken fears. *"These aren't just any footprints... Someone's been here, and they might still be nearby."*

Dea swallowed, the taste of anxiety rising in her throat. The realization settled heavily over her, the tension in the air thickening. The shadows, once mere illusions, now seemed to pulse with a quiet menace. The silence felt almost suffocating, as though the very walls were holding their breath, waiting.

A distant sound echoed through the oppressive silence of the mine, faint yet distinct—a rhythmic tapping, like metal striking against stone, reverberating through the cold air. The sound was steady, almost deliberate, as though the creator of it had all the time in the world to complete their work. It seemed to come from deep within the shadows of the tunnel, drawing Prex's attention immediately. He instinctively motioned for Dea to stay behind him, his hand resting on the hilt of his blade as a precaution, their every step muffled by the damp earth beneath them.

With cautious precision, they advanced, their movements slow and calculated, aware that the mine's ancient corridors held dangers unknown. The walls, slick with moisture and dust, seemed to close in around them as they made their way further into the heart of the mine. The sound grew louder, the rhythmic tap-tap-tapping like a heartbeat pulsing in the dark.

The tunnel gradually widened, and soon they found themselves at the edge of a cavern. It was vast, its ceilings lost to shadows, yet the walls of the space glimmered faintly with the shimmer of mineral deposits, reflecting the dim light that filtered in from somewhere far above. It was a strange, almost otherworldly glow, casting eerie reflections on the jagged stone surfaces.

In the center of the cavern, standing tall against the rough stone backdrop, was a solitary figure. They were completely still, their back to Prex and Dea, focused entirely on their task. The rhythmic tapping of a chisel against rock echoed through the cavern, sending small flakes of stone flying into the air with each precise strike. The figure was carving deep into the rock face before them, their hands moving with practiced, fluid motions. The sound was now unmistakably clear, each tap ringing out with sharp precision, as though the figure was not simply working, but creating something of great significance.

Prex's gaze remained fixed on the figure, a mixture of curiosity and wariness swirling in his chest. There was an almost unnatural stillness about the scene, the quiet of the cavern amplifying the tension that hung in the air. He glanced back at Dea, whose expression remained unreadable, but he could feel her presence close behind him, waiting for his lead.

The figure, unaware of their arrival, continued their task, seemingly oblivious to the world beyond the walls of the cavern. The sound of the chisel against the stone now felt almost like a command, pulling them further into the depths of the mine, urging them to discover whatever it was that had driven this mysterious figure to work in such isolation.

"Who's there?" Prex demanded, his voice sharp, slicing through the eerie silence that hung thick in the air. His words felt like an intrusion into a space that had long forgotten the presence of life. The figure froze, their body rigid, the chisel slipping from their grasp and clattering to the ground with an unnerving, metallic clang. The sound reverberated against the cold, damp walls of the cavern, the echo stretching long after the noise had ceased. Slowly, deliberately, the figure turned, their movements slow as if every inch of them were weighed down by something unseen. A dark hood obscured their face, casting it into shadow, but a faint gleam from beneath it caught the dim lantern light, revealing the sharp outline of a blade—a knife—held in a grip that spoke of practiced precision.

As the figure stepped forward, the lantern flickered, its light dancing across the rough stone of the cavern floor. The figure's presence seemed to absorb the light, their form barely visible except for the glinting edge of the weapon, which seemed almost to shimmer with a sinister promise of violence.

"Leave," the figure rasped, their voice low and guttural, as if it had been dragged from the depths of a dark well. The words were distorted, hollow, their tone carrying the weight of something far older than the figure itself. The voice didn't belong to any living person—there was an unnatural, otherworldly quality to it, like the remnants of a soul long forsaken. *"You don't belong here,"* the figure continued, the command hanging in the air like a tangible force, oppressive and cold.

Prex remained unmoving, his eyes narrowing as he gripped the revolver tighter in his hand, the cold steel a comforting weight. His stance was firm, unwavering, a soldier trained in the art of confrontation. *"We're not leaving without answers,"* he declared, his voice steady but resolute, refusing to be intimidated. His finger rested lightly on the trigger, though his instincts told him to wait, to listen.

The figure tilted its head slightly, the hooded face still hidden, but the sound of a laugh—cold, hollow, and unsettling—broke the silence. It reverberated off the walls, a sound so devoid of warmth that it sent a shiver crawling up Prex's spine. The laughter stretched, morphing into something almost mocking, like the echo of someone who had long since lost their humanity.

"Answers?" The figure repeated, its tone laced with cruel amusement. *"You think you'll find answers here?"* The laugh cut off abruptly, leaving an unnatural stillness in its wake. *"You won't find them here,"* it murmured, the words seeping into the cavern like poison. *"Only death."*

The knife in the figure's hand gleamed again in the dim light, and as it stepped closer, the very air seemed to grow heavier, thick with the promise of danger. Prex's heart beat a little faster, but his grip on the revolver remained steady. He was trained for moments like this, but something about the figure, the utter detachment in their voice, made his blood run colder than it had any right to.

"Who are you?" Prex asked, his voice breaking the stillness once more, but this time tinged with an urgency that betrayed his calm exterior. He needed to know what they were dealing with—this wasn't just some errant soul lost in the depths of the cavern.

The figure didn't answer. Instead, they stepped forward again, closing the distance between them, the gleam of the blade growing brighter. Prex's grip tightened on the revolver, but he didn't fire. Not yet. His eyes never left the figure, watching, waiting.

Before Prex could respond, a shadowed figure, cloaked in darkness, abruptly hurled something toward the ground with a swift, calculated motion. A deafening clang echoed in the cavern as the object hit the floor. Almost instantly, thick, pungent smoke erupted into the air, swirling violently and engulfing the entire space. The acrid fumes stung the air, and Dea found herself choking on the dense cloud, her breath ragged and labored as she desperately clung to Prex's arm, her fingers trembling with fear. She tried to blink through the haze, but her eyes burned with the sting of the toxic air, her heart pounding in her chest. She could barely make out the outlines of Prex's form, his arm around her waist, but his face was obscured by the smoke. Panic gripped her chest as she felt the disorienting weight of the darkness close in around them, the cavern suddenly feeling endless, as if they were lost in a suffocating void.

Minutes passed in the haze, though it felt like hours. The thick smoke that surrounded them refused to dissipate, and Dea felt her knees weaken beneath her. Just as she thought she might collapse, the oppressive cloud began to lift. The air, though still heavy, slowly cleared, and Dea's vision began to return, though she still squinted in the dim light.

But when the smoke finally settled, the figure was gone. Not a trace remained of the cloaked form that had appeared so suddenly before them. In its place, however, was something far more unsettling. On the rock face directly in front of them, carved into the cold, jagged stone, was a symbol—one they both recognized instantly.

It was the same grotesque design they had seen before: a circle with a jagged line running through it. The crude carving seemed almost alive in the flickering light, as though it had been etched there only moments ago. Dea's breath hitched as she gazed at it, a wave of unease washing over her.

Prex stood motionless, his sharp eyes fixed on the symbol. His jaw clenched as he studied it, the lines of his face hardening with anger. *"They're toying with us,"* he muttered, the frustration clear in his voice. His tone was low, edged with a dangerous calm that sent a chill through Dea's spine.

Dea's heart raced as she tried to steady herself, her voice trembling with uncertainty. *"What do we do now?"*

Prex's grip tightened on her arm, and without a word, he reached for the lantern. In one swift motion, he extinguished the flame, plunging them into total darkness. The cavern around them seemed to pulse with an eerie stillness, the silence deafening after the earlier chaos.

"We keep going," Prex said, his voice unwavering. *"They want*

us scared. They think this will break us. Let's show them we're not afraid."

His words, though spoken with determination, held a steely resolve that Dea could feel resonating within her. But as the weight of the darkness pressed in, she couldn't shake the feeling that whatever they were facing was much more dangerous than they had imagined. They had been marked, and the shadowed figure was just the beginning of something far more sinister lurking within the depths of the cavern.

The Key in the Darkness

The mine's suffocating darkness stretched endlessly, swallowing every inch of the passage with its oppressive grip. It seemed as though the shadows themselves clung to the walls, refusing to relinquish their hold. Yet, in the far distance, a faint glimmer of light pierced the gloom, a soft, ethereal glow that seemed to beckon them forward. Prex and Dea moved cautiously, their every step tentative, mindful of the treacherous ground beneath them. Their feet disturbed the thick blanket of dust that had settled over the years, a heavy layer that muffled their movements and lent an eerie stillness to the atmosphere.

The deeper they ventured, the more the temperature plummeted, the chill seeping into their bones with a cruel persistence. Each breath they took manifested as a visible puff of mist, a fleeting wisp that vanished almost as soon as it appeared. The air felt dense, as though it had been trapped within the mine's narrow corridors for centuries, thick with the weight of time and neglect. The silence that enveloped them was absolute, a suffocating stillness that seemed to press in on their ears, making each tiny sound feel amplified and unnatural. The occasional drip of water from the high, damp ceilings was the only interruption, its rhythmic plink-plonk echoing through the void like the ticking of an ancient clock, marking time in this forgotten place.

With every step, the tension in the air seemed to grow, an unspoken awareness that something lay just beyond the horizon of that fragile light. Neither Prex nor Dea dared to speak, their senses fully attuned to the faintest sound or movement, aware that the very nature of the mine seemed to whisper of secrets long buried and forgotten.

"What do you think that symbol means?" Dea whispered, her voice so soft it barely cut through the stillness of the night. Her wide eyes were locked on the mysterious emblem etched into the stone, the faint glow of moonlight casting an eerie pallor over its jagged edges.

Prex didn't immediately respond. His gaze remained fixed ahead, as though the symbol itself was the key to something far greater. His mind seemed distant, pondering the implications. After a long pause, he finally spoke, his voice low and steady, carrying a weight that suggested he already knew more than he was willing to share. *"It's not just a warning,"* he murmured, eyes narrowing in thought. *"It's a marker. A signal. Someone... someone wants us to follow."*

Dea frowned, the confusion on her face deepening. She stepped closer to the stone, trying to make sense of the swirling design. *"Follow to what?"* Her words trembled with uncertainty, but there was a spark of curiosity beneath her hesitation.

Prex's expression remained unreadable, his features hardened by years of experience with the unknown. He glanced back at her, his dark eyes flickering with a knowing intensity. *"That's exactly why we're here,"* he said, the words almost like a promise—quiet, but filled with a sense of purpose. *"To find out."*

Dea stared at the symbol once more, her mind racing. There was a certain familiarity in its intricate lines, but she couldn't place it. She wanted to ask more, to pry deeper, but something in Prex's tone told her that the answers wouldn't come so easily. This wasn't the first time they'd been led by a trail of cryptic signs, but this one felt different—more deliberate, more dangerous.

"Do you think it's a trap?" she asked, her voice barely above a whisper, fear creeping into her chest.

Prex's jaw tightened, and for a moment, the silence between them stretched thin. He finally exhaled a breath, his gaze shifting once more to the horizon. *"I think,"* he said slowly, each word deliberate, *"that it's more than that. Someone's waiting. And if we don't follow... we might miss our only chance."*

The weight of his words hung in the air, thick with the gravity of their situation. Dea looked back at the symbol, now realizing it was more than just an ancient relic—it was a call to action, a beckoning to a path that could lead them into the unknown. And despite the uncertainty swirling around them, despite the dangers that loomed, she knew they had no choice but to follow. The tunnel gradually expanded, opening into another cavern far larger than the last.

The air felt cooler here, thick with the scent of damp earth and ancient stone. The cavern's high ceiling stretched above like a shadowy void, and the uneven floor was scattered with jagged rocks, giving the room an unwelcoming, eerie aura. The walls, however, were a testament to the craftsmanship of a forgotten age. Massive shelves had been carved directly into the rock, their edges chipped and weathered by time, yet still bearing the weight of a collection of long-forgotten relics.

Old tools, their iron surfaces rusted and pitted with age, lay alongside broken lanterns whose glass was cracked but still faintly reflected the dim light from their torches. A jumble of scattered papers, some yellowed with age, others torn and brittle, littered the shelves like forgotten memories. The symbols and words scribbled upon them were almost indecipherable, as though time itself had conspired to erase the knowledge they once held.

At the heart of the cavern, a pedestal stood, its stone surface worn smooth by the passage of time. Intricate patterns had been painstakingly etched into the stone, swirling designs that seemed to pulse with an almost imperceptible energy. It was as though the very pedestal was alive, breathing with the weight of centuries, a silent sentinel guarding whatever secret lay within. Atop the pedestal rested a small, weathered box, its edges cracked and its surface marred by the years. The box was unlike anything Dea had ever seen, faintly gleaming under the torchlight despite its apparent age and neglect.

Dea approached the pedestal cautiously, her senses alert to every creak and whisper of the cavern. Her heart raced as her eyes darted around the room, scanning the shadows for any sign of movement or hidden threats. She could almost feel the weight of centuries pressing down on her, as if the very air in the room was thick with the presence of those who had come before.

"Do you think this is it?" she asked, her voice barely above a whisper, as though speaking too loudly might disturb the fragile silence of the cavern.

Prex, his jaw set with grim determination, nodded slowly. His hand hovered near his revolver, ready to draw at the slightest provocation. *"Looks like it,"* he murmured, his gaze never straying from the pedestal. *"But we can't afford to take any chances. Be careful."*

The words hung in the air like a warning, and Dea's fingers brushed lightly against the hilt of the dagger at her side. The sense of danger was palpable, as though the cavern itself was a trap, and they were but pawns in a game that had been set in motion long before their arrival. She took another step forward, her boots making barely a sound against the stone floor, and for a brief moment, all was still.

The box, the pedestal, the shelves of forgotten relics—everything seemed to pulse with a quiet, ancient power, as if the cavern had been waiting for them all along.

She reached out slowly, her fingers grazing the surface of the box with a tentative touch. The moment her skin made contact, a shiver ran through her. The box was colder than she had anticipated, a biting chill that seemed to seep deep into her bones, making her instincts flare with unease. It was as if the object itself exuded a strange energy, its icy presence causing her breath to momentarily catch in her throat. The carved symbols on the pedestal that held the box were intricate, their lines twisting and curling in such a way that they appeared to shift with every passing second. In the low, flickering light, the patterns seemed to dance—elusive, almost alive—pulling her gaze in with an almost magnetic force. The more she stared, the harder it became to look away, the patterns becoming deeper and more intricate, like a maze she couldn't escape.

"Dea," Prex's voice was sharp, slicing through the quiet tension that had settled in the air. His words were a firm command, as if he had recognized the subtle danger lurking within her entranced state. *"Don't lose focus."*

His voice grounded her, pulling her back from the spiraling depths of the strange carvings. She blinked rapidly, as though waking from a trance, her heart racing slightly as the oppressive weight of the room began to settle in again. She nodded silently, regaining control of her breath and steadying herself before carefully lifting the box from its pedestal.

It was lighter than she had imagined—surprisingly so—almost too light for its size, its hollow presence sending a fresh wave of suspicion coursing through her. She studied the rusted latch that kept it shut, its metal edges worn and tarnished by years of neglect. It seemed fragile, almost as if it might crumble under the pressure of a simple touch.

"Should we open it?" Her voice was barely above a whisper, the question hanging between them, heavy with the weight of uncertainty. There was a sharp pull in her gut, an instinct telling her that opening the box could lead them down a path they wouldn't be able to return from.

Prex gave a curt shake of his head, his eyes scanning the room with caution. *"Not here,"* he said, his voice laced with quiet urgency. *"We need to get out of this place first. It's not safe to do it now."* His gaze shifted back to her, the tension in his face clear. *"Let's move."*

Reluctantly, Dea allowed the box to fall back into her hands, the cool weight of it now a constant reminder of the unknown it contained. She could feel the eyes of the carvings on the pedestal still watching her, and with a last look around, she turned, following Prex out of the room. The air felt thicker now, as though something had shifted, and she couldn't shake the feeling that the box was not the only thing in that room waiting to be opened. As they turned to leave, a low rumble reverberated through the cavern, an ominous warning of the impending disaster. The ground beneath their feet quaked violently, sending a shower of dust and loose rocks tumbling down from the jagged ceiling above. The air grew thick with the stench of damp earth and the acrid scent of stone grinding against stone. Prex's eyes widened in alarm, and without a second thought, he grasped Dea's arm with a fierce urgency, yanking her toward the narrow tunnel they had just emerged from. His voice was raw, filled with panic. *"Move! Now!"*

They sprinted through the darkness, their boots pounding the uneven ground as the rumbling behind them intensified, growing into a thunderous roar that seemed to shake the very bones of the earth. The walls of the cavern seemed to warp and shift, closing in around them as if the mountain itself was alive and determined to swallow them whole. The oppressive darkness pressed down upon them like a physical force, suffocating and unyielding. Their breaths came in ragged gasps, the echo of their hurried steps lost in the chaos of the earth's fury.

The sound of falling rocks echoed through the tunnel, louder now, and they dared not look back. Every step they took seemed to lead them deeper into the heart of the storm, the tunnel narrowing, the air thickening with each passing second. Dea's heart raced in her chest, each beat a frantic reminder of the peril they were in. Her legs burned from the exertion, but she pushed herself harder, desperate to escape the crushing grip of the mountain.

Just as they neared the entrance, a deafening crash reverberated through the ground, a sound so powerful it seemed to tear through the very fabric of reality itself. The tunnel shook violently, and a cloud of dust erupted from the walls, choking them with its weight. They stumbled, disoriented, their feet slipping on the loose stones. Dea's vision blurred as the dust stung her eyes, but she forced herself forward, the cold rush of air from the open entrance urging her on.

With a final, frantic push, they burst out into the open, the daylight blinding them after the suffocating darkness of the cave. They tumbled to the ground, gasping for breath, their lungs burning with the effort. The echoes of the crash still reverberated in their bones as they lay on the cool earth, the distant rumble of the collapsing cavern a reminder of how close they had come to being swallowed by the very mountain they had ventured into.

Dea held the box close to her chest, her fingers trembling slightly as her heart thundered in her chest. The adrenaline coursing through her veins made everything feel sharper, more urgent. *"What the hell was that?"* she breathed out, her voice a mixture of disbelief and fear.

Prex, ever the composed one, surveyed the area, his revolver gripped firmly in his hand. His sharp eyes scanned the darkened treeline, seeking any sign of movement. *"Someone didn't want us taking this,"* he said, his tone cold, betraying no hint of surprise.

Before Dea could gather her thoughts, a voice sliced through the thick silence like a knife. *"You should've left it where it was."* The voice was low, gravelly, yet it carried an unmistakable weight of authority.

They both stiffened, turning in unison toward the source. From the shadows emerged a figure, their presence looming like an ominous storm cloud. The figure's face was hidden beneath the shadow of a wide-brimmed hat, casting an air of mystery and danger. A glint of metal caught the light — unmistakable. A weapon.

"Who are you?" Prex demanded, his voice sharper now, stepping protectively in front of Dea. His revolver was aimed, unwavering.

The figure chuckled softly, a chilling sound that seemed to reverberate in the cool night air. It was the kind of laugh that sent a shiver down your spine, as though they were fully aware of the power they wielded. *"Just someone who knows what you've gotten yourselves into."*

Prex didn't flinch, his hand tightening on the grip of his revolver. *"If you know so much, start talking,"* he said, his voice cold, a challenge.

The figure tilted their head slightly, as though considering Prex's demand. The pause stretched, thick with tension, before the figure spoke again. *"That box isn't just some relic. It's a key. And you're not the only ones hunting for what it unlocks."*

Dea's grip tightened around the box, her pulse quickening. The weight of the words settled heavily in her chest. *"Why does it matter to you?"* she asked, her voice strained but laced with a growing sense of urgency.

The figure's lips curled into something that might have been a smile — or a smirk. *"It matters to everyone,"* they replied, their voice carrying a foreboding edge. *"But some secrets are better left buried."*

In the blink of an eye, the figure's posture shifted, their hand jerking up, raising the weapon. Prex was faster. The sound of the gunshot cracked through the night like thunder, the bullet speeding toward the figure, forcing them to dive for cover with surprising agility.

"Run!" Prex shouted, his voice sharp and commanding. He didn't wait for Dea's reaction. Grabbing her hand with a force that didn't leave room for hesitation, he yanked her along as they sprinted toward the car.

The air was filled with the staccato rhythm of gunfire and shouted commands, the chaos of the moment surging around them. Every step they took felt heavier, laden with the significance of the box Dea clutched so tightly in her hands. It had become more than just an object — it had become a beacon for violence, a signal that some truths, some powers, were worth killing for.

Dea's breath came in sharp gasps as they reached the car, her mind still reeling. She didn't dare glance back, but the distant sounds of pursuit made her blood run cold. As the engine roared to life, Prex's grip on the wheel was unshakable, his jaw clenched in determination.

They shot off into the night, the headlights cutting through the darkness, but Dea's eyes were fixed on the rearview mirror. The mine, now a mere silhouette against the swirling dust and shadow, seemed to recede into the distance. Yet the feeling of being watched, hunted, lingered.

"What do we do now?" Dea's voice was barely more than a whisper, but the question felt as heavy as the box in her hands.

Prex didn't look at her, his eyes steely and focused on the road ahead. His knuckles were white around the steering wheel. *"We find out what this key opens,"* he said, his voice low, thick with determination. *"And we stay alive long enough to do it."*

Dea's stomach tightened. The journey ahead was uncertain, fraught with peril, but one thing was clear: *whatever lay ahead, the stakes had just become far higher than either of them could have imagined.*

Shadows of Eldridge Falls

The road stretched endlessly before them, an unyielding ribbon of cracked asphalt disappearing into the dark abyss of the night. It seemed almost alive, weaving its way through a dense forest that loomed ominously on either side, its ancient trees standing as silent sentinels under a shroud of shadows. The car's headlights carved twin beams through the oppressive darkness, their light catching fleeting glimpses of the woods. Branches twisted like skeletal fingers, their shapes shifting eerily, as if the forest itself were breathing, alive with an unseen presence. The occasional rustle of leaves, carried by a cold wind, hinted at creatures lurking just out of sight, adding to the uneasy stillness of their surroundings.

Prex's hands clamped onto the steering wheel with a force that turned his knuckles white. The strain etched on his face mirrored the tension radiating from his body. His jaw was locked in a grim set, the weight of unspoken thoughts pressing heavily on his mind. The rhythmic hum of the tires on the uneven road was the only sound, a monotonous melody that barely masked the thundering of his heartbeat. His eyes darted to the rearview mirror now and then, scanning the empty road behind them, his unease growing with each passing mile.

Beside him, Dea sat with rigid shoulders, her arms wrapped protectively around a weathered wooden box. Its surface was scarred with age, the grain darkened with the patina of years gone by. Her fingers traced its edges absentmindedly, as though seeking comfort from its solid presence. Yet the box offered no solace—only a heavy, foreboding mystery that weighed on her chest like a stone. Her mind was a tempest of questions and fears, each one more disconcerting than the last.

What secrets did the box hold? Why did it feel as though its contents pulsed faintly beneath her touch, like a heartbeat echoing through the wood? Dea's gaze flicked to Prex, searching for reassurance, but his expression remained impenetrable. A cold knot of dread twisted in her stomach as she shifted her focus back to the road ahead, watching as the headlights revealed more of the shadowed path, one ominous stretch at a time.

The air inside the car was thick with tension, an invisible force that seemed to grow heavier with each passing moment. It mingled with the faint smell of damp earth and the sharp metallic tang of old leather from the car's worn seats. Every so often, a shadow would dart across the edges of the headlights' beam, vanishing into the darkness before either of them could fully register it. The forest, with its gnarled trees and restless whispers, felt less like a bystander and more like an active participant in their journey—a silent observer biding its time.

Dea tightened her grip on the box, her nails digging into the worn surface as though holding onto it could anchor her spiraling thoughts. She longed to break the silence, to voice her growing fears, but the words felt lodged in her throat, too fragile to shatter the uneasy quiet. Meanwhile, Prex's gaze remained locked on the road, his lips pressed into a thin line, the only sign of his inner turmoil the occasional twitch of his fingers on the wheel.

They were headed somewhere—nowhere? The destination no longer seemed to matter as much as the journey itself, a haunting passage through a world that felt both familiar and foreign, like a half-remembered dream turned nightmare. And yet, they pressed on, the car's engine a low, steady growl against the oppressive night, as if challenging the darkness to reveal its secrets.

In the silence, the road seemed to stretch even longer, an unending liminal space between the safety of the known and the danger of the unknown.

"Where are we even going?" Dea's voice sliced through the heavy silence that had settled between them like an unwelcome guest. Her tone carried a mix of frustration and exhaustion, the weight of their predicament etched across her face.

Prex didn't look at her, his gaze fixed unwaveringly on the road ahead. *"Somewhere safe,"* he replied, his voice low but steady, though the weariness beneath his words was hard to miss. *"For now, that's all that matters."*

Dea let out a sharp, humorless laugh, shaking her head. *"Safe?"* she echoed, her disbelief thick in the confined space of the car. *"Safe doesn't exist anymore, Prex. Not with that thing."* She nodded toward the box resting heavily between them, its dark, enigmatic presence a silent reminder of everything that had gone wrong.

Prex's grip tightened on the steering wheel, his knuckles whitening as he spared her a glance. For a fleeting moment, his hardened expression softened, revealing the faintest trace of vulnerability. *"We'll figure this out, Dea,"* he said, his voice dropping just enough to sound almost tender. *"One step at a time. We have to."*

But his reassurance felt as insubstantial as smoke to Dea, dissipating before it could truly reach her. She sighed, her eyes drawn once again to the box. Its surface was carved with intricate patterns that seemed to defy explanation. The designs writhed in subtle, almost imperceptible movements, like shadows playing tricks on the mind—or perhaps something far more sinister.

Her fingers, as if moved by some unseen force, brushed against the carvings. The sensation was electric, a mix of cold dread and strange allure that sent a shiver coursing through her spine. She snatched her hand back instinctively, her pulse quickening.

"What is this thing, Prex?" she whispered, her voice trembling

despite her attempt to steady it. *"Why does it feel... alive?"*

Prex didn't answer right away, the question lingering in the air like an unspoken accusation. Instead, he pressed harder on the accelerator, the engine's growl filling the uneasy void between them. It wasn't until the road curved into the shadowy embrace of a dense forest that he finally spoke, his voice barely audible over the hum of the car.

"It doesn't matter what it is," he said, his jaw tightening. *"All that matters is keeping it away from them. As long as we have it, we're the ones in control."*

Dea's eyes narrowed, her fear momentarily eclipsed by anger. *"Control?"* she snapped, her voice rising. *"This thing is controlling us, Prex. Look at us—running, hiding, not knowing where to go or what to do. How is that control?"*

Prex didn't respond, his silence only fueling the growing tension. Dea leaned back in her seat, crossing her arms tightly over her chest as she stared out the window. The trees blurred into an indistinct wall of darkness, their towering silhouettes mirroring the oppressive weight pressing down on her.

The box, however, remained a steady presence. It sat there, unassuming yet foreboding, as though it were waiting—for what, neither of them could say.

Ahead, a sign materialized from the thick shroud of darkness, its grim presence amplified by the surrounding desolation. The weather-beaten board creaked softly in the night breeze, the faded words barely legible under the weak glow of the headlights: "Welcome to Eldridge Falls." Once a welcoming marker, it now stood as a forlorn relic of a better time, leaning perilously as if burdened by years of neglect and abandonment.

Prex instinctively eased off the accelerator, allowing the car to slow as they crossed into the town. The oppressive silence was unsettling, a stillness that seemed almost alive, pressing in on them like a heavy fog. The streets stretched out ahead, eerily deserted, their emptiness punctuated by the occasional whisper of wind carrying the faint rattle of loose debris. Shadows sprawled across the cracked pavement, distorted by the faint light of the few remaining streetlamps, their faint hum barely audible.

Dea leaned closer to the window, her eyes scanning the ghostly tableau before them. Most of the buildings lining the street were in various stages of decay—wooden shutters hanging askew, windows shattered like jagged teeth, and facades crumbling under the weight of time. The air carried a faint tang of mildew and rust, mingled with the unmistakable scent of damp earth.

"This place..." Dea's voice trailed off, her tone heavy with unease. *"It looks completely abandoned."*

"Not entirely," Prex countered, his gaze fixed ahead. He gestured toward the far end of the street, where a faint, flickering light broke the monotony of darkness. It emanated from a small diner, the only beacon of life amidst the desolation. The neon sign above its door struggled valiantly to stay lit, sputtering irregularly. The flickering letters spelled out "Maggie's," though some of the bulbs had long since burned out, leaving the name fractured and uneven.

The diner's glow cast a feeble halo over the cracked asphalt and nearby buildings, its light doing little to dispel the gloom. Yet it was enough to spark a flicker of hope—or perhaps apprehension—in the otherwise oppressive night.

Prex's grip on the steering wheel tightened as he maneuvered the car toward the solitary refuge. *"We can stop there,"* he said, his voice calm but tinged with caution. *"See if anyone's around. Maybe get some answers about this place."*

Dea nodded, though her posture remained stiff. Her fingers drummed against her thigh, a rhythmic, nervous tick that betrayed her unease. Outside, the world seemed to grow darker still, the shadows thickening as if the town itself sought to keep its secrets buried. The faint hum of the car's engine felt like an intrusion, a reminder that they were outsiders in a place that had seemingly forgotten the passage of time.

As they neared the diner, its worn exterior came into clearer focus. The once-bright paint was now faded and peeling, revealing layers of neglect. A solitary bulb above the entrance buzzed faintly, casting a sickly yellow light that barely reached the edge of the cracked sidewalk. Despite its dilapidated state, the diner exuded a strange allure—part sanctuary, part trap.

Prex parked the car just outside, the tires crunching softly against loose gravel. For a moment, neither of them moved, their eyes fixed on the dimly lit windows. Inside, faint shadows shifted, suggesting the presence of someone—or something—waiting beyond the glass.

ea hesitated, her fingers tightening slightly on the strap of her bag. *"And what if it's a trap?"* she asked, her voice low but edged with tension.

Prex's lips curved into a faint, almost imperceptible smile that hinted at a mix of confidence and recklessness. *"Then we spring it,"* he replied, his tone calm and deliberate, as if the very possibility of danger excited rather than deterred him.

They pulled the car off the road, parking under the cover of shadow a short distance from the diner. The soft hum of the engine faded into silence as Prex turned the key, leaving them with only the cool night air and the faint rustle of nearby trees. Stepping out, Dea shivered slightly, whether from the cold or the anticipation she wasn't sure. The air was thick with an eerie stillness, the kind that seemed to press down on them, amplifying every sound. The crunch of gravel under their boots echoed unnaturally loud as they moved toward the building, each step deliberate and cautious.

The diner loomed ahead, its worn exterior bathed in the dim glow of a single flickering neon sign. The red letters spelling out *"Open"* buzzed faintly, casting an unsteady light that danced across the cracked asphalt of the parking lot. Dea's eyes darted around, scanning the windows and the surrounding shadows for any sign of movement. Her instincts screamed at her to turn back, to suggest a more calculated approach, but she knew better than to voice it. Prex thrived on the edge of uncertainty.

He walked slightly ahead, his posture relaxed but with an unmistakable tension coiled beneath the surface. One hand hovered close to the worn leather holster strapped to his side, his fingers brushing the handle of his revolver. The subtle motion was enough to assure Dea that he was ready for anything. His other hand pushed the diner's door open, the hinges creaking loudly in the oppressive quiet.

The diner was a time capsule, a living remnant of a long-forgotten era. Its black-and-white checkered floors gleamed faintly under the soft hum of flickering fluorescent lights, each tile seeming to whisper stories of the countless footsteps that had crossed them over the years. The booths, lined with crimson vinyl, showed signs of wear — small cracks and creases that spoke of decades of conversations, laughter, and perhaps the occasional tear. Along one wall stood a jukebox, its chrome frame dulled by age, standing as a silent witness to a past when it had likely been the heart of the diner, belting out rock-and-roll hits and soulful ballads. Now, it looked more like an ornamental relic, long untouched and forgotten.

Behind the counter, a lone figure moved with an air of quiet efficiency. She was an older woman, her silver hair tied tightly into a neat bun that suggested both practicality and a sense of pride. Her hands were weathered, the kind of hands that had known years of hard work, as she meticulously wiped a glass with a faded, threadbare rag. Her sharp, observant eyes flicked toward the door as it swung open, catching the faint chime of a bell overhead. Her gaze, as sharp as a blade honed by time, settled on them with a mixture of curiosity and suspicion.

"Kitchen's closed," she announced, her tone brisk and carrying the faintest trace of a Southern drawl. Her voice was low, but there was an edge to it, a quiet firmness that left little room for negotiation.

"We're not here for food," Prex replied, his voice steady and unflinching as he stepped forward. His words seemed to hang in the air for a moment, as though testing the tension of the room. *"Just information."*

Her eyes narrowed ever so slightly as she studied him, her scrutiny as piercing as it was silent. Then, her gaze shifted to Dea, or more specifically, to the box she held tightly in her arms. The change in her expression was subtle but unmistakable. Her lips pressed into a thin line, and a shadow of something akin to unease flickered across her face before she quickly masked it with a hardened stare.

"You should leave. Now." Her words were like a command, clipped and resolute, carrying the weight of someone who had seen more than she cared to share. There was no hesitation, no room for argument in her tone, as though she was fully aware of what they sought and was equally certain she wanted no part in it.

Prex's jaw tightened, but he didn't move. The quiet defiance in his posture was clear, but he remained measured. The silence that followed her statement was heavy, charged with an unspoken tension, as though the diner itself was holding its breath, waiting to see what would happen next.

Dea stepped forward, her posture resolute and her voice unwavering. *"We can't just abandon this,"* she insisted, setting the intricately carved box down on the counter with a deliberate motion. The ornate patterns etched into the surface seemed to shimmer under the dim light, their eerie beauty demanding attention.

The woman behind the counter recoiled visibly, her eyes widening with a mix of dread and disbelief. She clutched at the pendant around her neck, a gesture of instinctive protection, and took a hesitant step backward. Crossing herself, she whispered, almost inaudibly, *"You... you brought that here?"*

"You recognize it," Prex interjected, his voice low and edged with a quiet intensity. His sharp gaze locked onto her as he leaned in slightly. *"Tell us what you know."*

The woman hesitated, her trembling hands betraying her mounting fear. She glanced between Dea, Prex, and the ominous box as if weighing the consequences of speaking against the perils of silence. Finally, her voice cracked through the oppressive stillness, a hoarse whisper heavy with foreboding. *"That box... it's cursed. It carries a darkness you can't comprehend. Wherever it goes, death and madness follow in its wake. You need to get rid of it—burn it, bury it, anything to sever its hold."*

Dea shook her head firmly, her expression unyielding. *"We can't do that,"* she countered, her eyes flickering with determination. *"Not until we understand what it unlocks. There's something inside, something important, and we need answers."*

The woman's face contorted with a mixture of fear and pity, her voice rising in desperation. *"You don't understand,"* she pleaded, her tone now laced with a near-hysterical urgency. *"Some doors are not meant to be opened. What lies beyond them is beyond mortal comprehension—chaos, despair, things no soul should ever confront."*

Prex exchanged a glance with Dea, his expression a mask of stoic resolve. *"We're not walking away from this,"* he said, his voice steady. *"Whatever's in there, we need to face it."*

The woman sighed deeply, her shoulders sagging as though the weight of the box's presence bore down on her. *"You've already made up your minds, haven't you?"* she muttered, her voice barely above a whisper. *"I hope you're ready for the consequences. Because once you open that box, there's no turning back."*

Her words hung in the air, heavy with ominous finality. The carved patterns on the box seemed to gleam brighter, as if mocking her warning, daring them to uncover its secrets.

Before anyone could press her for more information, the jukebox suddenly sputtered to life, its once-cheerful neon lights flickering erratically like a dying star. The familiar hum of the diner was drowned out by the haunting melody that spilled from the old machine. The tune was no ordinary song—it was jagged, discordant, and drenched in an eerie melancholy that seemed to worm its way into the bones of everyone present. The air grew heavy, suffocating almost, as if the melody itself carried an unspoken warning.

The woman's reaction was immediate and chilling. Her confident demeanor shattered like glass. Her olive complexion drained of color, leaving her as pale as a specter. Her wide eyes darted toward the jukebox, then to the darkened corners of the room, as if expecting shadows to come alive.

"They're here," she whispered, her voice barely audible over the escalating wail of the jukebox. The words hung in the air like

an accusation, drawing every eye to her trembling form.

Prex's hand moved instinctively to his revolver. He drew it with a sharp, practiced motion, the metallic click echoing through the tense silence. His steel-gray eyes narrowed as they scanned the room, searching for a threat he couldn't yet see. *"Who's here?"* he demanded, his voice low and steady, though there was an edge of urgency to it.

The woman didn't respond. Her lips parted as if to speak, but no words came. Instead, she took a step back, then another, her movements jerky and panicked. Her gaze flicked to the front door, then the back, calculating her escape. Without warning, she bolted toward the kitchen, her heels clattering against the linoleum floor. The door swung shut behind her, the small bell above it jingling faintly as she vanished into the night.

The jukebox's sinister tune grew louder, almost deafening now. The once-steady rhythm unraveled into a chaotic cacophony of notes that seemed to claw at the walls. The fluorescent lights above flickered in frantic staccato bursts, plunging the diner into an unsettling dance of light and shadow.

A chill swept through the room, an icy draft that made the patrons shiver despite the diner's usual warmth. Prex's grip on his revolver tightened as he shifted his stance, his senses on high alert. *"Everyone stay calm,"* he ordered, though his own unease was evident in the tension of his jaw.

The shadows seemed to deepen, stretching unnaturally toward the jukebox. It was as if the room itself was reacting to the melody, bending to some unseen force. For a fleeting moment, Prex thought he saw something—a flicker of movement, dark and amorphous, just beyond the edge of his vision. But when he turned, there was nothing there.

"Prex," Dea whispered, her voice quivering like a taut string about to snap. *"What's happening?"*

Her words were swallowed by the oppressive silence that had descended upon the room. Prex didn't answer, his jaw clenched so tightly that the tendons stood out sharply beneath his skin. Without a word, he grabbed her arm with a firm yet urgent grip, pulling her toward the door.

"We need to go. Now," he said, his voice low and clipped, each word laced with an urgency that sent a shiver down her spine.

The moment they stepped outside, the atmosphere shifted, an almost palpable heaviness settling over them. The air was thick, suffused with an unnatural energy that hummed just beyond the edge of hearing. Dea's breath hitched as her gaze darted around. The streetlights flickered erratically, casting fractured shadows that seemed to twist and ripple of their own accord.

Out of the corner of her eye, she caught glimpses of movement—shadows flitting across the edges of her vision. They were quick, too fluid and sinuous to be human, darting from one patch of darkness to the next. Her heart thundered in her chest as she clutched Prex's arm tighter.

"The car," Prex muttered, his voice barely audible over the sound of her ragged breathing. The vehicle was just a few steps away, yet the distance seemed to stretch endlessly, as though the ground itself conspired to slow them down. Each step felt labored, the weight of the air pressing down on them like an invisible hand.

They reached the car, and Prex yanked the door open, ushering Dea inside before sliding into the driver's seat. His hands trembled slightly as he turned the key in the ignition, the engine sputtering to life with a roar that seemed far too loud in the eerie stillness.

The headlights flickered on, piercing through the darkness, but what they revealed sent a chill racing down Dea's spine. Figures stood just beyond the reach of the light, their forms obscured by the shadows that clung to them like shrouds. They were unnaturally still, their faces hidden beneath an impenetrable veil of darkness. Yet their presence was undeniable, a foreboding weight that pressed down on the night.

Dea's eyes widened as she stared at them, her voice caught in her throat. *"What are they?"* she managed to whisper, barely audible.

Prex gripped the steering wheel tightly, his knuckles white.

"Don't look at them," he said, his voice sharper now, almost commanding. *"And whatever you do, don't open the door."*

"Hold on!" Prex growled, his voice sharp and laced with urgency, as he slammed his foot onto the gas pedal.

The engine roared like a caged beast set free, the tires screeching against the asphalt as the car surged forward. The blurred figures behind them disappeared into the thickening shadows of the night, but the ominous sensation of being pursued lingered heavily in the air. Dea's knuckles turned white as she clung tightly to the box resting on her lap, her heart thundering so loudly she feared it might drown out the car's engine.

The box felt heavier than its modest size suggested, as if the secrets it held carried a weight far beyond its physical form. This was no longer a simple chase for answers; they were now prey in a dangerous game, and the hunters were closing in.

"Where do we go now?" Dea's voice trembled, barely rising above a whisper. She didn't dare look back, her courage already fraying at the edges.

Prex's jaw tightened as his eyes darted to the rearview mirror, scanning the dark road behind them. The headlights of distant vehicles blurred into pinpricks of light, but the unease clung to him like a second skin. *"Somewhere they can't find us,"* he muttered, his tone grim and resolute. *"If such a place even exists anymore."*

The tension in the car was suffocating. The low hum of the engine and the faint rush of wind through the cracked window were the only sounds, amplifying the heavy silence between them. Prex's fingers tightened on the steering wheel, his knuckles mirroring Dea's grip on the box.

Dea finally glanced at him, her breath catching at the sight of his determined expression. The shadows playing across his face made him look more hardened, more desperate. *"Do you even have a plan?"* she asked, though the hope in her voice was thin.

Prex didn't respond immediately. His gaze flickered to the GPS screen, its dim light illuminating a snaking map of roads that felt endless. *"The plan is to stay alive,"* he said curtly. *"And to keep whatever's in that box out of their hands."*

A shiver coursed through Dea. She looked down at the mysterious object in her lap, the intricate carvings on its surface almost glowing in the faint light. She could feel its significance, a quiet hum that seemed to resonate with her pulse. Whatever this box held, it was worth risking lives for—both theirs and their pursuers'.

"They won't stop, will they?" she murmured, more to herself than to him.

Prex shook his head, his eyes never leaving the road. *"Not until they get what they want. Or we make sure they can't."*

The car sped onward into the night, the world outside a blur of darkness and fleeting shapes. Somewhere, out there in the shadows, danger followed relentlessly, and the only certainty was that their journey had just begun.

The Beacon and the Shadows

The tires of the car hummed steadily against the asphalt, the rhythmic sound almost hypnotic in its monotony. Yet, beneath that steady drone, an undercurrent of unease simmered, palpable in the tightness of Prex's jaw and the way his fingers gripped the steering wheel, knuckles white. The car's interior felt like a suffocating cocoon, the air thick with a tension that seemed to press down on every inch of space. Prex's eyes flickered nervously between the road ahead and the rearview mirror, as if expecting something—or someone—to appear out of the shadows. The fleeting glances were a subconscious habit, a futile attempt to dispel the gnawing sense of impending danger that clung to him like a second skin.

Dea sat beside him, her posture rigid and still, as though every part of her body had stilled in protest against the weight of the moment. Her eyes were fixed, not on the passing scenery, but on the box resting on her lap. The small, unassuming object appeared almost innocuous, but there was something about it now—something in the way it seemed to demand attention, even as it lay quietly in her grasp. The box, once a mere possession, had morphed into something much more. The unsettling events in the diner had somehow imbued it with a sense of foreboding, as if the air itself had grown heavier with the secrets it contained. Every bump in the road seemed to make the box feel more cumbersome, more burdensome, as if it were absorbing the fear and confusion that swirled around them both. The weight was no longer just physical; it had become metaphorical, a symbol of the choices they had made and the paths they were now forced to follow. Dea's fingers curled slightly around it, the edges of the cardboard digging into her skin as she sat motionless, lost in the swirling storm of thoughts that she couldn't quite voice.

Prex's jaw clenched again as he forced himself to focus on the road, but his mind kept straying back to the diner—the conversations, the looks exchanged, the words that were left unsaid but hung in the air like poison. He couldn't shake the feeling that they were being followed, that they were always a step behind something they couldn't quite understand. His foot pressed harder on the gas pedal, but even as the car picked up speed, the unease clung to him. The horizon in front seemed as distant and unreachable as ever, and the road beneath felt endless, winding, leading them further into a maze they might never escape.

"We can't keep running," Dea said finally, her voice slicing through the heavy, suffocating silence that had settled between them. Her eyes, wide and filled with a mixture of fear and resolve, fixed on the road ahead. *"We need to stop and figure out what they want. This can't go on."*

Prex's jaw tightened as he clenched the steering wheel with white-knuckled intensity.

"It's not that simple," he muttered, his voice low and edged with frustration. He glanced at her, the shadows of the night flickering across his face. *"Whatever's after us isn't human. You saw them... You felt them."*

Dea bit her lip, her hands gripping the seat beside her as if she could anchor herself to something more solid than the terror clawing at her insides.

"I did," she admitted, her voice trembling like a leaf in a gust of wind. The memory of those figures—silent, impossibly fast, their eyes glowing with a malevolent hunger—was enough to

send a cold shiver down her spine. She swallowed, forcing herself to stay calm. *"But we can't just keep driving, Prex. We're running in circles, getting deeper into the unknown. We need to make a decision, to come up with a plan."*

Prex's sharp exhale was full of impatience, his gaze flickering to the rearview mirror as if expecting those things to appear at any moment.

"Plans are useless if we don't know what we're dealing with," he said bitterly, shaking his head as though he were trying to shake off the weight of the reality they were facing.

"How do you plan for something you don't understand? We've seen their power, their speed... What are we supposed to do? We don't even know if there's a way to stop them."

Dea's thoughts were a chaotic whirlwind, each possibility more terrifying than the last. She tried to steady herself, focusing on the present, on the fact that they were still alive—for now.

"I know," she said softly, her gaze hardening. *"But running only gets us so far. Eventually, we'll run out of roads, out of options. We need to find out what they are, where they came from, what they want... and then maybe we'll have a chance."*

Prex fell silent, his fingers drumming anxiously on the steering wheel. The silence stretched between them, thick with uncertainty and fear, yet there was something else buried beneath it—something that urged them to keep moving forward, to not succumb to the paralyzing dread that threatened to take hold. Neither of them had answers, but there was no turning back now.

Dea whipped her head toward him, her gaze sharp and defiant, a fire blazing behind her eyes despite the fear that threatened to choke her words.

"Then let's find out," she said, her voice trembling slightly, but carrying an undeniable determination.

Before Prex could respond, the sound of tires screeching on the tarmac filled the air as a shadowy figure materialized out of nowhere, standing directly in the middle of the road. Prex's instincts kicked in immediately, and he slammed his foot down onto the brake pedal. The car lurched forward as it screeched to a halt, the tires locking up and sending a cloud of dust into the air. The headlights of the vehicle bathed the figure in an eerie, unnatural light, casting long shadows and illuminating the stillness of the night. Yet, the person did not even flinch—motionless as a statue, their silhouette barely distinguishable against the empty expanse of the road.

A chill crept up Prex's spine, but his face remained a mask of cold focus. He gripped the steering wheel tightly, his knuckles whitening as he stared at the figure with calculated suspicion. *"Stay here,"* he commanded in a low voice, his hand instinctively moving to the revolver at his side, fingers brushing the cold metal. He was a man who had seen enough to know when something was wrong, and this—this felt wrong in every possible way. He pulled the weapon from its holster, the click of the chamber echoing ominously in the silent night air.

Dea's eyes narrowed at his command, her lips curling into a small but fierce sneer. *"Like hell I will,"* she spat, her words laced with defiance. Without hesitation, she yanked open the car door and slid out onto the pavement, her boots hitting the ground with a sharp thud. She didn't wait for Prex's reaction; there was no time to waste. She was already moving, her every step deliberate and filled with a quiet resolve, each footfall punctuating the gravity of the moment.

The night air was heavy with tension, thick enough to cut with a knife. The figure stood unmoving, their face hidden in shadow, their posture unnervingly calm. The only sounds were the soft rustling of the wind and the distant chirp of insects. But in the space between them and the figure, an electric sense of danger simmered, a silent warning that neither Prex nor Dea could ignore.

Prex, eyes darting between Dea and the figure, exhaled sharply, his grip on the revolver tightening. He knew this could go south in an instant. But as he glanced over at Dea, already stepping toward the figure, he could see that she wasn't backing down—no matter the threat. And neither was he.

The figure that stood before them was a man, his clothes hanging in tatters, frayed at the edges, as if time itself had worn them thin. His face was obscured by the shadow of a wide-brimmed hat, the kind that spoke of an era long passed, and the brim cast a dark veil over his features. His frame was thin but muscular, the remnants of a life that had been hard, one that demanded endurance. There was an unsettling stillness about him, as though he had been standing in that very spot for far longer than was natural.

As Prex and Dea approached cautiously, their senses alert to every shift in the air, the man raised one gloved hand in a slow, deliberate gesture—a peaceful offering, though its hesitation spoke volumes. There was no hostility in the movement, only a faint air of wariness, as though he knew that peace in this world was fleeting, and often, fragile.

"I mean no harm," the man said, his voice deep and gravelly, roughened by years of exposure to harsh winds and the weight of time. It was the kind of voice that seemed to carry the echoes of ancient secrets, worn down by the years but still firm in its conviction. *"But you're treading dangerous ground."*

Prex, ever the skeptic, kept his gun trained on the stranger, his finger resting lightly on the trigger, though his instincts screamed for caution. There was something about this man—something that suggested he was far more than he appeared. *"Who are you?"* Prex asked, his voice cold, betraying no sign of the unease that gnawed at the back of his mind.

"Call me Elias," the man replied without missing a beat. His eyes were hidden, but his voice hinted at a wisdom, a burden, that made it clear he knew far more than he was letting on. *"And I know what you carry."* His eyes flicked momentarily toward the small box Dea was holding, the object of their mission, the very thing that had brought them here. It wasn't just any box; it was something far darker, far more important than they could have anticipated.

"That thing is a beacon," Elias continued, his voice low and filled with forewarning. *"It draws them."*

Dea's grip on the box tightened, the sensation of being watched now prickling at her skin. She glanced at Prex, his expression unreadable as he kept his weapon steady, but she could feel the shift in the air, a tension that had thickened since the man spoke.

"Who are they?" Dea demanded, her voice sharp and insistent. *"What do they want?"*

Elias's gaze, which had been locked on the box, flicked to the shadows beyond the car, where the faintest stirring seemed to suggest something lurking just out of sight, something waiting. His posture stiffened, and for the first time, a tremor of doubt crossed his expression. *"They are remnants of a forgotten war,"* he said, his words heavy, like the weight of an old and painful memory. *"Souls twisted by their own greed, hatred, and thirst for power. The kind of men and women who lost everything in their pursuit of domination, and in their death, they were condemned to linger in this world... a curse that binds them to the earth. That box... it's their anchor. It keeps them tethered here, in a place where they no longer belong."*

A chill swept over Dea, and she could feel the air growing colder, the shadows deeper, as if the very earth beneath them was exhaling a slow, mournful sigh. The box in her hands, so innocuous in appearance, had become something far more dangerous. It was a tether to something ancient, something monstrous, and it was drawing them in, inch by inch, whether they were ready or not.

"What exactly does it want with us?" Prex asked, his voice steady but the unease creeping into the edges of his words. His gun was still raised, but his mind was racing. He knew this man wasn't speaking without reason; every word carried weight, and it was clear that Elias had seen things—horrors that most could never comprehend.

"They want the box," Elias said, his eyes narrowing as his gaze flickered to the road ahead, where the shadows seemed to pulse with an unnatural energy. *"It's their tether to this world. Without it, they are trapped. But with it... they can return. And they will not stop until they've reclaimed it."*

A heavy silence fell between them, the only sound the distant hum of the wind and the occasional rustle of unseen things moving through the underbrush. Dea felt the weight of the box in her hands, its presence now more ominous than ever. She glanced at Prex, whose expression was grim, his mind already racing through the possibilities.

Elias lowered his hand slowly, as if realizing that any further movement might provoke a reaction he wasn't prepared to face. *"You're in their path now,"* he murmured, his voice carrying a quiet finality. *"And they won't be merciful."*

"Then why not destroy it?" Prex's voice cut through the air, sharp and demanding, as if the very idea of holding onto something so dangerous was inconceivable.

Elias, standing firm with an air of quiet authority, shook his head slowly, his gaze distant. *"It's not as simple as that,"* he said, his voice carrying a weight of experience that made his words land heavily in the silence that followed. *"Destroying it could unleash something far worse than you can imagine. The force that lies within that object is ancient, beyond our understanding. It has the potential to unravel everything, to open doors we can't close."*

Dea, who had been listening intently, let out a low, frustrated mutter, barely audible but thick with skepticism. *"Of course it could,"* she scoffed, rolling her eyes. *"So what exactly are we supposed to do, just sit here and wait for it to do its worst?"*

Elias turned toward her, his expression unchanged, as if her frustration was something he had expected. He gestured towards the dense woods that loomed in the distance, the treeline barely visible in the encroaching twilight. *"There's a place not far from here,"* he explained, his voice steady yet tinged with urgency. *"A sanctuary, hidden from their reach. It's a place of refuge, a temporary haven where you'll be safe, for a time. But you must trust me on this."*

Prex's eyes narrowed, his mistrust palpable as he stepped forward, his stance defensive. *"And why should we trust you?"* he asked, his words laced with suspicion. The tension in the air thickened, as though every word weighed heavily on the fragile trust between them.

Elias met his gaze without flinching, his demeanor calm but resolute. *"You don't have to trust me,"* he replied simply, his tone neutral, almost resigned. *"But if you choose to stay on this path, if you continue down this road without a plan, I can assure you, you won't survive the night. The forces you're dealing with are beyond your control. You're not ready for what's coming, not yet."*

For a moment, there was silence, the weight of Elias' words hanging in the air. Prex's jaw clenched, and Dea's brow furrowed in thought. Both were well aware of the danger they were in, but the idea of blindly following Elias into an unknown sanctuary stirred doubt.

"We don't have much time," Elias continued, his voice softer now but no less firm. *"The moment you hesitate, the moment you question your next move, it might be too late. So make your decision quickly."*

The wind rustled through the trees, carrying a chill that seemed to seep into their bones. The quiet urgency in Elias' voice left little room for debate.

Prex and Dea exchanged a long, silent glance, the weight of the decision hanging heavily between them, a silent understanding passing through their eyes. The tension was palpable, thickening the very air around them. Prex's grip tightened on his gun, his mind racing, but in the end, the cold, hard reality settled in. He couldn't keep holding onto it forever. Slowly, with a resigned sigh, he lowered the weapon, his fingers brushing the smooth metal of the barrel as it dropped to his side.

"Lead the way," he murmured, his voice strained but resolute.

Elias's gaze flickered briefly to Prex before he gave a small nod. Without a word, he turned and vanished into the shadows of the dense forest, his form melding seamlessly with the darkened trunks and gnarled branches. Prex and Dea exchanged one last, fleeting look, then followed him, their footsteps muted against the damp, sponge-like earth beneath them.

The box in Dea's hands grew heavier with every passing second, its coldness seeping through the thin fabric of her gloves, sending shivers up her arms. It was as though the weight of it was growing, the burden of their mission pressing against her chest, constricting her breath. The air around them was thick with the scent of damp moss and decaying leaves, a putrid sweetness that seemed to cling to their clothes, their skin. The underbrush was dense, and every so often, the sharp rustling of unseen creatures skittering through the brush would make them pause, their senses heightened, straining to catch any sound, any movement.

The forest was alive with shadows. They twisted and writhed between the trees, distorting the world around them, turning it into something unnatural, something unsettling. The dim light filtering through the canopy above seemed to do little to lift the suffocating gloom that wrapped itself around them like a second skin.

Hours seemed to pass as they pressed deeper into the wilderness. The path ahead was unclear, and at times, it felt as though they were walking in circles, the trees and foliage blurring together in an indistinguishable sea of green. But Elias moved with a purpose, his steps unerring, as though he knew the forest in ways that no outsider could comprehend. His silhouette flitted between the trees, an almost ghostly figure in the twilight, his presence barely a whisper in the wind.

Then, just when they thought they couldn't go any further, the dense foliage parted, revealing a clearing. The transition was abrupt, like stepping from one world into another. The air was somehow different here—colder, but fresher. In the center of the clearing stood a dilapidated cabin, its wooden frame sagging under years of neglect. The structure was shrouded in ivy and moss, as though nature had begun to reclaim it. Yet, despite its decay, there was an undeniable presence about the place.

From within the cabin's broken windows, a faint, golden glow flickered, casting an eerie warmth against the darkening sky. It was a stark contrast to the cold, suffocating shadows of the forest, and for a moment, Prex couldn't shake the feeling that something was wrong, that the light was somehow out of place, like it didn't belong here.

Elias stopped at the edge of the clearing, his posture tense but expectant. He turned to face Prex and Dea, his expression unreadable. With a subtle gesture, he indicated for them to enter, his eyes glinting with an urgency that made Dea's heart beat faster. The air felt charged, as if the world itself was holding its breath, waiting for them to make their move.

Dea felt the box grow heavier still in her hands, the coldness of it seeping deeper into her bones. She exchanged a quick, uncertain glance with Prex before they both nodded in unison. It was time. They had no choice but to step forward, to cross the threshold into the unknown.

Inside the cabin, the air was warm and thick with the scent of wood and burning embers. Despite the rustic surroundings, everything had a peculiar sense of order. Shelves, made of weathered oak, lined the walls, groaning under the weight of countless books, each one bound in rich leather or faded cloth. The shelves were also home to jars filled with dried herbs—some familiar, others unknown—each sealed with wax to preserve their potency. There were also various trinkets and strange artifacts scattered throughout, each one appearing to tell a story of its own. A small, ornate dagger rested in one corner, its handle worn from use. A polished crystal, casting rainbows across the walls, lay on a nearby shelf, seeming to hum with an energy that was almost tangible.

In the center of the room, a large stone hearth crackled with a fire, its warmth filling the cabin and casting dancing shadows on the walls. The flames flickered, their orange glow reflecting off the polished wooden floors, creating an almost hypnotic rhythm. The gentle, crackling sounds of burning wood seemed to calm the tension in the air, but there was a weight of something unspoken that lingered just beneath the surface.

Elias closed the door softly behind them, sealing them away from whatever might be lurking outside. His movements were deliberate, and his face, usually so composed, now seemed etched with a tension that was hard to ignore. He looked over

at Dea, his gaze hardening for a brief moment before he spoke.
"You'll be safe here," he said, his voice low but firm. *"For now."*
Dea carefully set the box down on a nearby table, her hands trembling slightly as the weight of its contents seemed to settle into the room. She could feel her pulse quickening, the questions burning on her tongue. Her eyes flickered to Elias, then to Prex, before she finally spoke.
"What's in this thing?" she asked, her voice cracking slightly.
"Why is it so important?"
Elias stood motionless for a long moment, his eyes flickering to the box and then back to her. There was something unreadable in his expression, a kind of sorrow or regret that made his words feel heavy, as if the very air in the room had thickened with the burden of his response. Finally, he exhaled sharply, the sound barely audible over the crackling fire.
"It's not what's in the box that matters," he said, his voice barely above a whisper, but with an edge of finality.
"It's what it keeps out."
Prex frowned, stepping forward with a confused look on his face.
"What does that mean?" His brow furrowed in suspicion, but Elias didn't meet his gaze. Instead, the older man turned toward the fire, the shadows of his face now more pronounced. There was a flicker of something—a brief glimpse of fear, or perhaps something darker—that seemed to pass across his features before he closed his eyes, as if bracing himself against an old memory or an unseen force.
"The box," Elias continued, his voice strained, *"is not just a container. It's a barrier. A prison."* His eyes opened again, meeting Prex's for the first time since their arrival.
"And it's only as strong as the forces that are kept at bay. Whatever you think you know about this world... about the things that lurk in the dark... It's not the whole truth. And that box," he said, nodding toward it, *"keeps the worst of it sealed away."*
The air grew heavier, charged with the unspoken threat that lingered in the corners of the room. Dea swallowed hard, her breath

catching in her throat as she glanced from Elias to the box. She could feel the weight of its presence now, as though it was more than just an object—it was a promise, a warning, or perhaps something more sinister that would make its presence known in due time. The fire crackled once more, but the sound now seemed distant, lost in the silence that stretched between them.

The fire in the hearth erupted with a violent intensity, its once-orange flames twisting and contorting into an unnatural shade of deep, eerie blue. The temperature in the cabin dropped sharply as the fire seemed to burn colder rather than warmer. A low, menacing growl reverberated through the wooden walls, a sound that was neither fully animal nor human, sending a wave of cold dread coursing through their veins. The noise seemed to emanate from the very earth itself, vibrating in their bones.

Elias stiffened, his eyes narrowing as he watched the flames dance with an unsettling rhythm. His hand instinctively reached for the hilt of the dagger sheathed at his side, though he knew it would offer little protection against whatever force had found them.

"They've found us," Elias muttered, his voice tight, strained with both urgency and resignation. *"We don't have much time. They're closer than I thought."*

Prex, already on edge, quickly reached for the revolver that rested against the wall beside him. His knuckles turned white as he gripped the handle, his jaw clenched in grim determination. *"What do we do?"* he asked, his voice low, yet tinged with the edge of panic that neither man dared show.

Elias didn't answer immediately. His gaze shifted, locking onto a weathered wooden shelf across the room. A faint, ethereal glow emanated from a jar resting there, its contents swirling with a strange luminescence, like liquid starlight trapped in glass. He moved toward it with a practiced calmness, though his every step was measured, as if the very air around him had thickened. He lifted the jar carefully, his fingers brushing against the cool glass. There was an ancient weight in his hands, a feeling that this was no ordinary item. It was a relic—a tool of last resort, one that had been passed down through generations. Elias unscrewed the lid, and the faint hum of the contents grew louder, almost as though the jar itself was alive.

"*We fight,*" Elias said, his voice steady now, though it carried the gravity of knowing just how much was at stake. His eyes met Prex's, unspoken understanding passing between them. "*And we pray that it's enough.*"

Prex nodded, his heart hammering in his chest. The growl from outside grew louder, more distinct, as if something—or someone—was drawing nearer. His instincts screamed at him to flee, but there was no escape. Not now.

With a quick, fluid motion, he clicked the revolver into place, his fingers brushing over the cold metal as his eyes never left the door. They both knew that the creature hunting them would not be deterred by mere barricades or walls.

Elias raised the jar, the glow intensifying as the liquid inside began to pulse in rhythmic waves. He muttered something under his breath, a chant in a language long forgotten by most, his voice barely audible over the growing growl outside.

The fire crackled once more, and the flames shifted in color again, now flickering between shades of red and gold as if responding to the ritual. The air thickened with tension, the very fabric of the cabin seeming to tremble under the weight of the approaching danger.

"*What the hell is that stuff?*" Prex asked, his voice hoarse as he kept his eyes trained on the door.

"*It's the last of a potion made from the heart of the old world,*" Elias replied, his gaze locked on the jar, his mind focused on the incantation. "*It's meant to hold back what's coming. But we need to be ready for anything.*"

The growl grew into a deafening roar, and without warning, the door burst open, sending splinters of wood flying across the room.

Veil of Forgotten Wars

The blue flames flickered and swirled in the hearth, their ethereal glow casting an unsettling, otherworldly light that flickered across the rough-hewn cabin walls. The fire seemed to burn with a strange intensity, its unnatural hues painting the space in shades of cobalt and indigo, as if it was more a creature of the night than a simple flame. Shadows, distorted and elongated, stretched across the timber walls, twisting in ways that made the air feel thick with anticipation. The cabin, once a quiet refuge in the dense forest, now felt alive, suffocating under the oppressive atmosphere that the fire seemed to conjure.

Elias moved with a quiet urgency, his every motion deliberate and fluid, as though he had rehearsed this dance a thousand times before. His long fingers swept across the cluttered shelves, grasping jars of various sizes, their contents unknown, their labels faded with age. Each item seemed to hum with its own subtle energy, an undercurrent of mystery surrounding every artifact. He moved swiftly but with practiced grace, pulling objects from their places and arranging them meticulously, as if the success of whatever ritual he was about to perform depended on the perfect alignment of every trinket and jar.

Prex and Dea stood frozen, caught in the eerie silence that followed the guttural growl that echoed through the cabin like the growl of some unseen predator. The sound reverberated through their bones, a deep, menacing vibration that set their nerves on edge. Their breath hitched in their throats as the hairs on the back of their necks stood on end. The growl lingered in the air, a sound that didn't seem entirely of this world, its source hidden in the shadows, just beyond their reach. The tension between the three of them grew palpable, and for a moment, the very air seemed to hold its breath, waiting for the next move in this strange and perilous dance.

As Elias continued his work, the faint crackling of the fire and the unsettling sound of his movements filled the otherwise silent room. Prex and Dea exchanged wary glances, their hearts pounding in their chests as they strained to make sense of what was unfolding before them. Every instinct screamed at them to turn and flee, but they remained rooted in place, drawn by some unseen force, their feet heavy with the weight of uncertainty. The cabin felt smaller now, its once familiar surroundings now infused with a sense of dread, the walls closing in as the fire's eerie glow grew more intense.

"Barricade the windows!" Elias barked, his voice sharp and commanding, cutting through the heavy air and snapping them out of their stupor.

The urgency in his tone ignited something within them, a primal instinct to survive. Prex's heart pounded in his chest, but he didn't hesitate. He sprinted across the room, his boots thundering against the wooden floor, and seized a heavy wooden table. With a strained grunt, he shoved it with all his might, the legs scraping loudly against the floor as he wedged it tightly against the nearest window. The rough surface of the table dug into his palms, but he ignored the sting, his eyes darting frantically around the room.

Dea, less composed than Prex, was frozen for a moment, staring at the approaching window. But the growing sense of danger shook her out of her paralysis. Her breath quickened, and her hands trembled with a mixture of fear and adrenaline. She bolted toward the bookshelf, her fingers brushing against the worn, dust-covered spines as she dragged it with force across the room. The bookcase groaned in protest, its heavy weight slowing her down, but she didn't relent. Every movement was desperate, each step fueled by the deepening terror.

The eerie growl from outside sent chills down their spines, low and guttural, reverberating through the walls like the roar of a hungry beast. The whispers followed, so faint at first they seemed like nothing more than the creaking of the house. But as the sounds grew louder, it became clear—they were not from the wind or the house settling. The whispers slithered through the cracks in the walls, a strange language, soft but insistent, like voices from another world, beckoning and threatening at the same time.

The air in the room grew heavy, thick with the tension of the moment. Prex's breath came in shallow gasps, his eyes wide with fear as he surveyed their makeshift barricade. But they weren't safe yet. The window, now partially covered, still offered a view of the terrifying unknown outside. He could see shapes moving in the distance, their outlines barely visible through the haze, creeping closer.

Dea's heart raced as she finished moving the bookshelf into place, her fingers shaking as she pressed it against the wall. She shot a nervous glance at Elias, her mind swirling with questions—*what were they up against? What were those sounds?*

Elias, standing at the center of the room with his back to the door, surveyed the scene with grim resolve. The walls were closing in, both physically and mentally. But they had no time for doubt. They had no time for anything but survival.

"What are those things?" Dea demanded, her voice trembling with a mix of fear and confusion. Her wide eyes darted between the shadowy forms gathering at the edges of the cabin, their shapes indistinct, almost ethereal. Each figure flickered like a candle in the wind, yet their presence felt so heavy, so undeniable.

Elias stood motionless, his face pale, a faint sheen of sweat glistening on his brow. *"Shadows of the past,"* he said, his tone grave and strained, as if the words themselves carried the weight of years lost. *"They're fragments of souls—lost, broken, wandering. Souls that once were, but no longer truly are. They are echoes of forgotten lives, cursed to wander the veil between worlds. And they are drawn here... to the box."*

"The box?" Prex echoed, a nervous edge creeping into his voice. He quickly wedged a heavy wooden chair beneath the doorknob, his hands shaking slightly as he worked to fortify the cabin's only exit. The ominous figures outside had grown nearer, their movements jerky and unsettling, as if they were uncertain of their own existence.

Elias' eyes flickered toward the box, which now sat on the floor between them—an innocuous-looking object, yet pulsating with an unseen power. His expression darkened further. *"The box calls to them,"* he continued, his voice barely more than a whisper. *"It offers them a promise, a lie—release from the torment they've endured for what feels like an eternity. They think that opening it will set them free."*

Dea felt a chill run down her spine as she clutched the box tighter against her chest. The air seemed to grow colder, and the shadows outside pressed in, their dark outlines sharpening in her vision.

"Release from what?" she asked, her voice faltering as the gravity of the situation began to sink in.

Elias hesitated, his eyes flickering between the box and the growing shadows at the door. He took a deep breath before answering, as if the weight of the truth might crush him.

"Release from an eternity of torment. They've been trapped, bound to this place, to their own suffering. Each soul that touches this cursed relic believes they're escaping, that they're escaping their pain... But opening the box won't free them." His voice dropped to a low murmur, as though fearing even the walls of the cabin might hear. *"It will unleash something far worse."*

Before Dea or Prex could question him further, the silence was shattered by a deafening bang—louder than thunder, sharper than any storm. The door, reinforced with the chair, buckled under the invisible pressure, shaking violently as if it were being struck by an unseen hand. The walls seemed to tremble, the air crackling with an oppressive energy. Dea's breath caught in her throat, her heart hammering in her chest.

The shadows outside had no physical form, but their presence was unmistakable. They were closing in, drawn to the box, drawn to the promise of release. A cold gust of wind swept through the cabin, extinguishing the dim light from the lantern, leaving them in darkness. Dea felt the air grow heavy, thick with a palpable dread. Every corner seemed to pulse with the anticipation of something terrible.

Dea's grip tightened around the box, her knuckles white as the tremors of fear coursed through her. Her heart pounded violently, echoing in her ears as the sounds of the banging intensified. She didn't understand what Elias meant by *'far worse,'* but the shadows outside were now so close, their forms swirling like smoke, as if they were waiting for a signal—a signal that would give them what they wanted.

"Stay close," Elias ordered, his voice a low, urgent command. The shadows were already clawing at the door, their ethereal tendrils slipping through cracks in the wood, curling like fingers desperate to touch the box. Dea knew the time for questions had passed. Now, survival was all that mattered.

"They're here," Elias muttered, his voice low and tense, barely more than a whisper, but laden with the weight of urgency. His hand trembled slightly as he uncorked an ancient jar, its surface smooth but worn, filled with a glowing amber liquid that pulsed faintly, as if it contained the heartbeat of something far older. He tipped the jar, letting the viscous fluid flow freely, and with steady precision, began tracing intricate, looping symbols onto the cold stone walls. The air around him seemed to hum with an energy that was both unnatural and powerful, the glowing liquid reacting to his every movement as though it, too, was alive.

"These wards will hold them off for a time," Elias continued, his voice growing more focused, *"but not long. We need to act*

quickly, or everything will be lost."

Dea's eyes widened as the faint glow from the wards bathed her face in a soft light, the growing sense of dread pressing against her chest. She swallowed hard, her breath shallow as panic began to rise.

"What do we do?" Her voice cracked, desperation seeping through the cracks of her usually calm demeanor. The weight of the moment settled heavily on her, the looming threat outside seeming to claw at her from the other side of the walls, invisible yet ever-present.

Elias turned to face her, his expression grave, the lines of worry etched deeply across his brow. His usual composure faltered slightly as he locked eyes with her, the severity of their situation making every word that much more profound. *"We need to sever their connection to the box,"* he said, his words deliberate, each syllable carrying the heavy burden of truth. *"That means understanding its origin. Only then will we have a chance of stopping what's coming."*

Prex, who had been standing silently in the corner, brow furrowed in thought, suddenly spoke up. His voice was sharp, cutting through the tension in the room. *"You know where it came from, don't you?"* His eyes were narrowed, his suspicion clear. There was something in Elias's demeanor, the way he hesitated before speaking, that made Prex's gut churn with unease.

Elias paused, the weight of the question seeming to hang in the air for a moment longer than necessary. His gaze fell to the floor, the shadows beneath his eyes deepening as he seemed to gather his thoughts. Finally, he nodded slowly, his voice tinged with a kind of sorrow that Dea had never heard before. *"The box is older than memory itself,"* he began, each word like a careful unveiling of a long-forgotten truth. *"It was crafted in a time when the lines between this world and the next were thin, almost nonexistent. A time when the veil between realms was not as strong, and the forces that lay beyond could slip through if given the chance. It was made as a prison—no, not just a prison, a containment for a power so dangerous, so terrifying, that its very existence threatened to unbalance the fabric of all that we know."*

He looked up then, meeting Dea's eyes with an intensity that sent a chill down her spine. *"That power was never meant to roam free. And now, somehow, they've found it. And they want to set it loose."*

Prex's face paled at the implication, his hand instinctively reaching for the dagger at his side. He knew the legends, the stories passed down in hushed whispers, and the mere mention of such an ancient force was enough to send a ripple of dread through him. *"But if the box is that old, why is it still here? Why hasn't it been destroyed?"*

Elias's lips tightened, his jaw clenched in frustration as though he himself had pondered that very question a thousand times. *"Because the prison was never meant to be broken,"* he said, his voice now laced with a mixture of regret and resolve. *"Whoever forged the box, whoever created it, knew that its purpose was sacred. They made it unbreakable, or so they thought. But there's always someone, someone willing to take the risk."* His hands trembled slightly as he completed the final ward on the wall, the symbols glowing with an eerie brilliance. *"And now, the consequences of their actions have caught up with us."*

Dea took a step closer, her eyes scanning the glowing runes, her mind racing with the implications of what Elias had said.

"So, we're not just dealing with thieves," she murmured, more to herself than anyone else.

"We're dealing with something... older than we can even comprehend."

Elias's eyes softened, a mix of pity and regret flashing across his features. *"That's right."* He turned back to the wall, his hands still tracing the symbols with a practiced, almost ritualistic precision.

"The box was never meant to be opened. And now that they have..." He trailed off, the words hanging heavy in the room like a suffocating fog.

"And now it's a beacon," Dea muttered under her breath, her

voice laced with bitterness. Her hands clenched at her sides, every muscle in her body tensed with frustration. *"Great. Just what we needed."*

Another deafening bang reverberated through the cabin, sending a shiver down her spine. The ground beneath them trembled, a violent shake that rattled the walls. Moments later, the piercing sound of glass shattering echoed through the narrow space, sharp and dissonant. Dea's eyes darted to the windows, and what she saw made her breath catch in her throat. The shadows outside were no longer still—no longer dormant. They twisted and writhed, their forms coiling and stretching like dark serpents, pressing against the cabin's fragile barriers as though testing their strength. Their movements were unsettling, as if they were alive, intent on breaking through, and Dea couldn't help but feel the oppressive weight of their unseen gaze.

"Elias!" Prex shouted, his voice laced with urgency. He was pacing back and forth, his hands gripping his hair as if trying to hold himself together. *"We're running out of time! We need to do something—NOW!"*

Elias, standing near a cluttered shelf at the far end of the cabin, didn't waste a moment. His eyes flicked to Dea, then to Prex, and then back to the thick layers of shadows gathering outside. His expression was grim, as if he too could feel the suffocating pressure of whatever was about to happen. In one swift motion, he reached for a worn leather-bound book resting on a dusty shelf. The book's edges were frayed, the cover cracked with age, but Elias seemed to regard it with a reverence that made Dea pause.

Without another word, Elias shoved the book into Dea's hands. His fingers brushed hers for a brief second, and she could feel the intensity of his grip, a silent warning in his touch. *"This,"* he said, his voice low but charged with an unmistakable urgency, *"will tell you what you need to know. But be warned—the answers you seek... they come at a price."*

Dea stared at the book, her fingers trembling slightly as she flipped it open. The pages were yellowed and brittle, their surface covered in intricate, swirling script that seemed to almost move on its own. Her eyes skimmed over the text, but it was incomprehensible—ancient symbols that danced before her like a riddle she couldn't solve.

"I can't read this!" Dea's voice was filled with frustration as she looked up at Elias. Her brows furrowed, and the heat of panic rose in her chest.

"What is this? Some kind of joke?"

"You don't need to read it," Elias replied, his voice steady, but there was a flicker of something else in his eyes—fear, perhaps. *"The box will guide you."*

At first, Dea didn't understand what he meant, but then she noticed the small, intricately-carved box sitting next to her. She hadn't noticed it before, its presence so subtle, yet now it seemed to pulse with an energy of its own, as though it was alive. It beckoned to her, its surface adorned with symbols that mirrored those on the pages of the book.

"The box," Elias continued, his gaze fixed on her. *"It reacts to your touch, to your intentions. It knows what you need to do, even if you don't understand yet. Trust it."*

Dea hesitated for a moment, her fingers brushing the edges of the box. Almost immediately, a surge of energy rushed through her, a strange warmth spreading from her fingertips up her arm. The box seemed to hum, its surface glowing faintly, and the pages of the book shifted, as if responding to the energy she had unleashed.

The shadows outside pressed closer. The air felt thick, and the sense of impending danger was more tangible now than ever. Dea could feel it—this was the moment. The answers lay just beyond her reach, but what would it cost her to find them?

The book trembled in her hands, and for a split second, she wondered if she was making a mistake. But there was no turning back now. The box had already chosen her, and she had no choice but to follow where it led.

"What does that mean?" Prex demanded, his voice cutting through the tension in the room. His eyes darted nervously be-

tween Elias and the symbols that now seemed to pulsate with an unnatural light. Elias, however, offered no response. His focus remained unwavering, his lips moving in a chant so deep and resonant that it seemed to come from the very earth itself.

The words, unintelligible and ancient, spilled from his mouth in a steady rhythm, their guttural cadence reverberating through the room. As he spoke, the air around them seemed to tremble, and the symbols etched into the walls, once faint and unremarkable, began to glow with an eerie intensity. The light spread, its hue shifting between shades of crimson and violet, casting long, twisting shadows that danced erratically across the cabin's decaying walls.

Prex took an involuntary step back, his heart hammering in his chest as the atmosphere grew thick, charged with a palpable energy. The very air felt alive, crackling with an unseen force that tugged at their senses, making the hairs on the back of their necks stand on end. Every breath seemed to grow heavier, laden with a pressure that pressed in from all sides.

Outside, the world had descended into chaos. The shadows that had once been mere shapes now writhed in the periphery, their forms shifting and twisting like dark tendrils of smoke. As the chanting grew louder, they began to howl in unison, their cries a haunting mixture of rage and despair. The sound was inhuman, a cacophony that reverberated not only through the cabin but through the very ground beneath their feet.

The floorboards beneath them creaked and groaned, as if the very foundations of the cabin were under siege. A tremor ran through the walls, and the entire structure seemed to shudder violently, as if caught in the grip of an earthquake. Dust and splinters fell from the ceiling, settling in the air like a fine mist. The trembling intensified, each violent shake reverberating in their bones, and Prex could feel his legs growing unsteady, as if the ground beneath him was no longer solid.

Elias remained oblivious to the chaos, his voice rising in pitch as he continued to chant, his words becoming more urgent, more frantic. The symbols on the walls flared with an unholy brilliance, the glow so bright it felt like they were being burned alive by the very energy that surged through the room. Every sound—every movement—seemed swallowed by the growing darkness that enveloped them.

And still, Prex could do nothing but watch in frozen terror, knowing that whatever Elias was doing, there was no turning back now.

"Prex!" Dea cried, her voice laced with panic as she clutched the ancient, worn book tightly against her chest. Her fingers trembled, her knuckles white from the force with which she held it. *"What do we do now? How do we stop this?"*

Prex didn't hesitate for a second. He moved toward her with swift, measured steps, his broad hand grasping her arm in a firm yet reassuring grip. His eyes, normally cool and calculating, burned with an intensity that was almost unnatural. *"We survive,"* he said, his voice low but resolute, carrying an edge of finality. *"That's what we do. No matter the cost, we survive."*

Outside, the chant of Elias had grown louder, reverberating through the wooden walls of the cabin. Each word he uttered was an incantation, a sound that seemed to claw at the very air around them. The floor beneath their feet quaked as though the earth itself was being pulled into the darkness. The sound of Elias's voice reached a fevered pitch, a crescendo that filled the cabin with a pulsating energy that seemed to press in from all sides.

Suddenly, a blinding light erupted from the center of the room, so intense that it swallowed the cabin whole. The walls, the floor, the very air itself seemed to distort as the light expanded, flooding every crevice with an unnatural radiance. Dea shut her eyes against the brilliance, but even through her closed lids, she could see the flickering patterns of the light dancing across her eyelids like a hundred thousand stars collapsing into one singular point. The shadows that had once lurked outside—sinister, shifting shapes that had long been a threat to their existence—began to wail, their voices rising in anguished screeches. The sound was chilling, an inhuman cry that seemed to reach deep into Dea's very soul. As the light grew, the shadows seemed to writhe, their forms twisting and dissolving into nothingness. For a moment, it felt as though the entire world was being torn apart by the sheer power of the magic that Elias had invoked.

Then, just as suddenly as it had started, the light began to fade. The air grew still, and the oppressive pressure that had once filled the cabin lifted as if it had never been there. The hearth that had once burned with an eerie blue fire now settled into its natural orange glow, the flames licking at the air in their familiar dance. The once-chilled air felt warmer, more breathable, and the cabin was eerily silent, save for the soft crackling of the fire.

Dea opened her eyes, her heart still racing, but the terror that had gripped her was now replaced with a sense of bewilderment. They had survived... but what had they truly faced? Prex's grip on her arm loosened slightly, but he did not let go entirely. His gaze shifted to the door, the only remaining indication of the danger that had surrounded them just moments before.

"It's over," Prex muttered, though there was a trace of uncertainty in his voice. *"For now."*

Dea nodded, though her mind raced with questions. What had Elias done? And what would come next? She had no answers, but one thing was certain—they had made it through the storm, and the world had changed forever.

Elias slumped against the cold, jagged stone wall, his chest rising and falling with labored breaths. His once-vibrant face was now ashen, his lips pale and drawn tight, as though the weight of the world had just been placed upon his shoulders. The fight had drained him, both physically and mentally. His eyes, usually sharp and calculating, now carried the hollow emptiness of someone who had seen the inevitable yet still couldn't quite escape its grasp.

"They're gone," he muttered hoarsely, his voice barely above a whisper. *"For now. But it's not over. They'll be back. Stronger than before."*

Dea, who had been watching him with a deep, almost maternal concern, knelt beside him, the lines of worry deepening across her brow. Her hands, delicate but firm, reached out to steady him, offering support in the only way she knew how. *"Are you okay?"* Her voice trembled slightly, though she tried her best to mask the anxiety that had been steadily creeping into her thoughts.

Elias raised a hand, brushing off her concern with an almost mechanical gesture. *"I'll be fine,"* he replied, though the weakness in his voice betrayed him. *"I've endured worse. But this... this is different."* His eyes flitted toward the darkened horizon as though sensing a storm on the cusp of breaking. *"This is just the beginning. They've found us once, and they'll find us again. We're not done yet."*

Prex, standing just a few paces away, was already preparing to act. His movements were sharp, calculated, his body tense, every muscle ready for the next fight. Without a word, he moved closer, offering a strong hand to Elias. *"Then we need to move. No more waiting, no more hesitation. We can't afford to stand still any longer."* His voice was calm, yet there was an edge to it that only came from someone who knew the stakes were higher than ever.

Elias, though clearly struggling, accepted Prex's help, his grip weak but resolute. *"The answers are in there,"* he said, his eyes locking onto the small, weathered book that Dea still held tightly in her hands. The book had become more than just a collection of pages; it was a key, a guide, and now, a dangerous burden. *"But be warned—every step you take toward the truth will push you further toward the edge. You'll come face to face with things you can't unsee. Things that might break you."*

Dea felt a shiver run down her spine as Elias's words hung in the air, thick with foreboding. She glanced down at the book in her hands, feeling the ancient carvings etched into its cover pulse with an energy that seemed to shift, even under the dim light of the moon. The carvings were intricate, the patterns complex and alien, as if the book itself were alive, watching, waiting. Her grip tightened instinctively, almost as if she could squeeze some form of strength from the weight of it.

"What's inside it?" Prex asked, his voice low and tinged with an undeniable curiosity. His eyes flickered between Dea and the box, aware that whatever lay within it could very well be their salvation—or their doom.

Dea hesitated for a moment, her thoughts swirling with doubt. She met Prex's gaze, her resolve settling like a heavy stone within her chest. *"I don't know,"* she confessed quietly. *"But I know one thing. We don't have a choice. We keep going. Whatever it takes. Whatever it costs."*

Prex's jaw tightened in a grim expression of determination. *"Then we move forward. There's no turning back now."*

With those words, they all stood in unison, as if an unspoken agreement passed between them in that moment. The air around them was thick with the promise of danger, the kind that could not be ignored. Stepping out into the cool embrace of the night, they found themselves enveloped by a vast, ink-black expanse of shadows that seemed to stretch endlessly into the horizon.

The silence was unnerving. The usual hum of the world—the rustling of leaves, the distant chirping of insects—was absent. It was as though the night itself had drawn in its breath, waiting for the next move. But the shadows, once an oppressive force, seemed to draw back slightly now, as if respecting the weight of the decisions that had just been made. They watched from a distance, gathering in anticipation, but did not advance. For now, the trio had been granted a temporary reprieve.

Dea's arms ached with the weight of the box, its secrets pressing down on her like an invisible force. Her fingers tingled where they grasped the corners, the wood cool against her palms. She knew that the truth held within it would not come easily, nor without consequence. But she also knew that there was no going back. Whatever was to come, they would face it together, or not at all.

Together, they disappeared into the night, each step taking them further into the unknown. The path ahead was shrouded in uncertainty, yet there was an undeniable resolve in their every movement. They were no longer running from the darkness;

they were moving toward it, ready to confront whatever truths awaited them, no matter how harrowing. The weight of their decision was heavy, but their determination was unshaken.
The journey had only just begun.

The Key to Oblivion

The forest stretched before them, an immense wilderness where the canopy above seemed to blend into an endless tangle of twisted branches and darkened foliage. Shadows swirled in the spaces between the trees, shifting and pulsing as though they harbored secrets of their own, waiting to be uncovered by the brave or the foolish. The air was thick with the scent of earth and damp leaves, and the sound of distant, unseen creatures echoed through the dense underbrush. It was a place that felt ancient, untouched by time, yet burdened with a weight of forgotten stories.

Prex stood at the edge of the forest, his gaze steady as he took in the path ahead. He adjusted the strap of his satchel, the leather creaking softly under his touch, and made sure his revolver was firmly nestled against his hip, its cold metal a reassuring presence. The silence seemed to press against him, almost tangible, as if the forest itself was waiting. The wind picked up, rustling through the leaves and whispering of things unseen, filling the air with a tension that seemed to settle deep in his bones.

Behind him, Dea moved with quiet steps, her fingers wrapped tightly around the ancient book she carried, its pages worn and edges frayed from years of use. The weight of it was both physical and emotional, a burden that felt as though it could drag her down at any moment. She held it close to her chest, the cover decorated with symbols long forgotten, symbols that burned with an almost ethereal glow whenever the moonlight touched them. The book had led them here, and though its pages held promises of answers, Dea couldn't shake the feeling that it also carried with it a darkness, a secret that they weren't yet ready to understand.

"Do you think we'll find anything here?" Dea's voice was a soft murmur, barely rising above the rustling of the leaves around them. Her words carried a weight of uncertainty, and her eyes flicked nervously between the trees, as though expecting something to emerge from the shadows at any moment.

Prex didn't immediately answer, his gaze focused on the winding path that disappeared into the heart of the forest. His face was a mask of stoic determination, yet his mind was far from calm. Elias had said the answers were hidden here, buried beneath the dense layers of the world's forgotten past, and the book had led them this far. But even as he stood there, something gnawed at him. The forest seemed too quiet, too still, and the very air felt thick with the weight of untold stories, like the land itself was holding its breath, waiting for something.

Without turning to look at her, Prex's voice cut through the silence, deep and steady. *"Elias said the answers were in the book. And the book led us here. Whatever we're searching for… it's here, Dea. We just need to trust it."*

He paused for a moment, his hand brushing the grip of his revolver before continuing, his tone unwavering. *"There's no turning back now."*

Dea nodded slowly, her fingers tightening on the book as though it might slip from her grasp if she didn't hold it tight enough. The forest loomed ahead, dark and impenetrable, and with every step they took, the weight of the unknown seemed to grow heavier, pulling them deeper into the mystery they had sought out.

Dea's brow furrowed, a shiver creeping down her spine as her sharp gaze swept over the dense forest that loomed before them.

She hesitated, her senses on edge. *"It feels... wrong,"* she said, her voice barely above a whisper. *"Like we're being watched. Every step we take, someone or something is keeping track of us."*

Prex, standing slightly ahead of her, didn't need any further urging. His eyes narrowed as he scanned their surroundings, the hairs on the back of his neck prickling. *"We probably are,"* he muttered, the words slipping out with a tone of cold indifference. His hand brushed lightly over the polished grip of his revolver, a gesture that spoke volumes of the unease building within him. *"Stay close, Dea. Don't stray too far."*

They moved forward cautiously, the weight of the forest pressing in on them from all sides. With each step, the air thickened, growing cooler and denser, as though the very atmosphere was aware of their presence. The canopy above stretched in endless layers, thick and unyielding, allowing only fragmented beams of sunlight to filter through. Those few rays barely touched the ground, casting the path ahead in an eerie, greenish hue, like the world had been drained of its color. The shadows seemed to deepen with every moment that passed, making the trees appear as silent sentinels, their twisted limbs reaching down as if to ensnare any intruders.

The silence around them was stifling, oppressive, and it felt as though the world itself had fallen into a suffocating pause. There were no birdsong, no rustling of leaves in the breeze, no distant calls of animals. It was as though the entire forest was holding its breath, waiting for something—someone—to make the next move. Only the occasional snap of a twig beneath their boots broke the stillness, and the sound was magnified in the unnerving quiet. Each step seemed too loud, too deliberate, but the air around them was thick with anticipation, an unspoken promise that danger lurked just beyond the veil of shadows.

As they walked through the dense underbrush, the air heavy with the scent of pine and damp earth, a soft but unmistakable hum began to emanate from the small wooden box Dea had clutched in her hand. At first, it was barely perceptible—like a whisper just beyond the edge of hearing. But soon, the sound intensified, and the carvings etched into the surface of the box began to glow faintly. The light was subtle at first, like the faintest pulse of moonlight reflected off still water, but it grew, spreading in ripples along the intricate symbols, casting an eerie, almost supernatural glow that illuminated the path ahead. The shadows around them seemed to twist unnaturally, stretching and contracting as if responding to the power within the box.

Dea came to an abrupt stop, her breath hitching as her wide eyes locked onto the glowing artifact. *"Prex... the box. It's... reacting."*

Her voice, though barely above a whisper, was laced with an unmistakable note of fear, and Prex, ever vigilant, instantly turned to her. His brow furrowed in concern as his gaze shifted to the box. *"What does it mean?"* His voice was calm but edged with an urgency that betrayed his curiosity and the undercurrent of caution he felt.

Dea, her fingers tightening around the box, shook her head slowly, as if trying to comprehend the inexplicable. *"I don't know,"* she admitted, her voice a mix of awe and fear. *"But it's never done this before... not like this."*

She took a hesitant step back, her instincts warning her that something was amiss. The glow continued to intensify, casting a pale light that seemed almost too unnatural, too pure. The trees around them stood in stark contrast, their dark silhouettes towering ominously against the glowing orb that now seemed to pulse with a life of its own.

Before either of them could fully process the implications of the box's strange behavior, a low growl echoed through the trees, sending a chill through the air. The sound was guttural, a deep vibration that resonated through the earth beneath their feet. It was a warning—an unmistakable sign that something was close, something dangerous.

Prex's reaction was immediate. His hand shot to the holster at his side, fingers curling around the cold, comforting grip of his revolver. He pulled it free in a smooth, practiced motion, his eyes narrowing as he scanned the darkening woods. The growl had faded, but its presence lingered, heavy in the air, thick with menace. His gaze flickered back to Dea, his face hardening with the realization that they were no longer alone.

"We're not alone," he murmured, his voice low and steady, though his posture was tense, ready for whatever might come from the shadows.

The wind stirred the trees, but it was the silence that followed the growl that made Dea's heart race. They were being watched. The box, still glowing softly in her hands, pulsed in time with the rhythm of her rapidly beating heart. The shadows around them seemed to shift, as though something—someone—was moving just out of sight.

Every instinct in Dea's body screamed at her to run, but she stayed frozen, her breath shallow as she waited for Prex to take the lead. There was no turning back now.

Dea's fingers tightened around the box, her knuckles pale from the pressure, as the low growls grew steadily louder. The sound seemed to emanate from all directions, a deep, throaty rumble that echoed through the dense underbrush of the forest. A sudden, sharp snap of branches breaking made her flinch, her heart racing.

The air around her grew cold, the once peaceful surroundings now thick with a sense of impending danger. The shadows, which had seemed harmless moments ago, began to shift and undulate, stretching out like dark tendrils. From the corner of her eye, Dea caught glimpses of shapes moving within the darkness—shapes that were almost human, yet undeniably wrong.

The creatures that emerged were tall and wiry, their bodies hunched and contorted in unnatural angles. Their limbs twisted and jerked, as though they were being manipulated by some unseen force. Their skin was an ashen gray, and their faces were gaunt and distorted, with jagged, wolfish features. But it was their eyes that truly unnerved her—glowing a sickly, unnatural yellow, like twin lanterns in the dark. They gleamed with malice and hunger, fixed on Dea and the box in her hands, as though they could sense its significance. The sound of their breath was harsh, rattling, as if it came from deep within their chest, unnatural and alien.

Dea's throat tightened in fear, her voice barely a whisper as she turned to Prex, her words shaking. *"What are they?"*

"Not friendly," Prex answered curtly, his expression grim. He moved quickly, positioning himself in front of Dea, his eyes scanning the surrounding forest with sharp precision. He gripped the sleek, black weapon in his hands, his finger ready on the trigger. *"Stay behind me,"* he ordered, his voice steady but laced with an undercurrent of tension.

Before Dea could respond, the creatures lunged forward in a blur of motion. Their movements were eerily fast, far quicker than any human could hope to match. Their limbs flailed wildly, as though they were driven by some uncontrollable hunger or rage. The sound of their feet slapping against the damp earth was drowned out by the violent growl that erupted from their throats.

Prex reacted in an instant, his weapon lifting with deadly aim. The first shot rang out, shattering the stillness of the forest. It hit one of the creatures square in the chest, and with a horrible, sickening scream, the creature collapsed to the ground. But instead of blood, a thick, black mist began to pour from its body, swirling and writhing in the air. Within moments, the creature was nothing more than a swirling cloud of darkness, dissipating into nothingness.

The remaining creatures hesitated, their glowing yellow eyes flicking toward the box with renewed focus. They shifted, their bodies swaying, as though contemplating their next move. A low growl rippled through the air, their hunger now palpable. The shadows around them seemed to deepen, as if the very forest was conspiring to conceal their intentions. The tension in the air was suffocating, and Dea could feel her heart pounding in her chest.

"Prex," she whispered, her voice trembling, *"What are they after?"*

Prex didn't answer immediately, his gaze locked on the creatures, his finger hovering near the trigger. His expression was cold, unreadable, but there was an unmistakable flicker of urgency in his eyes.

"They're after the box," he said finally, his voice grim. "And if they get it, we might not be able to stop them."

"They're after it," Dea muttered, her voice a breathless whisper as a cold shiver ran down her spine. The reality of the situation hit her like a brick, and her heart pounded in her chest, threatening to burst out. The glow of the box grew brighter, almost pulling her in, as if the object itself was beckoning the unseen pursuers.

Prex, never one to hesitate, quickly snapped into action. His gunshot echoed through the air, the sharp crack of it followed by a guttural growl from somewhere behind them. He turned to her, his face a mask of urgency and focus.

"Then we need to keep moving," he commanded, his voice steady but filled with tension. *"Go! I'll cover you!"*

Dea felt the weight of his words, the force of them pushing her forward despite the dread that gnawed at her insides. She hesitated for a fraction of a second, uncertainty gripping her, but then nodded. She didn't have a choice.

The pull of the box and the need to escape those shadows creeping at the edges of the trees were more than enough to spur her into action. Her legs burned as she broke into a full sprint, the path beneath her feet shifting with every step, twisting as if the forest itself were alive, shifting to trap her.

Behind her, the sounds of chaos erupted. Prex's gunfire continued to crack through the air, followed by the heavy, unnatural growls of creatures that couldn't possibly belong to this world. His shouts mixed with the heavy thud of pounding footsteps, urging her forward. *"Keep going, Dea! Don't stop!"*

But even as she sprinted, Dea couldn't shake the growing sensation that the forest was closing in around her, tightening like a noose. The trees, once silent and unmoving, now seemed to lean in, their gnarled branches reaching down like skeletal fingers. She gasped for air, the pressure on her chest mounting as if the very atmosphere had thickened to hinder her escape.

As her footfalls echoed in the stillness, the glow from the box intensified, casting an eerie light that illuminated the surrounding trees. Strange symbols appeared on the trunks, glowing faintly, as though the forest itself were marking her path. Each symbol seemed to pulse with an ancient energy, directing her deeper into the labyrinth of darkened woods. Dea followed their lead, her mind racing to make sense of it all, but the fear gnawing at her focus left little room for clarity.

Every corner she turned felt like a new twist in a dark and twisted game, each step pulling her further from safety, closer to the unknown. The oppressive darkness seemed to crawl toward her with every breath, the shadows stretching unnaturally long and thick. It was as if something unseen were reaching out, beckoning her into its grasp.

With each hurried breath, Dea pushed herself harder, but it felt as if the forest was closing in on her with every step. She couldn't look back; she could feel the ominous presence gaining on her. The whisper of leaves brushing against each other sounded like distant voices, a chorus of warnings that sent chills down her spine. The symbols on the trees grew more intricate, almost like a cryptic language that only the woods understood.

The path ahead continued to wind in impossible directions, growing darker and more foreboding, but Dea couldn't afford to stop. Not now. Not when she knew that the box was drawing them all closer, pulling them toward something greater—and far more dangerous—than she could imagine.

Finally, after what seemed like an eternity of running through dense, unforgiving foliage, Dea stumbled into a clearing. Her breath came in shallow gasps, her legs aching from the relentless sprint. At the heart of the clearing stood an ancient stone altar, its weathered surface covered in layers of moss and lichen. The altar was carved with intricate symbols, swirling patterns that seemed almost alive in their complexity. Each curve, each line appeared to tell a story, one that had long been forgotten by time. The glow from the box she clutched in her trembling hands intensified, casting an ethereal light that bathed the entire clearing in a soft, otherworldly glow. It was as if the box had been waiting for this moment, this place, for centuries.

Before Dea could fully process what she had found, a figure burst through the dense trees at the edge of the clearing. Prex, panting heavily, his clothes torn and bloodied, skidded to a halt just beyond the treeline. His revolver was still smoking from his frantic escape. *"They're right behind me!"* he yelled, his voice urgent and laced with panic.

Dea's heart skipped a beat as she quickly assessed the situation. She could hear the heavy footsteps of the creatures closing in, their growls growing louder, more menacing. Her hands, slick with sweat, trembled as she moved toward the altar. She could feel the weight of the box increasing with every step, as if it were becoming more alive in her grasp. As she reached the altar, she gently placed the box upon the stone surface, her eyes wide in both awe and terror.

"What do we do now?" Dea's voice quivered, though she tried to maintain control.

Just as she spoke, the ground beneath their feet began to rumble. It started as a faint tremor, barely noticeable, but it quickly grew into something far more intense. The earth itself seemed to groan, as if awakening from a long slumber. A deep, resonant hum vibrated through the air, low and vibrating in the bones, like the sound of the very earth itself speaking. The air grew thick, heavy, as if the atmosphere were charged with an unnatural energy.

The symbols on the altar and the box began to pulse with light, their patterns shifting and merging, flowing like liquid fire. It was mesmerizing, hypnotic, and terrifying all at once. The very fabric of reality seemed to bend and distort around them. Dea felt a chill crawl up her spine as the carvings seemed to reach out toward her, their energies calling her closer.

And then, they came.

The creatures emerged from the shadows of the forest, their forms barely distinguishable at first. Their movements were slow, deliberate, as if they were being pulled unwillingly toward the light. Their eyes glowed with a fierce, predatory hunger, but they hesitated, unsure of the power that now filled the clearing. They stopped just at the edge, their bodies tensed and poised, as if they feared crossing an invisible line.

Dea could feel the weight of their gaze, their hunger, but the light from the altar seemed to hold them at bay. It was as if the creatures were bound by something far older, something far more powerful than they had ever encountered. The tension in the air was palpable, thick with uncertainty.

Prex stood beside her, revolver in hand, his eyes darting between Dea and the creatures.

"What is this?" he muttered under his breath, his voice tight with fear.

Dea didn't answer. She couldn't. The only sound was the deep, rhythmic hum of the altar and the pulsing light that seemed to fill every inch of the clearing. Whatever was about to happen, whatever this place was, it was beyond their understanding. All they could do was wait, trapped in a moment suspended between past and future, unsure of what the next moment would bring.

Prex raised his revolver slowly, his finger poised on the trigger, his eyes narrowed with suspicion. He had been in enough dangerous situations to know that this moment was teetering on the edge of something catastrophic. But before he could take any action, Dea's hand shot out, gripping his arm with surprising strength.

"Wait. Look," she whispered urgently, her voice tinged with awe and a hint of fear.

Prex hesitated, his eyes flickering toward her, then following the direction of her gaze. The creatures, the ones that had been lurking in the shadows of the forest, had stopped at the very edge of the clearing. Their glowing eyes, once full of malice, now seemed mesmerized by the sight before them. They stood motionless, like statues carved from the very darkness of the night itself, staring intently at the altar.

One by one, as if guided by an unseen force, the creatures began to dissolve. It wasn't the kind of dissolution one might expect from something corporeal—there was no decomposition or decay. Instead, their bodies began to unravel, their forms disintegrating into swirling tendrils of black mist. The mist coiled upwards, drawn inexorably into the intricate carvings etched into the altar's surface. The symbols on the stone seemed to pulse, as though they were alive, greedily absorbing the mist, and the hum that had been faint before grew louder, more insistent, vibrating in Prex's chest.

The light from the mysterious box that lay upon the altar began to glow brighter, and the carvings shimmered as if responding to the gathering power. What had been a faint illumination was now a blinding, overwhelming flash, filling the entire clearing with an ethereal light that made the trees appear like phantoms, their forms stretching and distorting in the glow.

Prex squinted, shielding his eyes with one arm. The intensity of the light seemed to pierce through the very fabric of the forest, making the shadows flicker and dance unnaturally. It felt as though the world itself was holding its breath.

And then, just as abruptly as it had started, the light faded. The hum dwindled into a haunting silence that seemed to hang in the air, thick and unshakable. Prex blinked rapidly, his eyes adjusting to the sudden dimness. The creatures were gone—vanished as if they had never existed in the first place. The only sign of their presence was the lingering, faint scent of ozone that clung to the air.

The altar, once filled with the dark energy of the creatures, now lay utterly still. The box that had been atop it was open, its once-sealed lid now resting at an angle, its edges glowing faintly. Prex could hardly believe his eyes. Whatever had happened, it was clear that the box had been central to it all.

He stepped forward cautiously, his revolver still gripped tightly in his hand, his eyes darting around for any sign of danger. He couldn't shake the feeling that they were being watched, that something was still out there, lurking just beyond the edges of the clearing.

"What the hell just happened?" Prex muttered, his voice low and filled with disbelief.

Dea, her expression unreadable, approached the altar slowly. Her gaze was fixed on the object now resting in the open box. She reached out with a careful hand, her fingers brushing over the smooth surface of the object within. It was a key—no ordinary key, but a gleaming, ornate thing, its surface covered in strange, ancient runes. The key seemed to shimmer in the dying light, as though it were alive, its presence pulsing with an otherworldly energy.

Dea picked it up with reverence, holding it in her hands as if it were something sacred. She turned it over, studying the runes as her fingers traced the intricate markings etched into its surface. The key felt heavy in her palm, as though it carried the weight of a thousand secrets.

"I think..." she began, her voice soft, almost hesitant, as though she were speaking to herself. *"This is what the box was protecting. The key... it's not just a key. It's a key to something much bigger than we can understand."*

Prex eyed her, his gaze sharp and filled with suspicion. *"And what does it unlock?"* His voice was thick with unease, the tension in the air palpable.

Dea looked up at him then, her eyes meeting his with a steady, unwavering gaze. Her expression was one of resolve, her lips set in a firm line. There was no hint of doubt in her eyes, no second-guessing. She knew what had to be done. She had known since the moment the creatures had disappeared, since the moment the key had been revealed.

"We're going to find out," she said simply, her voice low but filled with an unshakable determination. It wasn't a question—it was a declaration.

For a moment, neither of them moved. The forest around them seemed frozen in time, the air thick with anticipation. The key in Dea's hand glinted faintly, as though urging them forward. Whatever lay ahead, Prex could feel it—feel it in the very marrow of his bones. There was no going back now.

The forest stood still, its ancient trees watching with quiet knowing, as if they had seen this moment unfold countless times before. The only sound was the distant rustling of the wind, and the faint hum of the now-quiet altar. Prex's hand tightened around his revolver, but there was no longer any real intention to use it. They had come too far for that. Whatever awaited them in the dark, they would face it together.

Dea turned her gaze toward the forest, her fingers still wrapped around the key, and nodded toward the unseen path ahead.

"We move forward," she said softly.

Prex's heart beat faster, but there was no fear now—only the grim resolve that came with knowing that whatever came next, they would face it head-on.

And with that, they began to walk into the unknown, the key glinting in Dea's hand, its runes whispering the promise of secrets yet to be uncovered.

Shadows and Sparks

The air hung heavy with the scent of damp earth and moss, a reminder of the recent rainfall that had soaked the forest floor. Prex and Dea moved away from the shadowy clearing, their pace brisk but measured, as if reluctant to disturb the fragile peace that seemed to hover around them. Prex's satchel swung lightly with each step, the weight of the key inside a quiet reassurance. The dense forest canopy filtered the waning light into dappled patches on the ground, and the once-ominous trees now seemed merely ancient, their twisted trunks and gnarled branches whispering of stories long forgotten. Yet, an eerie stillness clung to the air, as though the land itself had paused, waiting—watching.
"You okay?" Prex asked, his voice low but cutting through the oppressive quiet like a blade. He cast a glance toward Dea, his expression a mix of concern and weariness.
Dea gave a small nod, but her gaze remained locked on the uneven path ahead, her shoulders tense as if carrying an invisible burden.
"Yeah," she replied softly, though the word felt hollow. Her lips pressed into a thin line, betraying the unease she tried to suppress.
Prex studied her for a moment, noting the way her hands

clenched into fists at her sides, then relaxed again, as if wrestling with unspoken thoughts. He didn't press further. Instead, he let his eyes wander to their surroundings, scanning the shadows for any sign of movement. The silence wasn't comforting—it was unnatural, the kind that made the hairs on the back of his neck stand on end. Even the forest creatures seemed to have fallen into a reluctant hush.

Their boots crunched softly against the damp underbrush, the sound almost intrusive in the quiet. A faint breeze stirred the leaves above, carrying with it the faintest hint of something metallic—like the aftermath of a thunderstorm. Prex frowned but said nothing, his grip tightening slightly on the strap of his satchel.

The key was theirs now, but the unease in his chest told him that retrieving it had only been the beginning of something far greater—and far more dangerous.

"Just... trying to make sense of it all," she confessed, her voice tinged with a mix of exhaustion and lingering disbelief. *"What we saw back there... and what it could mean for us."*

Prex's steps slowed, his rugged features softening as he glanced over at her. The usual confidence in his demeanor was replaced by something gentler, something reassuring. *"We'll figure it out,"* he said, his voice steady, a quiet promise in his words. *"Whatever it is, we'll face it. Together."*

Dea paused, her eyes meeting his. For a moment, the weight of their shared burden seemed to lift, if only slightly. Her lips curved into a tentative smile, one that carried a flicker of hope amidst the shadows of uncertainty.

"Together," she repeated, the word rolling off her tongue like an unspoken vow. *"I like the sound of that."*

The silence that followed wasn't heavy with tension but rather filled with an unspoken understanding, a newfound connection between them. Each step they took through the forest felt synchronized, as though the rhythm of their hearts had somehow aligned. The dense canopy of trees began to recede, giving way to patches of silvery moonlight that spilled across the forest floor in scattered pools. The soft glow illuminated their path, casting long shadows that danced with each swaying branch.

Prex came to an abrupt halt, his gaze sharp and alert, as if he'd sensed something unseen. His hand brushed against Dea's arm, the touch light but enough to send a ripple of awareness coursing through her. She stopped beside him, her breath hitching as she followed his line of sight, though there was nothing immediately apparent in the dim light.

"What is it?" she whispered, her voice barely audible over the faint rustle of leaves in the gentle breeze.

He didn't answer right away. Instead, his fingers hovered near the hilt of his blade, his stance shifting subtly into one of readiness. But then his posture relaxed, and he turned to her, a faint, almost imperceptible smile playing at his lips.

"Nothing," he said after a moment, his tone laced with an unexpected warmth. *"I just wanted to make sure you were still with me."*

Dea let out a breath she hadn't realized she'd been holding, her tense shoulders easing as she offered him a wry smile. *"I'm not going anywhere,"* she said softly, the sincerity in her voice undeniable.

As they resumed their journey, the forest seemed less foreboding, the once-overwhelming shadows tempered by the quiet companionship they shared. With every step forward, the bond between them grew stronger, a silent reminder that, whatever awaited them beyond the trees, they wouldn't face it alone.

"Look," he said, his voice steady yet tinged with weariness, as he gestured toward the path ahead. The sight was breathtaking—a small, tranquil lake shimmered in the moonlight, its glassy surface mirroring the endless expanse of stars scattered across the night sky. The gentle glow of the moon bathed the surroundings in a silvery light, casting long, soft shadows that danced across the ground.

"Let's take a break," he suggested, his tone softening. *"We could use it."*

Dea hesitated for a moment, her gaze lingering on the water. The serenity of the scene seemed almost foreign, a stark contrast to the chaos that had become their lives. After a brief pause, she nodded. *"Yeah,"* she murmured, her voice carrying a faint trace of exhaustion. *"A break sounds good."*

They moved toward the water's edge, the crunch of their boots against the forest floor fading into the background as the soothing sounds of nature enveloped them. The soft rustling of leaves in the cool night breeze and the rhythmic lapping of the lake against the shore created an ambiance that was both calming and melancholic. Prex eased the heavy satchel off his shoulder, setting it down with deliberate care as though it held not just supplies, but the weight of their burdens. He lowered himself onto the grass, the tension in his body slowly giving way to the tranquility of the moment.

Dea sat beside him, her movements tentative. She stretched out her legs and leaned back slightly, her hands sinking into the cool, damp grass. Her fingers traced absent patterns against the earth, as though grounding herself in the moment. The silence between them stretched, not uncomfortable but laden with unspoken thoughts.

"Do you ever think about what life would be like if none of this had happened?" she asked suddenly, her voice barely rising above the whisper of the wind. There was a raw vulnerability in her tone, a yearning for something lost—a past that seemed impossibly distant.

Prex glanced at her, his brow furrowing slightly. He didn't answer immediately, his eyes drawn to the lake as if it held the answer to her question. The reflection of the stars seemed to ripple with their own stories, distorted yet beautiful.

"All the time," he admitted at last, his voice low. *"It's hard not to wonder, you know? What it would've been like to just... live. Without all this."*

Prex leaned back against the rough bark of the ancient tree, his gaze fixed on the sprawling canvas of stars above. The night sky seemed endless, a vast expanse of shimmering constellations, their light piercing through the velvet darkness. He exhaled softly, the cool night air carrying the weight of his thoughts as he spoke, his voice low and contemplative. *"Sometimes I wonder... but then I remind myself—if none of this chaos had unfolded, I might never have met you."*

Dea turned her head to look at him, her heart stuttering at the quiet sincerity in his tone. The faint glow of moonlight illuminated his features, casting shadows that only accentuated the earnestness in his expression.

"Do you really mean that?" she asked softly, her voice barely above a whisper.

Prex nodded, his eyes locking onto hers with an intensity that sent a shiver down her spine.

"I do," he said, his words laced with a quiet conviction. *"You've been my anchor in all this madness, the one thing that's kept me grounded. Without you..."* He paused, as if searching for the right words, then continued with a faint smile. *"Without you, I don't know if I'd have made it this far. You've given me something to hold on to, something worth fighting for."*

Dea felt her cheeks flush, a warmth spreading through her chest as his words settled over her like a gentle embrace. She turned away, unable to hold his gaze, but not before the corners of her lips lifted in a shy, almost reluctant smile. *"You're not so bad yourself, Prex,"* she murmured, her voice tinged with a playful lightness that belied the emotions surging within her.

For a moment, neither of them spoke, the silence between them filled with the soft rustling of leaves and the distant hum of nocturnal life. The world seemed to fade away, leaving only the two of them beneath the starlit sky—a fleeting moment of peace amidst the storm that surrounded their lives.

For a fleeting moment, the burdens of their mission dissolved, replaced by the profound stillness of their connection. The chaos of the world seemed to recede, leaving only the fragile sanctuary they had created between them. Prex hesitated, his hand trembling slightly as he reached out. His fingers brushed against hers—a fleeting touch that felt like a question, a tentative bridge between their separate storms.

Dea didn't retreat. Instead, she turned her hand over, letting their palms meet, her touch a silent acknowledgment. Her skin was warm, grounding, and Prex felt the weight of his uncertainties lighten in the contact. Her gaze softened, her voice barely above a whisper yet brimming with sincerity.

"I'm glad you're here," she murmured, her words tinged with a vulnerability she rarely showed. *"Even when everything feels impossible, you make it... bearable."*

Prex's breath caught as her words settled over him, their weight both humbling and comforting. His thumb moved in slow, deliberate strokes across her knuckles, as if memorizing the moment. His touch was gentle yet filled with unspoken promises. *"I'll always be here,"* he said, his voice steady despite the storm raging inside him. *"For you."*

The moment hung between them, delicate and unbroken, as though time itself had paused to honor their connection. The world around them faded into an indistinct haze, the distant hum of their surroundings melting away. All that remained was the space they shared and the magnetic pull drawing them closer.

Prex leaned in slowly, his breath mingling with hers as the distance between them shrank. His eyes searched hers, a silent plea for permission, for reassurance that this was what they both wanted. Dea's chest rose and fell rapidly, her heart thundering in her ears. She felt a sudden rush of warmth, an uncontainable surge of emotion that propelled her forward.

With a hitch in her breath, she closed the gap, their lips meeting in a kiss that was both delicate and charged. At first, it was a tentative exchange, like the first brush of sunlight after a storm—soft, testing, and filled with unspoken emotion. But as they surrendered to the moment, the kiss deepened, their hesitations melting away like snow beneath a rising sun.

Prex's hand moved to cradle her face, his fingers threading through her hair as if to anchor himself to her. Dea responded, her own hands finding their way to his shoulders, pulling him closer, grounding herself in the solidity of his presence. The kiss was no longer just an expression; it was a conversation, a promise, a shared declaration of everything they couldn't say aloud. When they finally parted, their foreheads rested against one another, their breaths mingling in the space between them. Dea's eyes fluttered open, meeting his with a mixture of wonder and trepidation.

"Prex..." she began, her voice barely audible, but the unspoken words lingered in the air between them, their meaning clear.

"I know," he whispered, his voice steady and resolute. *"Me too."*

And for the first time in what felt like an eternity, the impossible felt possible. Together, they could face anything. Together, they were enough.

As their emotions swirled in a tumultuous storm, the weight of their predicament began to crush them under its merciless reality. The relentless uncertainty of their survival loomed over them like a dark shadow, an oppressive reminder of the slim chances of escaping the nightmare they had found themselves ensnared in. Every fleeting thought of hope, every fragile thread that bound their hearts together, felt as though it was fraying, threatening to snap under the strain of their fear.

Dea's shoulders trembled, and her breaths came in shallow, ragged gasps as tears spilled down her cheeks, hot and unyielding. Her anguish was palpable, each tear carrying the unspoken fear that lingered in the corners of her mind. Prex, standing close yet equally shattered, instinctively pulled back ever so slightly, his own emotions clawing at him from the inside. His deep-set eyes shimmered with unshed tears, betraying the composure he so desperately clung to for her sake.

"I'm scared, Prex," Dea finally whispered, her voice cracking under the weight of her despair. The words tumbled out, raw and trembling, as though saying them aloud made her fears all the more real. *"I'm scared we won't make it. That we'll lose this... lose us."*

Her voice broke on the last word, and Prex felt something deep inside him splinter. He reached out with both hands, cupping her face as if trying to hold her together through sheer will alone. His thumbs moved instinctively, brushing away her tears in slow, deliberate motions, but they were helpless to stem the flood of emotions that poured from her.

"Dea," he murmured, his voice thick and unsteady as a single tear slipped down his cheek. *"I know you're scared. I'm scared too."* His words were soft, yet they carried the weight of his vulnerability, his fear, and his unwavering love for her.

He paused for a moment, his gaze locking with hers, searching for the courage to say the words that lay heavy on his heart. The silence between them was filled with the sound of their breathing, shaky and uneven, as if the air itself had become too dense with emotion to bear.

"But right now," Prex continued, his voice growing firmer, though still tinged with sorrow, *"right now, in this moment, we have each other. And no matter what happens—no matter how this ends—I want you to know that I love you, Dea. I love you more than anything, and I'll keep loving you, even if the world tries to tear us apart."*

His confession hung in the air, a fragile but unbreakable truth that seemed to wrap around them like a shield. Dea closed her eyes for a moment, leaning into his touch, feeling the warmth of his palms against her damp skin. Though the tears didn't stop, her lips trembled into a faint smile, a small beacon of light piercing through the darkness of their despair.

Dea's sob wavered, transforming into a shaky, bittersweet laugh as she tightened her grip on Prex's hands. Her trembling fingers clung to him like a lifeline, grounding her in the storm of emotions that raged within. She leaned into his chest, her voice soft yet resolute as she whispered, *"I love you too, Prex. More than anything in this world, more than I thought I ever could."*

Her words were a salve to his fractured heart, igniting a warmth within him that spread like wildfire. Their eyes locked, a silent understanding passing between them, and then their lips met once more. This kiss was unlike any before—a symphony of desperation, longing, and unspoken promises. It carried the weight of their struggles, the pain of their scars, and the hope of a future they refused to abandon. Each tear that slipped down their cheeks was a testament to their enduring connection, as though the essence of their love was etched into every shimmering drop.

The world around them seemed to fade, the darkness receding as they held on to each other. Their hearts beat as one, a steady rhythm that defied the chaos threatening to consume them. In that fleeting eternity, they were invincible—two souls bound together by a love so profound it seemed to bend the fabric of existence.

When they finally drew back, their foreheads pressed together, their breaths mingled in the cool night air. Prex's voice, though heavy with emotion, was unwavering as he spoke. *"We'll fight,"* he declared, his tone resolute and filled with quiet determination. *"No matter what comes our way, we'll fight for this—for us. Until the very end."*

Dea's eyes glistened as she nodded, her gaze fierce and unwavering. *"Together,"* she echoed, her voice a vow as unbreakable as the bond they shared.

The moment stretched between them, sacred and eternal, as if the stars above bore silent witness to their pledge. The heavens seemed to shimmer with approval, their light casting a soft glow over the couple. The key nestled in Prex's satchel stirred, emitting a faint hum that broke the stillness. Its ancient runes began to glow softly, pulsating with an energy that hinted at the trials yet to come.

Hand in hand, they turned to face the unknown. The path ahead was fraught with uncertainty, but they stepped forward with unwavering resolve. Whatever awaited them—perils, heartbreak, or triumph—they would face it side by side. Their love, fierce and unyielding, would be their guiding light, a beacon piercing through the encroaching shadows.

As they disappeared into the night, their silhouettes blurred by the dim starlight, the key's hum grew louder, its glow brighter. It was as if the universe itself had chosen them, weaving their fates into a story of love and resilience. And in the depths of their hearts, they knew: *together, they could withstand anything.*

The Test of the Veil

The path ahead wound into an impenetrable darkness, a suffocating veil that seemed to stretch endlessly. The only source of light was the faint, flickering glow emanating from the mysterious key tucked deep within Prex's satchel. Its soft luminescence cast eerie shadows that danced across the twisted trunks of the ancient trees surrounding them, as if the forest itself were alive, watching, waiting. The gnarled branches seemed to bend and sway unnaturally, their creaks and groans carrying an unsettling resonance, like whispers of forgotten souls.

With every cautious step, the weight of the journey seemed to press down harder on Prex's chest, the air growing thick and heavy. The forest, once silent and tranquil, now felt suffused with an oppressive tension, a silent, invisible force that seemed to grow stronger with each passing moment. The trees, with their crooked limbs, appeared to close in around them, their leaves rustling like hushed voices murmuring secrets long buried. The path beneath their feet, once clear and inviting, now seemed treacherous, the earth shifting with every movement, threatening to swallow them whole.

Each breath felt labored, the very air seeming to conspire against their progress. The oppressive stillness was broken only by the occasional snap of a twig underfoot or the distant hoot of an owl, but these sounds only served to amplify the sense of isolation. It was as though they were walking through an ancient, forgotten world, a place where time itself had stopped, and the rules of nature no longer applied.

Dea clung to Prex's arm, her fingers trembling slightly as she tried to steady herself. The earlier sense of determination she had fought so hard to hold on to now seemed fragile, slipping away in the thick, almost suffocating silence that surrounded them. The air was dense with an unsettling energy, as if the very atmosphere was charged with something ancient and foreboding. *"This place... it feels wrong,"* she whispered, her voice barely rising above the faint rustling of distant leaves. There was an undercurrent of dread in her words, a quiet recognition that something wasn't right, that they were trespassing on grounds better left undisturbed.

Prex, though equally affected by the palpable tension in the air, remained resolute. His jaw was clenched tight, eyes scanning their surroundings with an intensity that suggested both vigilance and patience. *"We're close,"* he replied, his voice low, steady. *"Whatever this key unlocks, it's not far now. We've come too far to turn back."*

With a purposeful stride, he led the way forward, and Dea reluctantly followed, her senses heightened with every step. The path grew narrower, the trees on either side forming an almost unnatural wall that seemed to close in on them, their twisted branches reaching out like skeletal hands. The silence deepened, broken only by the occasional crunch of dead leaves underfoot. Despite the eerily still night, Dea felt the weight of a thousand unseen eyes watching their every movement.

Finally, they emerged into a small clearing. The moon hung high in the sky, casting a ghostly pallor over the land. In the center of the clearing stood an ancient stone archway, its presence both majestic and intimidating. The stones, weathered by centuries of neglect, were etched with intricate carvings—patterns that seemed to pulse with a life of their own. The designs mirrored those they had seen on the mysterious box and the key, symbols that appeared to shift when glanced at too quickly, as though they were more than mere decoration. There was a deep, hidden meaning in these markings, one that neither of them fully understood, but both could feel resonating in their bones.

At the heart of the archway, framed by the aged stone, was a keyhole—a precise, almost perfect opening that seemed to hum with quiet anticipation. The artifact they carried, the key that had led them here, fit into the hole with an uncanny precision. The air around the archway seemed to thrum with an energy that intensified the closer they drew, as if the very ground beneath them was alive, waiting. Dea's breath caught in her throat as she reached for the key, her fingers brushing against the cool metal, and she could feel the pulse of something ancient stir within her chest.

Prex stepped forward, his eyes never leaving the keyhole. His fingers hovered just above it, a mixture of reverence and tension in the air. The moment had arrived.

"This is it," Prex declared, a sense of finality in his tone as he drew the key from his satchel. The object shimmered with an ethereal glow, its surface etched with ancient runes that pulsed with a soft, rhythmic light, almost as if it were alive—thrumming with anticipation. The key's intricate symbols seemed to shift and writhe in the dim light, their purpose undeniably clear, yet unknown.

Dea stepped closer, her gaze fixed on the archway before them. The stone structure loomed large, its edges worn by the passage of time, but still standing resolute. Shadows clung to the contours of the arch, making the space beyond appear as a dark, beckoning abyss. The air around them felt heavier, charged with an ancient energy that hummed in the silence. Dea's brow furrowed as she took in the mysterious threshold, her eyes narrowing slightly as she considered the unknown that lay on the other side.

"What do you think is beyond this gate?" she asked, her voice low, tinged with both curiosity and trepidation. Her fingers

brushed the hilt of her dagger, as if instinctively readying herself for whatever might come next.

Prex's gaze never wavered from the archway. He felt a flicker of unease in his chest, but he masked it with a calm exterior. He knew they had come this far, and turning back now wasn't an option. *"There's only one way to find out,"* he replied, his voice steady, though the weight of the moment pressed upon him. His hand gripped the key tightly, feeling its warmth seep into his skin. The vibrations from the runes grew stronger, as though the very fabric of reality was reacting to their presence.

As he approached the archway, the key seemed to hum louder, its glow intensifying. Prex hesitated for only a moment, but it was enough for Dea to notice. She met his eyes, searching for any sign of doubt. But Prex's face remained a mask of determination. With a final, resolute breath, he placed the key into the lock that had appeared, hidden within the arch's stonework. The runes on the key and the archway aligned, and a low, resonant click echoed through the air. The ground beneath them trembled slightly, as if the world itself was holding its breath.

"I suppose there's no going back now," Dea murmured, her voice barely above a whisper.

"No going back," Prex echoed, his fingers tightening on the key, ready to turn it.

He slowly inserted the ancient key into the weathered lock, its intricate designs glinting under the faint light. As the key turned, the carvings etched into the archway seemed to come alive. A soft hum resonated through the air, gradually growing louder until a deep, rumbling vibration shook the ground beneath them. The stone beneath their feet trembled as if awakening from a long slumber, and the archway itself seemed to pulse with an otherworldly energy.

The air around them grew thick with anticipation. A faint glow began to emanate from the archway, at first dim, then gradually intensifying into a vibrant, swirling dance of colors—deep purples, fiery oranges, and streaks of electric blue. The space within the archway shifted and twisted, transforming into a chaotic vortex of light and shadow, as if the very fabric of reality were bending and warping before their eyes.

Dea stood frozen, her heart racing, her breath caught in her throat. *"It's... magnificent, but also so overwhelming,"* she whispered, her voice barely audible over the tumultuous rumblings around them.

Prex turned to her, his face illuminated by the ethereal glow, his eyes filled with both awe and resolve. He reached for her hand, their fingers intertwining with a sense of silent understanding.

"We knew this moment would come. Are you ready?"

Dea felt the warmth of his hand, a steady reassurance in the midst of the unknown. She took a deep breath, her gaze never leaving the mesmerizing vortex.

"I think so," she replied, her voice strong despite the uncertainty swirling within her. Her grip on his hand tightened, her fingers pressing into his with determination. *"Let's do this."*

Together, they stepped through the portal, and the world around them seemed to fracture into a thousand fragments. A vertigo-like sensation gripped their senses, as though their bodies were being stretched and compressed simultaneously, their very souls pulled in multiple directions at once. The air buzzed with an invisible force, and a low hum filled their ears, growing steadily louder, almost like the heartbeat of the universe itself. Every step they took through the swirling vortex felt like both an eternity and a fleeting moment. It was as if time itself had bent around them, altering its usual flow.

When the overwhelming sensation finally eased and the world around them began to stabilize, they found themselves in an enormous, cavernous chamber. The walls seemed to stretch far beyond sight, their surfaces alive with an ethereal, shimmering glow. It wasn't like any light they had ever encountered—there was no source they could discern, no visible flame or bulb. Instead, the illumination appeared to emanate from the very stone itself, as though the walls were infused with some kind of ancient energy. The light flickered and pulsed, casting long, undulating shadows across the ground, giving the entire space a surreal and dreamlike quality.

The air in the chamber was thick with an electric charge, like the calm before a storm, tingling on their skin and vibrating in their bones. A strange, almost magnetic pull seemed to emanate from the center of the room, compelling them to move forward despite the overwhelming sense of awe and caution that held them in place. The atmosphere was dense with unspoken power, and every breath felt heavier, laden with an ancient, forgotten knowledge.

At the heart of the chamber stood an imposing pedestal, crafted from an unknown stone that shimmered faintly in the ambient glow. Upon it rested a crystalline orb, unlike anything they had ever seen. The orb was perfectly spherical, its surface smooth and flawless, refracting the surrounding light in dazzling patterns. It pulsed with a rhythmic, almost hypnotic glow, its faint illumination growing brighter and dimmer in time with an unseen pulse, as though the orb itself had a heartbeat. It felt as though it was alive, filled with a vibrant, unseen energy that resonated deep within their chests, drawing their gaze and attention in a way they couldn't resist.

Surrounding the pedestal were towering statues, seemingly carved from the same ethereal stone as the walls. The figures stood in solemn silence, their forms looming high above them, their faces hidden beneath deep, flowing hoods that obscured any trace of identity or expression. Their hands were outstretched toward the orb, their fingers splayed as if they were reaching for something just beyond their grasp, or perhaps offering something to the pulsating sphere. The statues' presence was both awe-inspiring and unsettling, exuding an air of ancient reverence. It was as if they had been standing watch for eons, guarding something beyond comprehension, their gaze fixed on the orb, never faltering.

The entire chamber seemed to hum with energy, the very walls vibrating with the power contained within the orb at the center. The silence was profound, broken only by the soft echoes of their footsteps against the stone floor. Yet, despite the stillness, there was a sense of something immense, something powerful, waiting to be discovered, as if the chamber itself was alive, aware of their presence, and watching them. The atmosphere was thick with mystery, and as they stood there, taking it all in, a deep, unspoken sense of purpose stirred within them, as though they were meant to be here, as though this place held the key to something much larger than themselves.

"This has to be it," Prex murmured, his voice reverberating through the cavernous space. His words seemed to carry weight, as though they too were a part of the profound discovery they had stumbled upon. His eyes gleamed with a mix of excitement and awe as he gazed at the pedestal ahead. The room, bathed in an eerie, otherworldly light, seemed to pulse with an energy that felt almost alive.

"The source of everything. The answer we've been seeking."

Dea's heart raced in her chest, each beat growing louder in her ears. She took a hesitant step forward, her gaze unwavering on the orb resting atop the pedestal. It glowed with a subtle, almost hypnotic radiance, its surface shifting in ways that defied explanation. There was something undeniably beautiful about it—a swirling dance of colors, like the very fabric of the universe was contained within. Yet, beneath the allure, there was an unsettling energy that clawed at her instincts.

"It's beautiful," Dea whispered, her voice barely audible in the vast, echoing chamber.

"But why does it feel so... dangerous?"

Her words hung in the air, heavy with the weight of uncertainty. The orb, though captivating, radiated an aura that unsettled her. She couldn't shake the feeling that this was more than just an artifact—it was something far more powerful, something that could either save or destroy them.

Before Prex could respond, a deep, resonant voice echoed throughout the chamber, filling the space with an otherworldly presence. *"You have come far, seekers. But the path to truth is fraught with sacrifice."*

Dea and Prex spun around in unison, their eyes scanning the

shadows, searching for the source of the voice. The voice seemed to come from all directions, as though it reverberated off the very stone walls, making it impossible to pinpoint its origin. A cold shiver ran down Dea's spine, and she instinctively took a step back, her hand instinctively resting on the hilt of her blade. And then, from the shadows, a figure emerged—one of the ancient statues that lined the chamber. Its stone face was worn with the passage of millennia, etched with deep lines that told stories of long-forgotten times. The figure's hood, which had once been obscuring its face, fell away to reveal eyes glowing with an eerie, unnatural light. The eyes seemed to pierce through the very fabric of their souls, as though they were being weighed, measured, and judged.

The figure's mouth moved again, its voice now a low, guttural rumble that vibrated the air around them. *"The path you seek is not one to be taken lightly. Many have come before you, drawn by the allure of power, only to be consumed by it. Are you prepared to pay the price for the truth you desire?"*

Dea felt the weight of those words settle over her, like a heavy shroud. The statue's glowing eyes never left them, its presence now tangible, pressing in on all sides. The room seemed to close in around them, the air thick with the tension of something ancient and primal. Dea's pulse quickened, but she held her ground, steeling herself for whatever lay ahead.

Prex, on the other hand, seemed less shaken. His eyes were locked onto the orb, a determination burning within them. *"We didn't come this far to turn back now,"* he said, his voice steady, though there was a hint of uncertainty beneath the surface. *"We have to understand. We have to know what this is."*

The statue's lips curled into a semblance of a smile, though it was hard to tell whether it was a gesture of approval or mockery. *"Very well, seekers. But be warned—the truth you seek will come at a cost. It always does."*

Dea's stomach churned, but she knew there was no turning back. The orb before them seemed to beckon, its pull growing stronger with each passing moment. The figure in front of them, a guardian of sorts, had spoken the truth, but Dea could only wonder: What would they have to sacrifice to uncover the secrets of this place?

"Who are you?" Prex demanded, his hand instinctively reaching for the revolver tucked at his side, his fingers tightening around the cold, metallic grip. His stance was rigid, his eyes narrowing with suspicion and caution.

"I am the Guardian," the figure responded, his voice echoing in the vast, dimly lit chamber. He stepped forward from the shadows, the light glinting off his ethereal form. *"Protector of the Veil. The orb you seek possesses the power to reshape entire worlds, but such power demands a heavy price."*

Dea's heart thudded in her chest, the weight of his words sinking deep within her. *"What kind of price?"* she asked, her voice trembling despite her attempt at composure. Her eyes flickered to the orb, its pulsating glow casting an eerie light on her face.

The Guardian's gaze shifted to Dea, his eyes seeming to pierce through her very soul.

"A bond as rare as yours is something to be cherished," he said softly, his voice betraying no hint of malice, only solemnity.

"But to claim the orb, one must be willing to sever it. Permanently."

Prex's eyes widened, and he immediately stepped forward, positioning himself between Dea and the Guardian. His jaw clenched, his mind racing as the implications of the Guardian's words took root.

"There has to be another way," he stated firmly, his voice unwavering but edged with frustration.

"There is not," the Guardian replied, his tone grave. *"The orb's power is not a gift to be wielded lightly. To control it is to forsake all else—your ties, your connections, everything you hold dear."*

Dea's breath caught in her throat as her mind raced through every possibility. She glanced at Prex, her heart aching at the thought of losing him, yet her eyes were also drawn back to the orb, its power calling to her like a distant thunderclap, impossible to ignore.

"We came all this way. We can't turn back now," she whispered, almost to herself, but loud enough for the Guardian to hear.

Prex shook his head, his eyes softening with concern but hardening with resolve. *"Not like this,"* he said, his voice raw with emotion. *"There's always another way. We'll find it."*

The Guardian raised a hand, and the very air around them seemed to shudder, the ground beneath their feet quaking as though the chamber itself had a heartbeat. The intensity of the orb's glow grew brighter, bathing them all in an almost unbearable light.

"Choose quickly, seekers," the Guardian's voice thundered, reverberating through the chamber like the toll of a distant bell. *"The Veil does not wait. Time slips away, and the decision must be made."*

Prex turned to Dea, his eyes searching hers with a depth of emotion that left no room for doubt. His hand found hers, gripping it tightly, his fingers cold but steady.

"I'm not losing you," he murmured, the words heavy with finality. *"Not for this."*

Tears welled in Dea's eyes, her breath hitching in her throat as she reached up to touch his face, her fingertips trembling against his skin. *"Prex..."* she whispered, her voice breaking. *"What if this is the only way? What if there's no other choice?"*

Prex's hand covered hers, his touch tender yet firm, as though grounding them both in the midst of a storm. His voice faltered for a moment, the weight of his love for her and the gravity of their mission almost too much to bear.

"Then we'll find another way. Together," he said, his words fierce with determination, as though the very force of his will could shape reality itself.

The orb's glow intensified, its light becoming blinding, searing through the dim chamber. The Guardian's voice grew louder, a warning, a judgment. *"Your indecision will doom you both,"* he intoned, his gaze shifting between the two, his expression unreadable, like that of an ancient being who had seen countless souls face such decisions. *"You cannot delay. The path you choose now will determine everything."*

Dea's heart ached with the weight of the decision before her. She could feel the pull of the orb's power, could almost taste the possibility of shaping the world to their will. But at what cost? She glanced at Prex, his expression resolute, and she knew that this wasn't just about the orb. It was about them—about what they had built together, the bond they shared. She reached for him, her hand seeking his, her fingers entwining with his as her heart waged war with her mind.

"We fight," she whispered, her voice steady despite the turmoil inside her. *"No matter what. We can't lose ourselves in the process. We have to keep fighting. Together."*

Prex's grip on her hand tightened, his resolve unwavering, his eyes burning with the fire of determination. *"No matter what,"* he echoed, his voice a promise, a vow carved into the very essence of his being.

The Guardian's gaze softened, and for the first time, there was a flicker of something resembling sorrow in his glowing eyes. *"So be it,"* he said, his voice barely audible amidst the growing tumult in the chamber. *"The path you have chosen is fraught with peril, and the stakes are high. But your bond may yet prove stronger than fate itself. Choose wisely, for the Veil does not forgive."*

With those final words, the chamber trembled once more, the orb's glow flickering in time with the Guardian's fading presence. The decision had been made. And now, they would face whatever came next—together.

The statues, once still and frozen in time, began to move. Their stone hands, intricately carved and firm, slowly lowered as the glowing orb's light faded to a faint shimmer. The once vibrant energy in the chamber seemed to dissipate, and the space grew eerily quiet, the electric hum that had filled the air now nothing more than a distant memory.

"What just happened?" Dea whispered, her voice quivering with confusion and fear, her wide eyes scanning the room, trying to make sense of the sudden change.

Prex, too, was unsettled. His gaze was fixed on the Guardian, the towering figure that had stood like a sentinel, its eyes glowing with ancient wisdom. His brow furrowed in concentration, as if trying to unravel the mystery of the Guardian's sudden shift in demeanor. *"Why did you let us go?"* he demanded, his voice steady despite the unease that gripped him.

The Guardian's form seemed to waver, its outline flickering between solid and ethereal, as if it existed in a place just beyond the grasp of reality. It took a step back, its shadow stretching long across the floor. The ancient being's voice, a blend of sorrow and warning, echoed in the vastness of the chamber. *"The Veil has tested you, seekers,"* it intoned, each word heavy with meaning. *"The answers you seek lie ahead, but beware—every choice you make will demand a price."*

The air around them seemed to grow colder, and with a final, fleeting glance, the Guardian melted into the darkness, its presence dissipating like mist in the morning sun. As it vanished, the very fabric of the chamber seemed to dissolve, the stone walls crumbling away as if they were never meant to exist. The once sturdy columns and ornate carvings crumbled into nothingness, leaving behind only a blinding light that swallowed everything in its path.

Before Prex and Dea could fully comprehend what was happening, they found themselves standing once more in the familiar, towering trees of the forest. The archway, which had once loomed behind them like a silent guardian, was now nothing more than a dark, lifeless frame, its energy extinguished. The pulse of magic that had resonated through the space was gone, replaced by the stillness of the night.

Dea, her hand shaking as she reached for Prex's arm, felt her heart race within her chest. The sudden return to the forest, with all its quiet mysteries, left her feeling disoriented and vulnerable. *"What now?"* she asked, her voice barely a whisper as the weight of their experience settled in. The uncertainty of the path ahead was more daunting than ever.

Prex's grip tightened on her, pulling her closer as if to shield her from the unseen dangers that lingered in the shadows of the forest. He could feel the tremor in her body, the fear that had taken root within her, but he refused to let it consume them. His lips brushed gently against her forehead, a gesture meant to reassure her, even as doubt clawed at the edges of his own mind. *"Now, we keep going,"* he murmured, his voice resolute, though his eyes betrayed the uncertainty he fought to suppress. *"Together, Dea. We keep going. Whatever comes next, we face it side by side."*

The weight of their journey ahead loomed before them, but in that moment, amidst the quiet whisper of the wind through the trees, they knew that whatever trials awaited them, they would face them together. And that, for now, was enough.

Veil of Shadows

The air hung heavy with an unsettling tension as Prex and Dea drew closer to the forsaken railway station, a once-majestic structure now enveloped in the weight of time's cruel neglect. Its towering, crumbling walls bore the scars of forgotten history, with cracked windows and rusted iron beams that seemed to groan beneath the strain of years left untouched. The once bustling echoes of travelers now seemed a distant memory, replaced only by a thick silence that wrapped around them like a suffocating fog.

As they stepped through the derelict archway, the faint rustling of wind whispered through the broken windows, sending stray tendrils of dust and shattered glass tumbling in the air. The remnants of the station's former grandeur were visible in the intricate, yet faded, carvings along the walls, now shrouded in the grey film of decay. Every step they took echoed in the vast emptiness, a hollow reminder of the station's former life.

Prex's hand clenched around the runed key, its ethereal glow casting an eerie light across the floor. The symbols etched into its surface pulsed faintly, as though alive with a purpose known only to the past. The glow illuminated their path, stretching long shadows that seemed to sway and writhe like sentient creatures in the dark. The labyrinth of old ticket booths and forgotten benches stood as silent witnesses to a time long past, their edges softened by years of dust and neglect.

Dea, feeling the weight of the place press down on her chest, leaned in closer to Prex. Her breath came in shallow, uneven bursts, and her fingers tightened around his arm. *"This place... it feels like a tomb,"* she murmured, her voice barely above a whisper, as if speaking too loudly would awaken something that slumbered within.

Prex's eyes, sharp and ever vigilant, swept over the desolate station, the flickering light of the key casting a faint sheen on his face. He muttered under his breath, his voice tinged with a dark understanding,

"It might as well be." His gaze lingered on the shadows that seemed to stretch into infinity.

"But if the map is right, the next clue is here, hidden somewhere in this forsaken place."

His words hung in the air, thick with mystery and foreboding, as they continued their cautious journey deeper into the heart of the abandoned station. Each step they took seemed to reverberate through the long-forgotten halls, disturbing the stillness that had claimed this place as its own. Whatever secrets the station held, Prex and Dea knew they were not alone in their search. The very walls seemed to whisper ancient, forgotten truths—truths that had long been buried beneath layers of dust and decay.

They stepped inside, their footsteps resonating with a hollow echo as they traversed the dimly lit, desolate station. The cracked tiles beneath their feet were stained with the remnants of time, the grime and dust of neglect thick in the air. The faint glow of the key in Prex's hand illuminated the darkness, its runes pulsing with a gentle, rhythmic light, as though they were alive, guiding him like a silent, unseen force.

As they moved forward, the oppressive silence hung heavily in the air, broken only by the soft hiss of the distant wind that sneaked through the cracks in the walls. The walls themselves seemed to whisper, their surfaces weathered and marked by years of abandonment, a testament to whatever had once flourished here. With every step, the atmosphere thickened, the weight of forgotten memories pressing down on them.

At the far end of the station, hidden behind layers of dust and shadows, stood a rusted door. It creaked on its hinges as Prex pushed it open, the sound of old metal scraping against metal reverberating through the vast emptiness. The door gave way with surprising ease, revealing the darkened passage beyond.

Beyond the threshold, the air grew cooler, and a pungent, earthy scent began to fill the space. Before them stretched a spiral staircase, its iron steps worn and twisted by years of decay. The railing, once sturdy, was now weak, its surface slick with corrosion. The staircase wound downward into the earth, its depth impossible to gauge in the dim light. The shadows seemed to beckon, swallowing the steps below as the faint glow from the key cast long, flickering shadows that danced along the walls.

Prex's heart quickened as he peered into the abyss beneath, the darkness seeming to pulse with an energy of its own, drawing him in. The air felt heavier here, charged with an ancient power that whispered secrets only the brave, or perhaps the foolish, dared to uncover. Each step closer to the staircase brought a sense of unease, as if the very ground beneath them held memories it longed to keep buried. Still, Prex took a deep breath, the faint glow of the key now their only guide, and descended into the unknown.

"This just keeps getting better," Prex muttered under his breath, his voice dripping with sarcasm as he cast a glance toward Dea. The dark humor in his words only barely masked the tension in his body.

Dea, however, managed a faint smile, her fingers tightening around his arm in a quiet show of reassurance. Her gaze flickered across the room as she spoke, her voice a soft murmur, yet filled with a quiet strength.

"At least we're together. That's something."

The pair moved cautiously down the staircase, each step resonating with an eerie echo that seemed to carry the weight of centuries. The chill in the air grew more pronounced, creeping beneath their clothes, biting at their skin. The dim glow from the key in Prex's hand illuminated the winding path ahead, casting long, dancing shadows that played across the stone walls. It flickered with a strange energy, a subtle reminder of the mystery that lay ahead.

As they descended deeper into the chamber, the air grew heavier, thick with an ancient presence, like the very walls had witnessed the passage of time in silence. The key's light brightened further, revealing the intricate carvings that lined the walls, their deep grooves and delicate etchings obscured by centuries of dust. Figures of long-forgotten gods and strange beasts seemed to watch them, their faces frozen in an eternal gaze. Some appeared almost lifelike, their stone eyes burning with an intensity that sent a shiver down Dea's spine.

At the heart of the room, standing on a raised stone platform, was a pedestal, its surface smooth and polished despite the centuries of neglect. Resting atop it was a small, ornate box. Its design was unlike anything they had ever seen—a blend of delicate, swirling patterns, some sharp and angular, others flowing like liquid metal. It glinted faintly in the pale light of the key, an aura of ancient power emanating from it. The box seemed to pulse with energy, almost as if it were alive, waiting to be touched.

Dea's breath caught in her throat as she gazed at the box, her heart racing with a mix of excitement and trepidation. *"Is this it?"* she asked, her voice barely audible, as if speaking too loudly might disrupt the fragile stillness of the chamber.

Prex didn't answer immediately. His eyes, narrowing in concentration, scanned the room, looking for any sign of danger or hidden traps. With a slow, deliberate motion, he nodded, his eyes fixed on the box. *"Only one way to find out,"* he said, his voice low but resolute.

Without taking his eyes off the box, he began to approach the pedestal, his every step measured. The silence of the chamber seemed to grow thicker, pressing in around them, as if the very air was holding its breath. His hand reached out toward the box, fingers trembling ever so slightly, not from fear, but from the weight of the decision they were about to make.

The instant his fingers brushed the surface of the box, the carvings on the walls began to glow, their intricate designs lighting up with an unnatural brilliance. The low hum that had been present in the background suddenly grew louder, vibrating through the stone beneath their feet, a resonating sound that seemed to come from deep within the earth itself.

A cold wind swept through the room, gusting from nowhere, and the temperature dropped drastically. It wasn't just cold—it was biting, a sharp chill that seemed to sink into their bones, as though the very essence of the room was turning against them. Dea's breath escaped in visible puffs, her face paling as the air grew increasingly frigid. She instinctively took a step closer to Prex, her body trembling not only from the cold but from the strange sense of impending danger that enveloped them.

The door behind them slammed shut with a deafening crash, its sound echoing through the chamber like the clap of thunder. The sudden noise sent a jolt of panic through Dea's chest. She spun around, her eyes wide in alarm, but there was no way out now. The walls had already begun to close in around them.

The shadows in the corners of the room seemed to shift, stretching and twisting unnaturally. As the last of the light from the key flickered, the shadows coalesced, forming shapes that were not quite human. They moved with a purpose, their dark figures growing larger, their eyes glowing like burning coals in the darkness. Their presence was overwhelming, suffocating, as if they had been waiting for this moment, lurking just out of sight, biding their time.

Dea's heart pounded in her chest as she took a step back, her hand instinctively reaching for Prex's arm. *"What... what are they?"* she whispered, her voice trembling with fear.

Prex didn't answer immediately, his eyes fixed on the shadows, his muscles coiled in readiness. *"I don't know,"* he said quietly, his voice tight with the knowledge that whatever came next, they were not prepared for it.

The hum grew louder, vibrating through their very bones as the shadows closed in, their eyes burning with an intensity that could only be described as malevolent. The air was thick with a sense of dread, and in that moment, Dea realized that the box they had come for was not the only thing that had been waiting for them in this forgotten chamber.

"Not again," Prex muttered, his voice low, edged with frustration. He swiftly drew his revolver, the cold metal of the weapon gleaming under the dim light as he aimed it toward the writhing shadows that seemed to crawl toward them. His grip was steady, but his eyes never left the eerie dark forms that twisted and undulated with a malevolent energy. Every inch of his body was prepared for a fight, every muscle taut with anticipation.

Dea stepped forward, her usual confident stride faltering just slightly as she felt the weight of the moment settle on her shoulders. Her voice, though trembling, held an undeniable firmness as she spoke,

"Wait. Let me try something."

The words hung in the air for a heartbeat, uncertainty and determination mixing within her. The shadows seemed to pause, sensing the shift in the air. With a steadying breath, Dea raised the key high above her head. The old, ornate artifact was warm in her hands, its surface gleaming with an otherworldly light. As soon as she lifted it, the glow intensified, filling the space around them with a soft, ethereal radiance. The shadows, previously moving with relentless aggression, seemed to hesitate, their fluid motions faltering as if they were struggling to resist the pull of the key's power.

Dea's lips parted as she began to speak. The language that flowed from her mouth was alien, a strange cadence of sounds that seemed to resonate in the very air around them. It was as though her words were not merely spoken, but woven into the fabric of reality itself. The ground beneath them seemed to tremble slightly, and the shadows, once chaotic and uncontrolled, began to recoil. Their twisting forms writhed in response, as though the very nature of their being was being undone. The key's light grew stronger, and the shadows, unable to withstand its force, dissolved into wisps of smoke, vanishing into the nothingness from which they had come.

A deep hum, almost imperceptible, vibrated in the air, and the intricate carvings that had lined the walls seemed to dim, their eerie glow flickering before fading into complete darkness. The oppressive weight that had settled over them lightened, and for a moment, silence reigned.

Prex lowered his revolver, his breath coming in quick, shallow bursts. His eyes, wide with disbelief, scanned the empty space where the shadows had once loomed. He could feel his heart still hammering in his chest, but there was no immediate danger now. He looked at Dea, his gaze filled with a mix of awe and something deeper, something he couldn't quite name. *"What did you just do?"* he asked, his voice barely a whisper, as though the magnitude of the moment hadn't quite settled in.

Dea lowered the key, her hands trembling slightly as the glow around it began to fade. She glanced down at it, as though seeing it for the first time. Her mind was still racing, trying to comprehend the power she had just unleashed.

"I... I don't know," she confessed, her voice softer now, as if speaking too loudly would shatter the fragile calm that had descended. *"It just... felt right."*

Her words held an unspoken weight, a vulnerability that Prex hadn't expected. He took a step toward her, his movements slow, deliberate. Before she could react, he pulled her into a tight embrace, his arms encircling her with an intensity that seemed to speak volumes. His heart was still pounding, but it was no longer out of fear; now, it was the rush of adrenaline from the unexpected power that had just been unleashed. His chest pressed against hers, and for a moment, they stood there, caught in the quiet aftermath.

"You keep surprising me, you know that?" Prex murmured into her hair, his voice rough with emotion he couldn't fully express. Dea smiled, her face pressed against his chest, her body still shaking slightly from the intensity of the moment. The fear,

which had once gripped her so tightly, now felt distant, momentarily forgotten in the warmth of his embrace. She let out a soft laugh, the sound light and free, as if she were letting go of all the tension that had built up inside her.

"You're not so bad yourself," she replied, her voice a whisper of playfulness, though she still couldn't entirely shake the feeling that she had just tapped into something far beyond her understanding.

In that moment, as they stood together amidst the fading echoes of ancient power, a new understanding passed between them. The weight of their shared journey, the dangers they had faced, and the connection that had formed between them in the heat of it all was undeniable. Neither of them fully understood what had just happened, but one thing was clear: they were no longer just allies, but something more, something that neither of them could have predicted. And in that unspoken bond, they found a moment of peace amidst the chaos.

Their moment of quiet contemplation was shattered by the distinct sound of the box's lid clicking open. Both Dea and Prex turned in unison, their eyes drawn to the artifact before them. Slowly, the lid began to lift, revealing something that gleamed with an otherworldly brilliance: *a small vial, its contents shimmering like liquid gold.* The light reflected off the surface in a mesmerizing dance, casting faint shadows on their faces.

Dea took a step forward, her gaze fixed on the vial, as if it held the answers to everything they had been searching for. *"What is it?"* she asked, her voice barely above a whisper, filled with both awe and uncertainty. The air around them seemed to hold its breath.

Prex reached out cautiously, his hand trembling slightly as it closed around the vial. His brow furrowed in concentration, and his dark eyes narrowed in thought. *"I think it's what we've been looking for,"* he replied, his voice steady, yet laced with a hint of hesitation. The vial pulsed softly in his hand, as if responding to his words.

Dea's heart raced in her chest, her breath caught in her throat as she stepped closer, the weight of their shared journey pressing down on her. Her eyes locked with Prex's, searching for reassurance.

"Do you think it can save us?" she asked, her voice carrying a mixture of hope, fear, and desperation. They had faced countless trials, walked through darkened paths, and encountered horrors they had never imagined. Could this tiny vial hold the key to their survival, to the salvation they so desperately needed?

Prex studied the vial for a long moment, the golden liquid swirling within, almost as if it were alive. His gaze softened, and he looked at Dea, the intensity of their shared experience reflected in his eyes.

"I don't know," he said, his tone heavier than before. *"But it's the best chance we've got."* The words hung in the air between them, carrying an undeniable weight. The uncertainty was undeniable, but the flicker of determination in his voice was unmistakable.

They stood in silence for a few moments, the air thick with the gravity of the situation. The vial, glowing faintly in Prex's hand, seemed to pulse in time with the beat of their hearts. The uncertainty of the future loomed large before them—an unknown road that stretched far beyond their sight, filled with dangers they couldn't begin to comprehend. And yet, despite the fear, despite the unanswered questions, they stood together, united in their resolve.

In that moment, the future was as elusive as the light that flickered in the vial, shifting with each passing second. The journey ahead was shrouded in uncertainty, but one thing was clear: *they would face it together. No matter what trials awaited them, no matter how impossible the odds seemed, they would not be defeated. The weight of their journey, of the sacrifices they had made, pressed down on them, but it did not break them. Together, they would move forward—into the unknown, hand in hand, ready for whatever came next.*

The Labyrinth's Whisper

The vial of golden liquid shimmered faintly in the flickering light, casting intricate patterns on the stone walls as Prex and Dea ascended the spiraling staircase. Each step seemed to press harder against their feet, as though the very stone beneath them resisted their departure. The low hum of the chamber they had just left lingered in the air, a reminder of the secrets it harbored, of the mysteries that still swirled within its darkened depths.

Prex's grip on the vial tightened, his fingers almost white against its smooth surface. Despite its small, delicate appearance, the vial seemed to grow heavier with every movement, as though it carried the weight of an ancient curse or a power that could shake the very foundations of the world. The golden liquid inside swirled lazily, reflecting the light with an otherworldly glow, but Prex knew better than to trust its beauty. There was a force within it that could not be ignored.

Dea, walking a few paces behind, glanced up at him, her eyes wide with a mixture of uncertainty and determination. Her breath came in shallow bursts as they climbed higher, the silence between them thick with unspoken thoughts. Finally, she spoke, her voice breaking the heavy quiet.

"Do you think we're safe now?" she asked, the words a mere

whisper that seemed to hang in the air longer than necessary, as though the question itself feared being answered.

Prex turned his head slightly to glance back at her, his face obscured by shadows. His eyes, though hard with resolve, held a flicker of something else—something far more vulnerable. He opened his mouth to speak, then paused, his thoughts briefly clouded by the weight of what they had just uncovered, the danger still lurking on the edges of their journey.

"Safe?" Prex finally replied, his voice low and steady, carrying the weight of experience. *"No. Not yet. Not until we know what this... thing truly is."* His eyes drifted back to the vial, his gaze narrowing as he thought of the risks they had taken, of the unknowns still out there. *"But we're closer to answers than we've ever been. That's worth the risk, don't you think?"*

Dea fell silent, her brow furrowing as she looked ahead, her mind racing with questions that still had no answers. They continued their ascent, the faint creak of the staircase beneath their feet the only sound to accompany them. The further they climbed, the heavier the air seemed to grow, laden with the unspoken weight of what lay ahead. What awaited them at the top of the stairs, and would they be prepared for the truth they sought? Only time would tell.

They stepped cautiously into the decaying station, the air heavy with the musty scent of long-forgotten places. Faint rays of dawn filtered through the shattered windows, casting pale, jagged streaks of light across the rusted metal and broken stone. The station had once been a bustling hub, but now it was a hollow shell, crumbling beneath the weight of time and neglect. Its silence was unnerving, as though the very walls had been abandoned by sound. The outside world was still, too—a strange, suffocating stillness that seemed to hold its breath, waiting for something to happen.

Prex, ever vigilant, moved with purpose, his boots echoing softly on the cold, cracked floor. He led the way to an old, weather-beaten bench tucked against the far wall. The bench, once a place for weary travelers, now looked like an artifact of a forgotten era. They paused here, both of them winded, the tension of their journey pulling at their muscles.

Dea, always the more reflective of the two, turned the vial over in her hands. Her fingers traced the delicate etchings on the surface, patterns that seemed to shift and shimmer with an eerie life of their own. The vial felt like it contained something more than just liquid—something ancient, as though the very essence of it was alive, watching them with an unspoken awareness.

"It feels alive, doesn't it?" she murmured, her voice almost reverent. *"Like it's watching us."*

Prex's eyes narrowed, his brow furrowing in concern. He stood a little straighter, though the weight of the revolver in his hand didn't lessen his unease. He had lived through countless dangerous situations, but something about this felt different—more dangerous, more uncertain. He glanced over his shoulder, scanning the shadows that lingered at the edge of the room. The dim light did little to reveal what was hidden there, but Prex knew better than to underestimate the darkness.

"Let's hope it's on our side," he muttered, his voice low, almost a growl, as he looked down at the vial in her hands. He wasn't sure what they had uncovered, but one thing was certain—it wasn't something to be taken lightly. Not in this place.

The stillness around them stretched on, thick and suffocating, until a sudden, sharp noise shattered the fragile calm—a metallic clang from somewhere deep in the shadows. The sound was deafening in its suddenness, a jarring interruption that made the hairs on the back of Prex's neck stand on end. His instincts kicked in, and without a second thought, he was on his feet, his revolver raised and ready, the cold metal gleaming in the pale light.

Dea tensed beside him, her breath quickening. She gripped the key tighter in her hand, her knuckles white with the pressure. The key, an unassuming piece of metal, now felt like the most important object in the world. It was their only hope, their one thread of security in a place that offered none. She held it as if it could ward off the darkness, as though it might somehow protect them from whatever was lurking just beyond the reach of the light.

Prex's eyes flicked across the room, darting between the fractured beams of light and the deep, impenetrable shadows. The air was thick with tension, and even the faintest movement seemed to hold the promise of danger. But there was no sound now—nothing but the echo of their own breathing. He waited, muscles coiled, his senses stretched taut like a bowstring, ready to snap at any moment.

"Stay alert," he whispered to Dea, his voice barely more than a breath.

She nodded silently, her gaze fixed on the darkness, her grip tightening on the key. The silence pressed in around them, thick and oppressive, and for a moment, it felt as if the station itself was waiting—waiting for something to happen. Waiting for them to make the first move.

"Who's there?" Prex's voice rang out, calm but sharp, a contrast to the subtle tremor that ran through his taut muscles. His stance remained resolute, his hand resting lightly on the weapon at his side, ready to strike at the slightest provocation. His gaze swept over the shadows, searching for any movement, any sign of threat.

A figure emerged from the dimness, their form draped in a long, flowing cloak, their face shrouded by the deep folds of a hood. They moved with uncanny poise, each step purposeful and measured, betraying no hint of haste. As they entered the flickering light, their hands rose in a gesture of cautious surrender, fingers splayed as though to show they meant no harm.

"Easy now," the stranger's voice, smooth and controlled, carried through the still air, tinged with an unfamiliar accent. It was soothing yet edged with an unmistakable authority, as if the words themselves demanded peace.

"I'm not here to harm you."

Prex's eyes remained locked on the figure, but the hand near his weapon tightened, his finger hovering over the trigger. His grip was steady, his body rigid with the weight of caution.

"Then why are you sneaking around like a thief in the dark?" His voice was laced with suspicion, the accusation hanging in the air like a thick fog. *"What's your game?"*

The stranger's lips twitched in the barest of smiles, a quiet chuckle escaping them—soft, almost like a whisper of wind through a broken window. *"I wasn't sneaking,"* they replied, their tone almost too calm, as though they were explaining something obvious. *"I was waiting. Watching. Observing. You've made quite the impression, you know. Few make it this far. Most never even get close to the truth. But you, you've come much further than I expected."*

Dea, who had been standing silently beside Prex, took a cautious step forward, her eyes narrowing with wariness. The light caught the sharp edge of her features, casting faint shadows across her face.

"Who are you?" she asked, her voice like steel, firm and unyielding.

The stranger didn't answer immediately. Instead, they stood for a moment, as if considering the question carefully. Then, with a deliberate and slow movement, they lowered their hood, revealing a face that was both striking and unsettling. The features were angular, sharp, with high cheekbones and a strong jawline, a face that seemed carved from stone. Their hair, long and flowing, was streaked with silver, the strands catching the light like strands of moonlight woven through the dark. But it was their eyes that held attention—their eyes were a piercing shade of blue, so intense they seemed to bore straight through the veil of flesh and bone, to peer deep into the heart of those they gazed upon.

"Call me Caspian," the figure said, their voice now carrying a subtle weight, as though the name itself had significance. They surveyed Dea and Prex with a look that suggested they were being measured, evaluated. *"And if you're holding that vial, it means you've uncovered a piece of the truth,"* they continued, their words deliberate, laden with meaning. Their gaze flicked to the vial in Dea's hand, a silent acknowledgment of its impor-

tance.

Dea held the vial tighter, instinctively, the weight of Caspian's gaze pressing down on her like a physical force. *"What truth?"* she demanded, her voice tinged with both curiosity and caution. *"What do you know about this?"*

Caspian took a step closer, their movement smooth, almost predatory. The faintest smile danced on their lips, but it didn't reach their eyes. *"The truth is a rare thing,"* they said, their voice soft but rich with hidden knowledge. *"Many search for it, but few ever grasp it. You've already come further than most. That vial—"* Caspian paused, letting the silence hang for a moment, *"—it's a key. A fragment of something far larger. Something many have sought for centuries."*

Caspian gestured toward the worn bench beside him, his gaze intense yet calm. With a purposeful motion, he took a seat on the opposite side, the weight of his presence more pronounced in the stillness that enveloped the air between them. The faint flicker of distant torches cast an eerie glow on his face, highlighting the somber expression etched upon it.

"The liquid you carry, the one you guard so fiercely, is not merely a cure. It's far more than that," Caspian began, his voice low, almost reverent. *"It is a key. A key that unlocks not only the secrets of your past but the very forces that have relentlessly pursued you both."* He paused, letting his words sink in. *"But with such power comes a price—a cost that may be more than you're prepared to pay."*

Dea exchanged a glance with Prex, a mixture of confusion and caution flickering in her eyes. The vial, so simple in appearance, suddenly felt infinitely heavier in her hand. *"What kind of cost?"* she asked, her voice barely above a whisper, as though speaking too loudly might make the truth too real.

Caspian leaned forward, his eyes darkening as he spoke. The flicker of the torchlight seemed to dim, drawing their focus to him. *"The liquid you carry doesn't simply heal or protect. It takes something from you each time you use it. It's a trade—a trade of memories, of pieces of your very soul. The more you rely on it, the more it demands from you."*

Prex's brow furrowed, his jaw tightening as he processed the weight of Caspian's words. *"And what happens when there's nothing left to take?"* he asked, his voice sharp with the edge of frustration and fear.

Caspian's eyes, for the first time, seemed to soften with a sorrowful understanding. He remained silent for a long moment, as though the answer itself was too painful to voice. Finally, he spoke, his tone quiet but laced with unspoken depth. *"When the liquid has taken everything, there will be nothing left but the shell of who you were. A hollow vessel, unable to remember who you were or why you fought."* His voice trailed off, the silence stretching uncomfortably between them. It was as though the very air had grown heavy with the implications of what he had just revealed.

Dea's gaze dropped to the vial in her hands, her fingers trembling as they curled around the small glass bottle. The liquid inside, so clear and deceptively innocent-looking, now seemed like a poison—a slow, inevitable poison. She felt a coldness spreading through her chest as the enormity of the choice before her began to crystallize.

"So, it's a choice then," she murmured, more to herself than to anyone else. *"Save ourselves... or lose ourselves."*

Caspian nodded slowly, his expression hardening into one of resolve. *"Every decision you make from here on out will shape the path you walk. And each path carries its own burden. The more you rely on the liquid, the more you sacrifice. But... the path ahead is dangerous. It is fraught with peril, and the stakes could not be higher. But it is also the only path that will lead to your freedom—the only way to end the endless pursuit that has haunted you both."*

Prex stood silently, his fists clenched at his sides as he digested Caspian's words. His mind raced with a thousand thoughts, none of them offering any comfort. The decision weighed heavily upon him, the cost of each choice spiraling in his mind like a relentless storm. He looked at Dea, and their eyes met in mutual understanding—neither of them ready to face the truth, but both knowing they had no choice.

The stillness that lingered between them was palpable, filled with the unspoken realization that they were no longer just fighting for survival. They were fighting for something much deeper—something that neither of them could fully comprehend just yet. But whatever it was, they knew they couldn't turn back now.

Prex stood rooted to the spot, his revolver still resting at his side, fingers clenched around the handle. He wasn't one for idle chatter, especially not when things had escalated this far. His eyes narrowed, studying Caspian carefully.

"And what's your stake in this? Why help us?" The question was direct, probing. Prex had learned to trust his instincts, and they told him there was more to Caspian's involvement than met the eye.

Caspian, for his part, merely smiled, a subtle twist of his lips that hinted at both amusement and something darker lurking beneath the surface. *"Let's just say I have a vested interest in seeing this through,"* he said, his voice smooth, as if every word had been carefully chosen.

"You're not the first to walk this path, but you might be the last." There was an eerie finality in his tone, the kind that sent an unspoken warning crawling up Prex's spine.

The air grew thick with the weight of his words. It wasn't just a statement; *it was a threat, veiled in the guise of a cryptic observation.*

Prex didn't like it, but there was little he could do now. He could feel the tension rising between them, an unspoken acknowledgment that none of them had the luxury of turning back.

Dea, standing next to him, seemed equally affected. Her hand trembled slightly as she slipped it into Prex's, seeking the reassurance of his touch. The vulnerability in her expression was undeniable, but so was her resolve. She wasn't going to let whatever lay ahead break her. And with Prex by her side, she knew she wouldn't have to face it alone.

"What do we do now?" Her voice was barely above a whisper,

but it carried the weight of a thousand unspoken questions.

Caspian didn't answer immediately. Instead, he rose from his seat, his movements graceful and deliberate. There was something unnervingly calm about him, as if he had seen everything this world had to offer and had already made peace with it.

"Follow me," he said simply, his voice steady as he turned towards the exit. *"There's something you need to see."*

Prex exchanged a glance with Dea, the unspoken communication between them clear. She gave a slight nod, her hand tightening around his. They didn't have a choice. Whatever was coming, they had to face it. Reluctantly, but resolutely, they followed Caspian through the dimly lit station and out into the fragile light of dawn.

The world outside felt different, as though the very air had shifted in their absence. The city seemed quieter, as if holding its breath, waiting for something—or someone. The once-familiar streets now seemed alien, distant. The familiar sounds of the bustling metropolis had been replaced by a strange, almost oppressive silence that seemed to echo with the ghosts of their past decisions.

Prex stole a glance at Dea. Her face was pale, the color drained from her cheeks, but there was a spark in her eyes—a flicker of determination that wasn't there before. Whatever awaited them now, whatever danger loomed on the horizon, they would face it together. And for Prex, that was enough to keep moving forward.

The vial in Prex's jacket pocket felt heavier than before, as though it had gained weight in the short time since they had last checked it. It pulsed faintly, a soft vibration that seemed to resonate in his bones, as if it too was aware of the significance of the moment. The mysterious substance inside was no longer just a tool to be used; it had become a key to something larger, something far beyond their understanding. Whatever it unlocked, Prex could sense that it was only the beginning.

They walked in silence, the weight of the world pressing down on them with each step. The labyrinth of their journey was far from over, and yet, with each passing moment, the walls seemed to close in around them. The whispers of the past grew louder, clawing at the edges of their minds, pulling them deeper into a web of secrets that had been carefully spun long before their arrival. They had thought they were just players in a game, but now, they were starting to realize that they might be part of something far more dangerous, far more intricate than they could have ever imagined.

As Caspian led them down the winding streets, his back straight and his pace unhurried, Prex couldn't shake the feeling that they were being watched. The city had a way of revealing its true nature to those who dared to look too closely, and right now, *it felt like the city was alive—waiting, observing, judging.*

The Shifting Sands of Memory

The air, thick with the faint tang of salt, wrapped around them as they ventured closer to the coastline. The horizon stretched out like an endless canvas, painted with hues of amber and lavender as the sun began its descent. The ocean, vast and tumultuous, seemed alive with the rhythm of its waves crashing relentlessly against the jagged, weather-beaten rocks. The sound was both violent and melodic, a symphony of nature's fury that resonated in the core of one's being, as if the sea itself were singing a song older than time.

Prex's fingers tightened instinctively around the vial he carried, its contents glowing with a faint, ethereal golden hue. The liquid inside shimmered like liquid light, casting strange reflections on the darkening sand. The weight of the vial seemed heavier than its physical mass, as though the very air around them was charged with anticipation. In the twilight, it glowed with an otherworldly aura, casting faint shadows that danced and flickered, mirroring the rhythmic motion of the waves. Prex's gaze was fixed on the vial, his mind awash with thoughts he wasn't yet ready to voice aloud.

Beside him, Dea walked in silence, her presence a quiet contrast to the chaotic beauty of the world around them. Her fingers absentmindedly traced the edges of an ancient key that hung from a leather cord around her neck. The key, worn by time but still unmistakably crafted with an intricacy that spoke of forgotten ages, seemed to pulse gently in her touch, as if it recognized the moment that was approaching. The air itself seemed to bend and hum around the key, a faint vibration that sent a shiver down her spine.

"Why here?" Prex's voice broke the silence, low and strained, barely above a whisper. His eyes flicked from the vial to the dark expanse of the ocean before them, his mind struggling to process the weight of the task at hand.

Dea's gaze never wavered from the horizon, but her lips curled into a faint, knowing smile. She had asked the same question countless times in her mind, and yet, she already knew the answer. But it was Caspian, who had been a step ahead of them, who finally responded.

Caspian turned, his tall figure cutting a silhouette against the dying light. His features were chiseled and stern, but there was a glint of something deeper in his eyes—something that spoke of wisdom borne of hard-won experience. He studied them both for a moment, his voice carrying the weight of untold truths.

"The answers lie beneath the surface," he said, his tone deliberate, as if weighing each word before he spoke it. His gaze swept across the vast expanse of the ocean, the surface of which now gleamed with the first hints of moonlight. *"The ruins you seek... are hidden in the depths."* His words seemed to linger in the air, hanging like a heavy fog, as if the very ocean itself were listening.

He turned back toward the horizon, his posture tense, and his voice dropped to an almost conspiratorial whisper. *"But be warned—once you enter, there's no turning back."*

His words were as much a warning as they were a promise, and as he spoke, the air around them seemed to shift. The wind picked up, and the distant crash of the waves sounded louder, more intense. The ocean, which had once seemed like a peaceful force of nature, now felt like something far more unpredictable and dangerous. It beckoned them, calling them into its depths, and yet, there was an unspoken understanding between them all—there would be no return from this journey. The past would remain behind, and what lay ahead was a future shrouded in uncertainty.

Dea's eyes shifted toward Prex, her expression a mixture of curiosity and uncertainty. Her brow furrowed slightly, but she kept her voice even. *"And what exactly are we looking for here, Caspian?"*

Caspian raised one hand toward the horizon, his fingers pointing toward the turbulent sea where the setting sun cast long, jagged shadows across the water. His gaze was intense, yet distant, as if peering into something far beyond the visible. *"A chamber,"* he said, his voice carrying the weight of ancient secrets. *"One that's been sealed for centuries, hidden beneath the depths of this very coastline. Within it lies the final piece of the puzzle we've been chasing for so long."* He paused, letting the gravity of his words settle in the cool evening air. *"But it is not just a matter of uncovering the chamber; it's what guards it—what protects it—that makes this perilous."*

Prex narrowed his eyes, stepping closer to Caspian, his curiosity piqued. *"Protected? By what? You mean there are still more of those... things?"* His voice carried a slight edge, a wariness earned from previous encounters with the strange and deadly creatures that had stalked their every step on this journey.

Caspian nodded gravely, his face unreadable as the last rays of sunlight glinted off his dark hair. *"Yes. But they are not what they once were. These were once human—like you and me. Bound to these ruins by their own choices, their own actions. Their spirits linger in the remnants of this place, cursed to guard the chamber, to ensure that only those truly worthy can pass."*

A shiver ran down Dea's spine, and though the air around them was warm, she felt a coldness creep into her bones. *"And what makes us worthy, Caspian? What guarantees we won't become like them?"*

Caspian's eyes softened, and for a moment, the hardness in his demeanor seemed to crack. *"That, Dea, is not for me to decide. The chamber itself will determine if we are worthy or not. It will judge us for who we are, for what we've done, and what we are willing to sacrifice."*

Dea felt a weight settle in her chest. The thought of facing something ancient, something that could judge them so utterly, unsettled her. But they had come so far, and there was no turning back now. The answer—whatever it was—lay ahead.

Without another word, Caspian began to lead the way down a narrow, winding path that cut sharply into the cliffside. The sound of the ocean's waves crashing against the rocks below grew louder with each step, the rhythmic pounding of the water seeming to echo in Dea's chest. The path was treacherous, uneven, and barely wide enough for their feet to find purchase. Loose stones skittered underfoot as they descended, the danger of the path almost as palpable as the mystery that loomed before them.

Finally, they reached the base of the cliff, where the ground leveled off, and a small, weathered boat bobbed gently in the surf. Its wooden frame, scarred by years of exposure to salt and wind, seemed frail yet sturdy, its surface slick with the sheen of ocean spray. Caspian stepped into the boat first, his movements sure and practiced, steadying the vessel against the pull of the tide. The wood creaked under his weight, but it held firm.

Prex followed, his usual bravado subdued for the moment. He carefully stepped into the boat, his eyes scanning the waters as if searching for any sign of movement beneath the surface. Dea hesitated, her gaze drifting toward the crashing waves that stretched endlessly into the distance. She could feel the weight of the ocean, of everything that had come before them, bearing down on her. Yet, there was no turning back.

With a final, steady breath, she stepped into the boat, her boots scraping the edge of the wood as she settled beside Prex. The boat rocked gently, its old timbers groaning in protest against the tide, but it remained afloat, steadying itself with the grace of something that had weathered countless storms.

Caspian grasped the oars, the motion practiced and smooth as he began to row. The boat drifted away from the shore, moving deeper into the open water. The sun, now a mere sliver on the horizon, cast long shadows across the water, and for a brief moment, it felt as though they were floating on the edge of time itself.

As the boat carried them farther from land, Dea's mind swirled with questions, but Caspian said nothing more. His focus was solely on the path ahead, his quiet determination filling the air between them. The chamber, the spirits, the tests—they were all ahead. What awaited them, Dea couldn't say. But one thing was certain: *the journey was far from over.*

The journey across the water unfolded in eerie silence, the only sounds the rhythmic lapping of the boat against the darkened waves. A dense air of tension lingered between them, unspoken, yet heavy with the weight of uncertainty. The vial they carried, its contents glowing faintly with an ethereal light, cast shimmering patterns across the water's surface. The luminescence twisted and undulated with the movement of the boat, sending fragmented shadows that danced like phantoms on their faces, altering their features with every flicker.

Dea, her brow furrowed in concentration, reached out instinctively to take Prex's hand. Her fingers curled around his with a firm, unwavering grip—an anchor in the sea of tension. *"Whatever happens, we face it together,"* she murmured, her voice low but resolute. Her eyes, though filled with uncertainty, shone with a fierce determination. The faint glow of the vial seemed to mirror her resolve, casting an almost protective aura around them.

Prex turned his gaze to meet hers, his eyes piercing in the dim light. His expression was unreadable for a moment, but then a subtle change softened his features, replaced by a fire that seemed to burn brighter with every passing second. He nodded, the silence stretching before him as he held her gaze. *"Together,"* he affirmed, his voice thick with the same unspoken promise. No matter the danger, no matter the trials ahead, they would not falter.

As they neared the jagged outcrop of rocks, the boat's pace slowed, its keel scraping gently against the water. The rocky formations ahead seemed to loom like silent sentinels, sharp and unforgiving, yet beckoning them forward. Beneath the water's surface, faint outlines of what appeared to be ancient stone structures emerged in the gloom. The stones, covered in barnacles and moss, looked almost like ruins from another age. Their shapes, vague and distorted by the shifting waters, seemed to pulse with an unnatural rhythm, as if they were alive—watching.

Caspian, who had been silent for some time, finally broke the stillness. His voice was steady, but there was an edge of urgency to it. With a sharp motion, he pointed toward a narrow gap in the rocks ahead. *"There,"* he said simply. The opening was barely wide enough for the boat to fit through, a slim passage between the towering rock walls that seemed to grow darker as they approached. The water here was turbulent, swirling around the jagged edges like an ominous warning. It was a treacherous path, one that would require careful navigation.

Dea's pulse quickened, the boat now inching toward the gap. The tension in the air seemed to thicken, wrapping itself around them like a tightening noose. She squeezed Prex's hand a little harder, as if grounding herself for what lay ahead. They had come this far—there was no turning back now.

As they stepped into the submerged passage, the water seemed to freeze, its once lively ripples fading into an unnatural stillness. The air thickened, as if each breath carried an invisible weight, charged with an ancient energy that made the hairs on the back of their necks rise. The glow from the vial in Dea's hand flared, casting long shadows against the damp walls and revealing intricate carvings that adorned every surface. The symbols, worn by time but still sharp in their detail, told tales of forgotten legends—scenes of blood-soaked sacrifices, fierce battles that shook the earth, and moments of despair so deep they seemed to echo through the very stones.

Their footsteps were muffled by the water as they moved deeper into the passage. The faint sound of dripping water from above only added to the eerie silence, punctuated only by the soft hum of the vial, which seemed to pulse in rhythm with their own heartbeats. Each turn of the corridor revealed more carvings, each one more foreboding than the last, until the narrow tunnel gave way to an enormous cavern, its scale unfathomable. The air inside the cavern felt different—cooler, yet charged with a mysterious energy that made the hairs on their arms stand at attention.

High above, the ceiling stretched out into an abyss, disappearing into darkness. From the vast expanse above, clusters of glowing crystals hung like frozen stars, their pale light spilling down in jagged beams, illuminating the cavern in an ethereal glow. The walls were adorned with more ancient symbols, their meanings lost to time but seemingly just as alive with secrets as the path that had led them here. At the heart of the cavern, standing like an ancient sentinel, was a massive stone door. Its surface was covered with the same intricate runes as the key Dea held in her hand, as though the stone itself had been carved to mirror the very shape of the mysterious artifact.

Caspian, his expression hard as stone, stepped out of the boat with deliberate care, his feet sinking slightly into the soft earth beneath the water's surface. His gaze flicked to the cavern, his shoulders tensing as though bracing for something unseen. *"This is as far as I go,"* he said, his voice low and steady, carrying a weight of finality. *"The rest is up to you."*

Prex and Dea exchanged a brief, knowing glance, their gazes filled with a mixture of determination and uncertainty. There was no turning back now. The cavern seemed to pulse with the same tension that swelled in their chests, drawing them toward the stone door, which stood like an ominous gatekeeper to whatever lay beyond. Each step they took toward it felt like a step deeper into a forgotten history, a history that was about to reveal its darkest secrets.

As they neared the stone door, Dea felt a strange sensation—a hum, subtle at first, but growing stronger in her hand. The key she carried began to vibrate, the low resonance spreading up her arm, sending a shiver down her spine. The vibrations matched the rhythm of the runes on the door, as if the key and the stone door were speaking to one another in a language older than time itself.

Dea hesitated. The key's vibrations grew more intense, urging her forward, but a knot of uncertainty twisted in her stomach. She could feel the weight of the moment, the heavy silence pressing against her, making her breath catch in her throat. The key seemed to pulse with life, as if it had a will of its own. The door before them was more than just stone—it was a barrier, a threshold, and Dea was holding the key to unlocking it. The question remained—was she ready to face what lay on the other side?

"It's okay," Prex said softly, his hand resting gently on Dea's shoulder, offering a sense of calm amidst the growing tension. *"We've come this far, we can handle whatever comes next."*

Dea nodded, her heart pounding in her chest as she took a deep breath, gathering her courage. With a steady hand, she slid the ancient key into the intricately carved lock of the door. The moment the metal touched the surface, the runes etched into the door seemed to come alive. They shimmered and pulsed with a strange energy, their light flickering in rhythmic sync with the deep hum that resonated from within the walls themselves.

A tremor rumbled through the ground, subtle at first but quickly growing stronger. The door creaked, its heavy frame shuddering as if it were a reluctant guardian being coaxed open. Slowly, inch by inch, the door began to swing open, its movements grinding with an unsettling sound. Beyond it lay a long, shadowy corridor, its depth lost to the encroaching darkness. The air grew colder as the gap widened, and a palpable sense of foreboding swept over them.

The sudden drop in temperature sent a shiver down Dea's spine, and as if on cue, a faint, almost inaudible murmur swept through the air. The whispers were distant at first, a mere ripple of sound, but as they stepped closer, the voices began to grow clearer—too clear for comfort. They spoke in strange tongues, their words teasing at the edges of comprehension, yet always out of reach. Prex's instincts kicked in immediately. His hand shot to the holster at his side, drawing the revolver with a smooth, practiced motion. He held the weapon steady, his eyes narrowing as they scanned the shifting shadows.

"Stay close," he murmured, his voice low and steady, though the tension was unmistakable.

Dea gave a curt nod, her own senses alert, her every nerve on edge as they stepped cautiously across the threshold. The moment they crossed into the corridor, the darkness seemed to swallow them whole, wrapping around them like a suffocating cloak. The air felt thick, almost as if the very space itself was alive and watching, waiting.

The whispers grew louder, a cacophony of voices that echoed off the jagged stone walls. They seemed to swirl around them, intertwining with the soft, almost melodic hum of the ancient structure. The words remained elusive, slipping just beyond their grasp, like whispers in a dream that vanished the moment you tried to remember them. But there was a sense of urgency in the voices, an unspoken warning that set the hairs on the back of Dea's neck standing upright.

The corridor stretched endlessly before them, winding like a serpent through the heart of the unknown. The walls, once solid and unyielding, seemed to shift and breathe, contracting and expanding with each step they took. Every turn they made brought them deeper into the labyrinth, and the oppressive darkness seemed to close in tighter around them. The air felt heavier, as though the very weight of the corridor was pressing down on their shoulders, suffocating them with its ominous presence.

Prex's grip on his revolver tightened as his eyes flickered to every shadow, every movement in the corners of his vision. *"Keep your guard up,"* he muttered, his voice low but sharp, cutting through the eerie silence that had begun to settle like a thick fog around them.

Dea could feel her pulse racing, her breath shallow and quick as the whispers grew louder, their cadence now a chaotic chant that seemed to seep into her very soul. The walls, once solid and imposing, now felt like they were closing in, bending and warping with each step they took. The path before them was no longer a mere corridor—it had become a living, breathing entity, a twisting maze of shadows and whispers, guiding them toward an unknown, inevitable destination.

The further they ventured, the more the air seemed to thrum with dark energy, as if the very stones were imbued with a power older than time itself. And in the distance, just beyond the reach of their sight, something waited. Something watching.

Veil of Sacrifice

The chamber fell into an eerie, suffocating silence as the orb's radiant light gradually waned, casting long, creeping shadows that seemed to stretch and writhe across the cold, stone walls. The once vibrant glow now flickered weakly, its pulse growing fainter with each passing moment, as if it were drawing its last breath. Prex and Dea stood rooted in place, their bodies rigid with tension, their breaths shallow and quick, the weight of what they had just done settling upon them like an invisible shroud. Their hearts hammered within their chests, a frantic rhythm that mirrored the ominous stillness surrounding them.

The guardians, those ancient, ethereal beings, stood motionless in the periphery, their figures almost ghostly in the dimming light. Their translucent forms flickered unnaturally, as though they were caught between two realms, their presence an unsettling mix of fragility and immense power. The faint glow that clung to their figures was the only source of illumination, casting fleeting reflections that danced erratically on the walls, like flames disturbed by a sudden breeze.

Dea's voice, when it finally broke the silence, was barely more than a whisper, trembling with fear and uncertainty. *"What happens now?"* she asked, her words hanging in the air like fragile, unsaid thoughts. Her eyes darted nervously between Prex and the looming guardians, unsure of what fate had in store for them. For a long moment, there was no response. The guardians remained as they had been, silent and imposing, their eerie stillness almost mocking. Then, with a fluid, unsettling motion, the lead guardian stepped forward. Its form shifted and rippled, the edges of its body warping like mist curling in the wind, never fully solidifying. Its face—if one could even call it that—remained veiled in an ever-changing swirl of mist, the features hidden beneath an impenetrable veil of shadow.

"You have chosen to surrender your essence," the lead guardian intoned, its voice both ancient and otherworldly, a deep resonance that seemed to echo from the very core of the earth itself. The words were deliberate, weighed down with the gravity of the decision Prex and Dea had made. *"The price will be exacted,"* it continued, its tone cold and unwavering, as though the inevitability of the consequences had already been sealed long before they had entered this forsaken chamber.

A shiver ran down Dea's spine, and she instinctively took a step back, her body trembling. *"W-what price?"* she stammered, the question hanging in the air, thick with dread. She clutched the hem of her cloak tightly, the fabric cold against her clammy skin. The guardians' words had left her feeling hollow, as though they were merely the harbingers of something far darker to come.

Prex, ever the more composed of the two, swallowed hard, trying to maintain some semblance of control. His mind raced, but there was no escaping the heavy certainty in the guardian's words. The price would be exacted, and neither of them could yet comprehend the full weight of that statement. The guardians' presence, the pulsating dim light of the orb, the very air itself seemed to thicken, pressing down on them like the ocean's depths.

"Your essence is now forfeit," the guardian continued, its form undulating in the air, as though its very words were a tangible force that could alter reality. *"There will be no turning back. The sacrifice you have chosen will forever alter the course of your*

fates."

The chamber seemed to grow colder, the walls closing in on them, as if the very stones themselves had begun to tighten their grip on their souls. Dea's hands trembled as she reached out toward Prex, seeking comfort in the only presence she had left, but even his steady gaze could not dispel the chill creeping into her bones.

The lead guardian's misty face shifted, though its eyes, if they existed at all, remained hidden. The cryptic words it spoke next were final, unyielding, as though uttered from a place beyond time itself. *"Now you will pay the price for your choices,"* it said, its voice growing quieter, but carrying with it an undercurrent of finality. *"Your destinies are sealed, and nothing will save you from what awaits."*

And with that, the chamber descended back into an oppressive silence, the weight of their fate pressing heavily upon them.

Prex tightened his grip on Dea's hand, his fingers like iron bands, unwavering in their resolve. His gaze, fixed and intense, never wavered from the mysterious, glowing orb in the guardian's outstretched hand. There was no turning back now.

"We're ready," he declared, his voice steady yet laced with the weight of what was to come.

The guardian's ancient eyes seemed to acknowledge the finality of their decision, and with a slow, deliberate motion, it extended its arm further. The orb, pulsating with an ethereal glow, responded instantly, its light intensifying, swirling with energy. A soft hum emanated from the orb, growing louder and more resonant, as though the very fabric of time was bending to its will. Prex could feel the electric charge in the air, a palpable force that seemed to vibrate through his very bones.

Then, without warning, a brilliant beam of light erupted from the orb's core, its power unfathomable. The beam surged forward, wrapping itself around Prex and Dea in a cocoon of warmth and blinding brilliance. It was as if the very essence of the universe had reached out to embrace them, offering both protection and challenge in its grasp. The warmth seeped into their skin, flooding their senses with an overwhelming surge of energy. Every fiber of their being seemed to hum in resonance with the force that encased them.

As the light enveloped them completely, their surroundings began to fade away. It was as if the world itself had been torn asunder, leaving only the two of them in an infinite expanse. The air shimmered with the energy of the moment, and they could feel the weight of history itself pressing down upon them. Then, without warning, a cascade of memories rushed forth like fragments of a shattered mirror, each one shimmering and elusive, swirling around them in a kaleidoscope of moments.

The memories came in flashes—brief, disconnected images that danced in and out of focus, as if the very fabric of time was unraveling before their eyes. Faces, places, and events—some familiar, some distant, all blending together in a dizzying whirlwind. Prex saw the face of a woman he had once loved, her eyes filled with sorrow. Dea caught a fleeting glimpse of a child she had never known, a child who seemed to reach out to her from a time long past. The memories collided, merging and splitting, forming a tapestry of their shared destinies.

With every flash, the sense of time grew more fluid, more malleable. Past and future collided, bending and twisting, until it was impossible to discern where one began and the other ended. And all the while, the orb's light remained, unwavering in its brilliance, a beacon guiding them through the maelstrom of memories and possibilities.

Prex's breath quickened, but his grip on Dea's hand never faltered. This was their journey—one that would test them in ways they could never have imagined. And as the memories continued to flood their minds, they knew with an unwavering certainty that nothing would ever be the same again.

Prex stood frozen, his eyes gazing upon the shattered remnants of what was once his childhood home. The faint echoes of laughter lingered in the air, the sound of his siblings' joyous voices fading like distant music. He could almost feel their presence, a warmth that had once filled the halls, a comfort long since lost.

His father's stern yet loving gaze seemed to pierce through the veil of time, his protective yet unsentimental manner reminding Prex of the man who had shaped him. Those quiet moments, wrapped in a sense of security and familial bonds, now seemed like fragments of a distant dream, slipping away faster than he could grasp them.

He clung to these fleeting memories with all his might, each image a thread to the person he once was. The image of his father, the faintest sound of his mother's voice calling him to dinner, the feeling of his siblings running alongside him in the fields—they were all pieces of a puzzle he couldn't complete. His heart ached with the desire to keep them intact, to preserve a part of himself that was beginning to fade into nothingness. But despite his efforts, the memories slipped further out of reach, like shadows retreating in the light of dawn.

Dea's memories wove themselves into his own, threads of her past intertwining with his. He could feel the warmth of her mother's gentle lullabies, their soft melodies echoing in the back of his mind, bringing with them a sense of comfort and safety. The scent of wildflowers in the fields where she once ran, laughing freely under the sun, filled the air, mixing with the faint aroma of rain-soaked earth. It was a time of innocence, a time before the weight of the world pressed down on her shoulders. Yet, even as the beauty of those memories washed over him, there was an undeniable tension, a sense of fear and determination that underpinned her every action.

Dea's heartache, her relentless pursuit of the truth, pulsed through the shared memories like a deep, steady drumbeat. Prex could feel the anguish she carried—the pain of losing something precious, the desperation to uncover the answers that had eluded her for so long. He could sense her longing for clarity, her wish to understand the forces that had shaped her life. And yet, with every passing moment, those very memories seemed to slip further from her grasp, like sand running through the cracks of her fingers, elusive and fragile.

Tears welled in Dea's eyes, her emotions raw and unrestrained as she felt the pull of her fading memories. She reached out, as though trying to capture them, to hold them close. But the harder she tried, the faster they dissolved, slipping from her mind like smoke on the wind. The grief of losing her past was overwhelming, the weight of it pressing down on her chest as though the very air itself had turned oppressive.

And then, the light grew brighter, overwhelming in its intensity. It swirled around them, an ethereal glow that seemed to consume everything in its path. The memories, once so vivid and clear, began to blur, merging together in a whirl of colors and shapes. Prex and Dea cried out, their voices intermingling in a shared anguish, their pain now one and the same. The familiar images of their lives, their loves, and their struggles melded into a single, indistinguishable blur.

It was as though the fabric of their existence was being torn apart, the delicate threads of their memories unraveling in a final, agonizing moment. The orb—the source of all their hopes and fears—pulsed one final time, its glow blinding. Then, in a moment of unbearable tension, it shattered, exploding into a thousand shards that scattered into the air. Each fragment was a fleeting memory, each one dissolving into nothingness, leaving behind only the echo of their existence. The light faded, the air grew still, and all that remained was the emptiness where their pasts had once been.

In the silence that followed, Prex and Dea stood, breathless, their hearts heavy with the weight of what had been lost. The memories were gone, consumed by the light, and all that remained were the fragments of who they had once been—fragments that would never be whole again.

When the light faded into an eerie stillness, the chamber fell into a profound silence. The once-vibrant glow that had filled the space now dwindled, leaving behind only the faintest traces of its earlier brilliance. Prex and Dea, drained and fragile, collapsed to their knees, their bodies trembling uncontrollably. Sweat glistened on their skin, and the effort of whatever trial they had just undergone left them gasping for breath. Their hands, still entwined from the ordeal, shook as they struggled to regain composure. The guardians, standing as silent sentinels, watched them with unblinking eyes, their forms flickering like the last embers of a long-dying fire, their presence both comforting and foreboding.

The lead guardian, a towering figure draped in shadows, spoke with a voice that resonated like the whisper of ancient winds.

"It is done," it declared, its words imbued with an authority that seemed to reverberate through the very walls of the chamber.

"The path forward is yours to walk."

Dea, her head still clouded with the remnants of the strange energy that had filled the room, turned her gaze towards Prex. Her eyes, wide with both fear and hope, searched his face for any sign of recognition, any hint that he still remembered what they had once shared.

"Prex... do you remember?" she asked, her voice trembling as though the very air between them could shatter at any moment.

Prex's eyes flickered, his brow furrowing in confusion as he struggled to make sense of the whirlwind of emotions and fragmented memories that swirled within him. He paused, his thoughts clouded by the fog of uncertainty.

"I remember you," he murmured, his voice barely a whisper.

"I remember... us. But everything else... it's like a dream I can't quite grasp. A dream that slips through my fingers every time I try to hold onto it."

Dea nodded, her heart heavy with the same sense of loss. Her memories, once so vivid and clear, now felt like distant echoes reverberating from a time she could no longer touch. She placed a hand gently on his arm, her touch grounding him.

"Me too," she whispered. *"But we're still here. Together. And that's enough for now."*

The guardians, unmoved by the exchange, stepped aside in perfect unison. Their movements were deliberate, their presence unwavering. As they parted, a hidden passageway was revealed, its entrance bathed in a soft, golden glow that seemed to pulse with life, inviting them forward. The warmth emanating from it was almost tangible, promising both comfort and danger in equal measure.

The lead guardian, its eyes glowing with an eerie, unfathomable light, spoke once more. *"Your journey continues,"* it intoned, its voice now laced with an unsettling finality.

"Beyond this passage lies the truth you seek. But beware, for the truth you uncover may not be the one you desire."

Prex, still feeling the weight of the trial upon him, turned to Dea, his hand finding hers once more. The touch was familiar, grounding, a silent promise that whatever awaited them, they would face it together. With a deep breath, he helped her to her feet, the movement slow and deliberate. Their fingers intertwined as they stepped forward, the passageway looming before them, its golden light growing brighter with every cautious step they took.

As they walked, the air around them began to shift. The cool, sterile atmosphere of the chamber gave way to a warmth that seemed to wrap around them like a comforting embrace. The faintest scent of blooming flowers teased their senses, mingling with the distant, almost imperceptible sound of running water, as though nature itself was calling them forward. The walls of the passageway shimmered with an otherworldly glow, their surfaces adorned with intricate patterns that seemed to pulse in time with the rhythm of their own hearts.

With every step, the weight of the unknown pressed heavier upon them, but there was a sense of resolve that began to grow between them, a silent understanding that they could not turn back. Ahead of them, the light beckoned, promising answers, but also veiling dangers they had yet to comprehend. They moved forward, their bodies exhausted, their minds clouded, but their spirits bound by an unspoken bond that no darkness could ever sever.

Together, they ventured deeper into the glowing passage, their future uncertain, but their journey—whatever it may hold—now irrevocably set in motion.

As they emerged from the dense, shadowed passageway, the

world unfolded before them like an awe-inspiring vision. The landscape stretched out infinitely, bathed in the golden glow of a setting sun. A sprawling city of unimaginable beauty lay ahead, its towers shimmering like liquid crystal, their sharp spires rising toward the heavens. The streets, paved with smooth, reflective stones, wound through the metropolis like veins of light. Tall, graceful trees lined the avenues, their branches heavy with luminous fruit that pulsed softly with an otherworldly glow, casting iridescent hues over everything.

The air was thick with a serene energy, almost tangible, as if the very atmosphere vibrated with life. It was the kind of place one could only dream of, a place untouched by time, a sanctuary of unimaginable peace and power. Every inch of the city seemed to hum with quiet vitality, as though the city itself was alive, breathing, watching.

Dea, her heart pounding with excitement and disbelief, took in the sight with wide, awestruck eyes. The beauty of the place overwhelmed her senses, leaving her speechless for a moment. She could barely find the words to express what she was feeling, her mind struggling to comprehend the reality of the scene before her.

"Is this... real?" she breathed, her voice barely above a whisper, as if speaking too loudly might shatter the illusion.

Prex, standing beside her, could hardly believe his own eyes. His gaze swept over the city, his mind racing as he tried to process the enormity of what they had uncovered. The air around them crackled with a strange, undeniable energy. He nodded slowly, his voice filled with a mixture of awe and certainty. *"It has to be. This is what the guardians were protecting all along. This is the place... the heart of everything."*

They stepped cautiously into the city, their footsteps reverberating softly against the smooth, glass-like surface of the streets. The city was silent, yet it felt alive with presence, the inhabitants—ethereal beings of pure light and energy—watching them from a distance. These beings radiated a gentle, almost divine light, their forms shifting and flickering like flames caught in the wind. Their eyes, if they could be called eyes, were pools of light, deep and infinite, yet their expressions remained unreadable. They didn't move, didn't speak, but their attention was palpable, hanging in the air like a heavy mist.

Dea felt a chill crawl down her spine. There was something about the beings' silent gaze that felt both comforting and unnerving, as if they were observing not just their actions, but their very souls. Yet, she also felt no malice, only an overwhelming sense of peace—like being in the presence of something ancient, something greater than themselves.

They pressed onward, following the winding streets toward the center of the city, drawn by an unseen force. In the distance, they could see the towering spire that dominated the city's skyline, its surface covered in the same intricate runes that adorned the key and the box they had discovered. The spire seemed to pulse with energy, as though it was the source of all the light and power in the city. Its presence was imposing yet magnificent, an unmistakable symbol of the city's purpose.

Prex and Dea approached the spire cautiously, their hearts racing with anticipation. The closer they got, the more they could feel the air thickening with energy, as though the very fabric of reality around them was shifting, bending in response to their presence. When they reached the base of the spire, they paused, staring up at its immense height. The runes glowed softly, casting an ethereal light on the ground beneath them.

As they entered the spire, the world around them seemed to shift again. The atmosphere inside was vast, the chamber stretching upward into infinity. The walls of the spire were lined with swirling constellations and shimmering images that shifted and danced in the air, as though the stars themselves had gathered to form the very architecture of the room. The ground beneath their feet was covered in intricate patterns, the designs pulsing in time with their footsteps, guiding them toward the center of the chamber.

At the heart of the room stood a pedestal, simple yet majestic in its design. Atop the pedestal rested a second orb, identical to the one they had found earlier, but this one pulsed with a different kind of energy—one that was deeper, more ancient, more powerful. The orb glowed with an inner light, shifting from brilliant white to deep, calming blue. It seemed to beckon them, calling them to approach.

Dea felt a surge of hesitation. She wanted to reach out, to take the orb and uncover its secrets, but there was a gnawing fear in the pit of her stomach. *What if this orb took something from them? What if it drained them as the first one had? What if the cost was too great?*

Prex, sensing her hesitation, stepped closer, his presence a steadying force beside her. He reached out, placing a hand over hers in a silent promise of support. *"We've already given so much. Whatever this is, whatever price it demands, we'll face it together."*

Dea looked into his eyes, her gaze filled with trust and determination. She nodded, her fear dissipating, replaced by a renewed sense of resolve. Together, they had faced the unknown before. Together, they would face it again.

With a deep breath, Dea reached out and placed her hand on the orb. Prex followed suit, his fingers brushing against hers as they both connected with the pulsing energy. The moment their hands made contact, a surge of raw, indescribable energy coursed through their bodies. It was as if the very fabric of the universe had jolted, and everything around them coalesced into a single, vivid vision.

The chamber around them disappeared, replaced by a swirling sea of constellations, galaxies, and shimmering lights. The images shifted and reformed, merging into a single, clear image—a map, etched in glowing symbols, with one particular symbol standing out. It was the same symbol they had seen before, the one that had appeared on the key, the box, and now, here, on the map. It was the final piece, the missing link they had been searching for.

Prex's heart raced as he recognized the symbol.

"That's the final piece,"

He whispered, his voice thick with emotion. *"We're close. So close."*

Dea, her eyes shining with a mixture of triumph and exhaustion, smiled. Her hand tightened around his, a silent declaration of her unbreakable resolve. *"Then let's finish this. Together."*

The orb's light began to fade, its pulsing energy dimming as the images in the chamber slowly returned to their calm, serene stillness. The overwhelming surge of power slowly ebbed away, leaving them standing together in the center of the vast chamber, their hearts still racing but their minds clear.

They stepped back from the pedestal, their bond stronger than ever. The city of light and crystal, the guardians, the orb—all of it had led them here, to this moment. And whatever challenges lay ahead, they knew that they would face them together, unyielding in their determination, their trust in each other unshakable. The path ahead might be uncertain, but as long as they stood side by side, they could conquer anything.

The Final Threshold

The air in the city of light seemed to hum with an unspoken promise, as though the very atmosphere was charged with energy, waiting for something to unfold. Prex and Dea, with determination etched on their faces, made their way through the silent streets, each step resonating with the weight of their mission. The cobblestone roads stretched out before them like veins of ancient stone, guiding them toward their destination. Shadows of towering structures loomed on either side, their jagged silhouettes barely visible in the dim glow of the fading twilight.

There was something otherworldly about the city, an ethereal quality that hung in the air like a heavy mist. The beings that inhabited this place—beings of light, of shadow, of something in between—watched their every movement. Yet, they made no sound, spoke no words, and offered no guidance. Their eyes, glowing faintly with an inner fire, followed Prex and Dea from every direction, but there was no malice in their gaze—only an intense, unwavering scrutiny. It was as if the city itself was observing them, measuring their every action, their every breath.

"This is it," Prex murmured, his voice low, barely more than a whisper that seemed to blend with the soft hum of the air around them. His hand gripped the key with a sense of finality, his fin-

gers wrapped tightly around the smooth metal, as though its very presence could anchor him in the midst of the overwhelming uncertainty. The key felt heavy in his palm, but its weight was nothing compared to the burden of what lay ahead. His heart raced, but he pushed the fear aside. The map, etched deep into his memory, had led them here, to this very spot. There was no turning back now.

Dea stood beside him, her figure a silhouette against the strange, glowing landscape. Her eyes, usually so full of fire, were now clouded with a mixture of awe and apprehension. She gazed up at the towering gate before them, its presence imposing, almost regal. The structure was massive, made of an obsidian-like material that seemed to absorb the surrounding light. The gate was adorned with intricate, shifting runes—symbols that pulsed and flickered like the heartbeat of the very world they stood in. Each rune seemed to be alive, a constant dance of light and shadow, as if the gate itself was a living, breathing entity.

The gate stood before them like an ancient sentinel, its surface alive with movement, the symbols rearranging themselves in a fluid, seamless flow. Dea hesitated for a moment, her breath catching in her throat as she reached out, her fingers trembling slightly as they made contact with the cold, smooth surface of the gate. The instant her skin brushed against it, the runes flared to life. A brilliant flash of light erupted from the symbols, flooding the air around them with an otherworldly glow. It was as though the gate recognized her touch, responding with a power that sent a shiver down her spine.

For a brief moment, the light intensified, blinding in its brilliance, and then, just as quickly, it dimmed, the runes returning to their faint, steady glow. The pulse of energy that had surged through the air ebbed away, leaving only the eerie stillness that had surrounded them since their arrival. Dea stood frozen, her hand still resting lightly on the surface of the gate, the faint hum of energy vibrating beneath her fingertips. She looked at Prex, her expression unreadable.

"This is it," she whispered, her voice barely audible over the

silence. The words held a weight, a finality that hung between them like an unspoken agreement. They had come so far, endured so much to reach this moment, but the true test was just beginning.

"It's reacting to us," she murmured, her eyes shifting to Prex, who stood a few paces away, his focus entirely on the enigmatic gate before them.

"But it needs something more."

Her voice was tinged with uncertainty, as if she could feel the very air around them thickening with anticipation. The gate had been silent for so long, its ancient mechanisms dormant, as though it had waited for this precise moment. The runes etched along its surface shimmered faintly, as if alive, pulsing rhythmically in response to the energy they had unwittingly summoned. But despite its subtle movements, something was amiss—something that prevented it from fully unlocking.

Prex didn't speak right away. Instead, he reached into the folds of his cloak, his hand emerging with the key. It was an ornate object, unlike anything either of them had ever seen. The handle was made of smooth, dark metal, twisted into shapes that seemed to dance with arcane symbols, while the head of the key was adorned with intricate runes that seemed to shift and change as he held it. The very air around the key seemed to hum, a low vibration that resonated through the stones beneath their feet.

Holding it aloft, Prex inspected the runes, his brow furrowed in concentration. The symbols shimmered and shifted as his fingers brushed them, almost as if they were testing his touch, feeling the depths of his intentions. When he nodded, satisfied with his findings, he stepped forward, his boots silent on the ancient stone floor.

He moved with careful deliberation, as though the slightest misstep might unravel the fragile thread of connection they had begun to weave with the gate. With a swift, practiced motion, he slid the key into a small, unassuming slot that had previously been hidden in plain sight. The slot materialized as if it had been conjured by the very presence of the key, the surrounding stone

shifting and groaning as it revealed its secret.
The key fit perfectly, the intricate design aligning with the symbols etched around the gate.
The moment the key made contact, the atmosphere around them seemed to change. The gate groaned, a low, resonant sound that seemed to vibrate through the bones of the earth itself. The runes along the edges of the gate flared to life, casting ripples of light across the darkness that surrounded them. The once-muted symbols burned bright in a cascade of blinding light, each rune flickering as if it were being awakened from a long slumber. The vibrations intensified, humming in their chests as the air thickened, charged with the raw power of something ancient and forgotten.
And then, with a final, earth-shaking creak, the gate slowly began to open.
Beyond the threshold lay an immense, inky void, an infinite expanse that seemed to stretch into eternity. The darkness was absolute, swallowing everything in its path, yet scattered throughout the void were faint, distant glimmers of light. These lights flickered like the stars in a faraway sky, suspended in the blackness, their origins impossible to determine. They seemed alive, pulsing softly with an ethereal glow, as though they were watching, waiting for something—perhaps for them.
A narrow path emerged, cutting through the void like a fragile ribbon of light. It was suspended in mid-air, floating as if held by some invisible force, and stretched forward into the nothingness. The stones that formed the path were faintly illuminated, glowing with a soft, gentle radiance that seemed to beckon them forward. It was as if the path had been waiting for them, for this precise moment, offering no resistance as they moved toward the distant platform that shimmered faintly ahead.
The platform itself hovered, distant yet tangible, its edges blurred by the haze of darkness surrounding it. It pulsed with a faint light, like a heartbeat, rhythmic and steady, as though it were a lifeline in a vast sea of shadow.
Prex's grip on the key tightened, and he turned toward his com-

panion, his voice low but filled with a sense of awe. *"This is it,"* he said. *"The path to what we've been searching for."*

Dea hesitated, her gaze lingering on the endless expanse ahead. Her voice trembled as she broke the silence.

"Do you think this is the end?"

Prex, standing beside her, let out a slow, deliberate breath. His hand tightened around the hilt of his sword, an unconscious action borne from the tension coiling within him. He shook his head, his features grim yet reflective.

"It's the beginning of something," he said quietly, his words laden with uncertainty. *"I just don't know what."*

They stepped forward, their feet sinking slightly into the soft, ethereal mist that rose around them. Each movement felt slow, deliberate, as though the very ground they walked upon was unwilling to let them go. The air around them shimmered, the void stretching infinitely in every direction. There was no up, no down—just an endless sea of darkness that seemed to pulse with a life of its own.

With every step, the weight of their journey seemed to press down on them more heavily. The burden of all they had endured, the countless sacrifices they had made, and the love they had shared, swirled in their minds like a whirlwind. Memories, sharp and vivid, collided with one another, each one a jagged piece of their past, threatening to overwhelm them. Dea's heart clenched as she recalled their losses—the faces of those they had left behind, the paths they had crossed and lost, the unspoken promises now faded into the void.

Halfway across the path, the air thickened, the darkness began to shift unnaturally. The once still void began to ripple, as though it were a living, breathing thing. Faint whispers echoed from the depths, too soft to make out, but laden with a malevolent presence. Shapes began to take form, coalescing from the blackness like smoke curling in the wind. At first, they were faint, fleeting, like mere shadows of something larger. But then, they solidified—clearer, sharper, and unmistakable.

Dea's breath caught in her throat as her eyes widened, the realization crashing over her like a wave.

"Prex... do you see them?" she whispered, her voice barely audible, as though speaking any louder might shatter the fragile moment.

Prex froze mid-step, his eyes narrowing in disbelief. His fingers twitched involuntarily, a sense of danger prickling at the back of his mind. He stared at the figures, his pulse quickening as the shapes in the void morphed into something far more familiar. They were... him. And they were her. But not quite. The doppelgängers that had emerged from the darkness were twisted, distorted versions of themselves—familiar, yet unrecognizable. Their faces were hardened, twisted into expressions of anger and despair, eyes black with bitterness.

The figures moved, stepping onto the path, blocking their way. They were not content with merely existing as mere reflections; they were now tangible, solid beings, and they exuded a palpable malice. Their every movement was a cruel mockery of the real Prex and Dea, their faces twisted in cruel imitations of what should have been a reflection of love and understanding.

Dea's heart skipped a beat as she took a step back. The figures before them mirrored their every action, their every breath, their every hesitation. But in their eyes, there was no recognition—only hostility, the purest form of hate. She felt a coldness seep into her bones as the twisted mirror image of herself took a step forward, a cruel smile curving its lips.

"This is not just a reflection," Dea whispered, her voice trembling. *"They're us, but... they're not."*

Prex clenched his jaw, his hand tightening around his weapon. The sight of their doppelgängers was not just unsettling—it was an assault on everything they had fought for.

"No," he muttered under his breath. *"They're the things we fear to become. The parts of ourselves we've hidden away... and the things we couldn't protect."*

The doppelgängers advanced, their footsteps heavy and resolute. Every move they made seemed to bring with it a surge of dark energy, as though the very void itself was feeding them. The path ahead, once seemingly endless, now felt like a dead end. The air grew colder, and the oppressive weight of the darkness pressed down even harder.

Dea's heart pounded in her chest, and she could feel the bitterness rising in her throat. She glanced at Prex, their eyes meeting for just a moment, before she took a deep, steadying breath.

"We have to face them," she said, her voice a mixture of fear and determination.

Prex nodded, his features hardening. *"We don't have a choice."*

They took a step forward together, their resolve hardening with every breath. The path ahead was no longer just a journey; *it had become a trial. And they would face it together.*

"You think you can escape your past?" The voice of the mirror Prex hissed through the darkness, venom dripping from every syllable. The words reverberated through the air like the harsh crackle of lightning in a storm. His eyes, hollow and filled with contempt, locked onto Prex, who stood trembling, yet unwavering. *"You think you deserve a future? You believe you're worthy of something beyond this endless cycle of failure?"*

The mirror Dea stood nearby, her form twisted in mocking symmetry to the woman she once was. Her laughter, cold and bitter, echoed in the empty expanse of the room.

"You've sacrificed everything, but it's never enough. You've fought and bled, only to fall time and again. Do you really think that this time will be different? You will fail, just like before, just like you always do."

Prex felt the weight of the words crushing down on him. The haunting taunts of his reflection resonated deep within his core. No, he thought fiercely. Not this time. He refused to succumb to the dark tide of despair that had threatened to drown him for so long.

With renewed resolve, he reached out, grasping Dea's hand in his. His fingers trembled, not with fear, but with the fire of a determined spirit. *"We've come too far, Dea. Too far to let these twisted reflections drag us back into the shadows. We're not the same people we were before. We won't let them win."*

Dea's gaze flickered to him, and for a brief, fleeting moment, she saw the same flicker of defiance in his eyes. She tightened her grip on his hand, the unspoken bond between them strengthening, becoming a tether to the light that seemed so far away.

"No," she whispered, her voice full of quiet fury. *"We're not. And we'll show them that we're not going to break."*

The mirror Prex and Dea were no longer just reflections—they were grotesque, shadowed versions of their former selves, stepping forward with unnatural grace. Their movements were swift and fluid, almost too perfect, as if they were not bound by the same limitations as their counterparts. With an eerie synchronization, they lunged at Prex and Dea, their forms gliding through the air like specters, their strikes precise and cruel.

Prex blocked one of the mirror Prex's attacks, his muscles straining against the power of the blow. He could feel the sharp sting of doubt gnawing at the edges of his resolve, threatening to unravel everything he had fought for. The venomous reflection sneered, its eyes gleaming with an almost predatory satisfaction.

"You're weak, Prex. You always have been."

Dea was locked in a brutal clash with the mirror Dea, her own strength tested to its limits. Each strike felt like an echo of the past, the weight of her own guilt and regrets manifesting in every blow. Her reflection smirked, her laughter like shards of glass cutting through the silence.

"You'll never escape the things you've done. You'll always be haunted by them."

But Dea refused to falter. Her mind, once clouded with the suffocating fog of her own insecurities, had cleared. She knew what she had to do. She knew that she had already paid the price for her mistakes, and it was time to stop running from them. With a roar, she pushed her mirror image back, her heart pounding with a raw, primal strength.

The fight raged on, each movement now a clash of willpower and spirit, more than physical strength. Every blow felt like a confrontation with their deepest fears and insecurities. They fought not just to survive but to prove to themselves that they were more than the sum of their past failures. The mirrors seemed to flicker with each strike, their forms growing more unstable with every ounce of energy Prex and Dea poured into the battle.

Ahead of them, the platform they had been aiming for began to pulse with an intense, radiant glow. The light was blinding, cutting through the thick veil of darkness that had surrounded them, filling the space with a warmth that was both foreign and familiar. It was a beacon of hope—one they had almost forgotten existed. Prex and Dea, though exhausted and battered, could feel the pull of the light drawing them forward, their spirits renewed with the promise of something greater, something beyond the endless shadows.

The mirror doppelgängers, once so sure of their dominance, faltered. Their forms flickered like dying embers, their solid shapes dissolving into the air like smoke in the wind. Desperation crept into their movements, their once-unbreakable resolve cracking beneath the weight of the light. They stumbled, their unnatural grace faltering as they attempted to maintain their hold over their counterparts.

But it was too late.

With one final, unified effort, Prex and Dea surged forward, their combined strength a beacon of defiance against the dark. The light from the platform flared, enveloping the room in a brilliance so pure, so intense, that it seemed to erase the very essence of the shadows. The mirror doppelgängers screamed, their voices distorted by the power of the light, as they disintegrated into nothingness, leaving only the echo of their existence.

Breathing heavily, Prex and Dea stood together, their hands still clasped tightly. The darkness had been pushed back, but not vanquished entirely. It lingered, waiting for another chance to strike. But for now, they had won. For now, the future was theirs to claim.

Dea seized the moment, her hand trembling slightly as she reached for the pendant that hung from her neck, its delicate chain glistening faintly in the dim light. The pendant, a gift from a long-forgotten time, held the power of her past, and as her fingers closed around it, a surge of energy pulsed through her. She pressed it firmly against the mirror image of herself, the light from the pendant emanating in soft, rippling waves that spread across the mirrored doppelgänger's form. The reflection wavered, flickering like a candle in a gust of wind, before dissolving completely. The haunting expression of the figure, once twisted in torment, softened as if finally finding peace. It was as though the burden of its existence had been lifted, and for the first time, it seemed at rest.

Prex, still standing beside her, took a breath and shifted his gaze to his own mirrored counterpart. He drew his revolver, his fingers steady despite the weight of what was at stake. The revolver glowed with an eerie, ethereal light, a manifestation of the forces they had unleashed throughout their journey. With one swift motion, he aimed it at the mirror Prex, the cold, calculating doppelgänger staring back at him with eyes that held the echoes of regret and rage. He fired.

The shot rang out with a resonating boom that seemed to reverberate through the very fabric of reality. The mirrored figure shattered into a thousand pieces, each fragment glowing with an otherworldly light before it was consumed by the vast void around them. As the last of the doppelgänger's form vanished, the path ahead of them cleared. It was as though the very air had shifted, leaving them with no barriers between them and whatever lay beyond.

Breaths ragged and unsteady, they stumbled forward, each step bringing them closer to their uncertain fate. The platform ahead loomed like a distant star, its glow now so bright that it threatened to blind them. With no more words needed, they stepped onto it. The moment their feet touched the surface, the light enveloped them completely, wrapping around them like the arms of some ancient, unseen force. The world around them melted away in a blur of brightness, leaving only the sensation of weightlessness as they were pulled toward an unknown destination.

When the light finally faded, they found themselves standing in a tranquil garden, a place of surreal beauty that seemed almost too perfect to exist. The air was thick with the scent of blooming flowers, and the soft rustling of leaves created a symphony of sounds that soothed their weary souls. The trees towered above them, their branches heavy with blossoms of every imaginable color, each petal shimmering in the gentle breeze. A crystal-clear stream meandered through the garden, its waters sparkling like liquid starlight, reflecting the vibrant hues of the flora around it. Time seemed to stand still in this place, and for a fleeting moment, it felt as though they had stepped beyond the confines of the world they knew.

At the heart of the garden stood a figure cloaked in golden light. The radiance radiated from them like the sun itself, casting an ethereal glow that made it impossible to discern the figure's features. The light was blinding, yet not harsh; it was warm, welcoming, as though it had been waiting for them all along. The figure stood tall and regal, their presence commanding and serene, their face obscured by the brilliance surrounding them.

"You have proven yourselves," the figure spoke, its voice not just heard, but felt—an echo that resonated deep within their hearts. The tone was melodic, rich with a power that was both ancient and timeless. *"You have faced your fears, your past, and your sacrifices. The trials you endured were not mere tests; they were the forging of your souls. The choice is now yours."*

Prex's voice was hoarse, thick with the weight of his journey. *"Choice?"* he rasped, his words barely escaping his lips. *"What choice?"*

The figure extended its hand slowly, and in its palm, two orbs of radiant light appeared. The orbs hovered just above the figure's outstretched fingers, each pulsing with an intensity that spoke of infinite possibilities. One orb was a soft, soothing blue, its light calm and serene, while the other was a vibrant, fiery red, crackling with energy and an undeniable allure.

"One will restore what you have lost," the figure intoned, its voice carrying a profound sense of finality. *"The other will guide you to the ultimate truth. But be warned: each path holds its own burden, and each choice will alter the very course of your exis-*

tence. Choose wisely."

Prex and Dea stood in silence, their gazes meeting. The weight of their journey, the sacrifices they had made, the lives they had touched and lost, all of it pressed down on them like an invisible force. But in that moment, they knew that whatever lay ahead, they would face it together. The bond between them was unbreakable, forged in the crucible of their shared experiences.

Dea stepped forward, her movements deliberate, her voice steady despite the storm raging within her. *"We choose together."*

Prex nodded, his hand finding hers, his grip firm and reassuring. Together, they reached for one of the orbs, the decision made not through words but through the connection they shared. As their fingers brushed the surface of the glowing orb, the garden seemed to shimmer, the light around them intensifying until it was almost unbearable. The energy pulsed, growing brighter and brighter, until the world around them was consumed by it, leaving only an infinite sea of light.

The Light Beyond

When the brilliance that had swallowed them up finally began to recede, Prex and Dea stood in a place that seemed beyond comprehension, a realm where the very laws of nature felt suspended. The sky above them shimmered like a living, breathing entity, a cascade of vibrant colors that swirled and shifted in an endless dance, a celestial tapestry in constant motion.

It was as though the heavens themselves had come to life, each hue more vivid than the last, radiating a strange and palpable energy that seemed to resonate in their very bones. The ground beneath their feet was unlike anything they had encountered before—a smooth, crystalline surface that rippled like liquid glass, reflecting the distorted images of the ever-changing sky above.

The air was thick with a profound, almost sacred stillness, a quiet that hummed with the sound of something far greater than them, as though the entire cosmos were holding its breath. It was a silence that was both oppressive and peaceful, filled with the weight of an ancient presence. There was no wind, no scent, no noise—only an all-encompassing serenity that seemed to hang in the space between each heartbeat.

Dea's grip on Prex's hand tightened involuntarily, as though the reality of this place was too much to fully comprehend. Her voice was barely a whisper, as though speaking too loudly might shatter the delicate balance of this strange world.

"Where are we?" she asked, her gaze searching the ethereal landscape for any sign of familiarity.

Prex's eyes flicked nervously over their surroundings, his heart racing with a mixture of awe and trepidation. Every instinct screamed that they were no longer in the realm they had known, that they had crossed into something both ancient and eternal.

"I don't know," he admitted, his voice strained with the gravity of the moment. "But this... this is it. This is where it all leads."

Before them, from the swirling depths of the kaleidoscopic horizon, a figure began to materialize, its form emerging like a phantom from the very fabric of the world around them. The golden-cloaked being they had encountered in the garden was now fully present, its presence more immense, more overwhelming than ever before. The light emanating from it seemed to stretch and twist, casting long, ethereal shadows that rippled and danced with an almost sentient life of their own. The air hummed with an energy that felt as though it were resonating directly with their souls, stirring something deep within them that neither of them had ever known existed.

"You have chosen," the figure intoned, its voice reverberating with an almost divine clarity that echoed in the very fabric of the air around them. It was not a mere voice—it was a sound that carried with it the weight of the ages, the power of the universe itself. "Now, the truth will be revealed."

The figure's words hung in the air like a promise, an invitation to a journey that neither Dea nor Prex could have anticipated. The weight of their choice, the gravity of the path they had just stepped onto, was suddenly more real than anything they had ever experienced. In the blink of an eye, the golden figure's light intensified, bathing them in a warmth that was both comforting and all-consuming. Yet, it was not a warmth of flesh or blood—it was the warmth of a truth far beyond their understanding, a truth that seemed to transcend time itself.

Dea's heart beat in her throat, her hand trembling in Prex's grasp as she instinctively took a step forward, her eyes locked on the being before them. There was a pull in the very air, a magnetism that drew them to it, urging them to come closer, to learn what was to come. The choice they had made—their decision to face whatever lay ahead together—was no longer just a choice. It was a declaration of their resolve, their trust in each other, and in whatever this place was to reveal.

As the figure extended its glowing hand toward them, the shadows around it deepened, and the light flared brighter, casting strange, elongated reflections on the crystalline ground beneath their feet. The air itself seemed to hum louder, vibrating with an ancient force that they could neither name nor comprehend. The moment was heavy with significance, and yet, for all its weight, it was strangely serene.

Prex's chest tightened, the enormity of the moment crashing down on him. His pulse raced, his every instinct telling him to proceed with caution. And yet, there was no hesitation in his eyes. Not anymore. Whatever the outcome, whatever truth lay beyond this moment, he and Dea would face it together. Always. Dea, her eyes brimming with a mixture of determination and fear, spoke softly but with unwavering clarity.

"We choose together," she said, her voice carrying the strength of everything they had endured, everything they had fought for. Prex nodded silently, his hand closing over hers with a firm, resolute grip. Together, they reached for the orb in the figure's hand, the path to the ultimate truth unfolding before them, their journey now irrevocably tied to the fate that awaited them.

And as their fingers brushed the orb's surface, the world around them seemed to shudder, the light intensifying until it consumed everything in a blinding flash.

The orb they had chosen, now suspended in midair, began to glow with an almost palpable energy. Its radiant light grew brighter with each passing second, enveloping them in a soft, ethereal warmth that seemed to hum with the very rhythm of the universe. Within its translucent core, images began to emerge—flickering like fleeting memories, each one vivid yet fleeting.

Scenes from their journey played out before them: the faces of enemies vanquished, the quiet moments of reflection, the struggles and triumphs that had shaped them. But it was not just their present that filled the orb.

Fragments of their past, long-buried and forgotten, flickered and intertwined with those of their future, casting shadows of possibilities both bright and terrifying.

As the visions accelerated, twisting and blending together, the orb's light intensified to a blinding brilliance. For a moment, it felt as though time itself had frozen, the very air thick with anticipation.

Then, in a single, overwhelming flash, the light erupted in a burst so blinding that it seemed to consume everything around them. They were momentarily engulfed in a sea of pure, unrelenting light—heat radiating from its core—until, as quickly as it had appeared, it began to recede.

When their senses returned, the blinding light had dissipated, leaving only a profound silence in its wake. Both Prex and Dea stood motionless, their hearts pounding as they took in their new surroundings. Before them, rising from the earth like a colossal monument, stood a door—towering and imposing.

Its surface was a mosaic of intricate carvings, each line and curve seemingly alive, shifting and pulsing with an energy of its own. The door seemed to breathe, its contours ebbing and flowing as if it were made of liquid light, rippling with an intelligence beyond comprehension. The patterns etched upon it were cryptic, a language they could not decipher, but they instinctively knew that they had seen these designs before—perhaps in the very visions they had just witnessed.

Prex's fingers curled around the familiar object in his hand—the key. It seemed to hum in tune with the door's pulse, its weight anchoring him in the moment. The key was not merely a physical object; it felt like a symbol of everything they had endured, a vessel carrying the culmination of their trials. Its surface was worn and smoothed from the countless times it had been held, but now, in the presence of the door, it felt inexplicably heavy—

laden with the significance of their choices, the sacrifices they had made, and the unknown path that lay ahead.

With a steady hand, Prex approached the door, his heart thrumming in his chest as Dea stood beside him, her presence a silent, unwavering pillar of strength. Together, they gazed at the door, knowing that whatever lay beyond would be the final test of everything they had fought for.

The air was thick with tension as they prepared to face whatever would come next. The garden, once a sanctuary of peace, now felt like an arena where destinies would be forged. The choice they had made, one that transcended time and reason, was no longer just a decision between two paths. It was the key to unlocking the ultimate truth—and to discovering the very nature of their existence, their past, and the future that awaited them.

With a final, unspoken exchange between them, Prex stepped forward. The key, glowing with an inner fire, found its place in the lock, as if waiting for this moment. The door creaked, its massive frame shifting ever so slightly, and for the first time, they felt as though the weight of their journey had brought them to the precipice of a new beginning.

"This is it," Prex whispered, his voice a mixture of awe and dread. *"The end... or the beginning."*

Dea stood beside him, her gaze unwavering as she stared at the ancient door that now lay before them. Its surface was etched with cryptic symbols, worn and weathered by the passage of time. But it wasn't the door itself that demanded their attention. It was the palpable weight of destiny hanging in the air, thick with anticipation. She stepped closer, a soft breath escaping her lips as she placed a hand on the cold metal.

"Whatever it is, Prex," she said, her voice steady yet filled with resolve, *"we face it together. We've come this far. We can't turn back now."*

Her words were like a lifeline to him, pulling him from the overwhelming uncertainty that gnawed at the edges of his thoughts. Prex met her gaze, his eyes hardening with determination. He knew that whatever lay beyond this door was the culmination of everything they had endured—the trials, the dangers, and the choices that had brought them here. He could feel the weight of the key in his hand, heavy with the gravity of their decision. With a silent nod, he inserted the key into the lock, feeling it click into place.

The moment the key turned, the door groaned in protest, its ancient mechanisms protesting the intrusion. A low hum vibrated through the floor, the very air around them thickening with energy. For a moment, they stood there, suspended in time, as if the door itself was holding its breath.

Then, with a deafening creak, the door slowly began to open. The air shimmered, swirling in a tempest of invisible forces, and a powerful surge of energy rippled outward, pulling them into the depths of the chamber beyond.

The world around them twisted, disorienting and surreal, as they were swallowed by the unseen force. When the spinning ceased, they found themselves standing in an enormous chamber that stretched endlessly in every direction. The space was cavernous, its walls lined with mirrors that seemed to breathe with an unnatural life. These weren't just ordinary mirrors, though. As they gazed into them, they saw not just their physical forms reflected, but something deeper—something far more personal. The mirrors, it seemed, were attuned to their very souls.

Prex's breath caught in his throat as he looked into one of the mirrors. It wasn't his face that stared back at him, but his inner self—his determination, his unwavering devotion to Dea, and the battle scars of the countless sacrifices he had made.

His reflection flickered, showing flashes of the pain and the guilt he had carried with him throughout his journey. But amidst the darkness, there was a faint, but undeniable, glimmer of love. His love for Dea, the one constant that had kept him going through every trial, every obstacle. It was a strength that anchored him, giving him purpose even in the face of overwhelming odds.

Beside him, Dea's gaze was fixed on another mirror. As she peered into its surface, the reflection that greeted her was one of quiet resilience. She saw herself not as the world saw her, but as she had truly become—the woman forged by pain, by loss, and by an unyielding hope that had never once faltered. The mirror revealed her inner strength, the fortitude that had pushed her forward, even when everything seemed lost. But it also showed the softer side of her—a side that was vulnerable, that feared losing everything she held dear. And yet, despite it all, there was an unmistakable sense of peace in the reflection. A peace born from the unwavering trust she had in Prex, and in herself.

The mirrors held them captive in their gaze, forcing them to confront the truths they had long hidden, the fears they had buried deep within their hearts. The chamber seemed to pulse with a life of its own, as if the very air was charged with the weight of these revelations. The energy around them hummed, a low, melodic vibration that seemed to resonate with their very souls.

For a long moment, neither of them spoke. They stood in silence, absorbing the full weight of what they were seeing. They had faced countless dangers, fought against impossible odds, and endured the most unimaginable hardships. But now, in this moment of clarity, they were forced to confront not just the world around them, but themselves. The reflection in the mirrors was not just a reminder of their past; it was a testament to who they had become. And more importantly, it was a reflection of the choices they were about to make.

The chamber stretched out before them, vast and silent, its walls adorned with intricate carvings that shimmered faintly in the dim light. At the heart of the room, atop a towering pedestal of stone, rested the crystal sphere. Its surface was smooth and flawless, yet it seemed to pulse with life, a rhythmic thrum that resonated in the very air, as if attuned to the beating of their own hearts. The sphere's glow shifted between shades of violet and gold, casting long, strange shadows across the floor, and in its core, there was a flicker—a faint glow that seemed to beckon them forward.

From the shadows emerged the figure, its form now dimmer, the golden light that had once been blinding reduced to a gentle, radiant glow. Its presence still commanded reverence, as though the very air around it held its breath. The figure raised its hand, the motion slow and deliberate, as it spoke in a voice that resonated deep within them, vibrating through the very bones of their being.

"This," the figure intoned, its voice carrying a weight that seemed to press down on them, "*is the Heart of All Things. It holds within it the power to reshape reality itself, to mend what is broken, or to reveal the ultimate truth. But take heed, for such power is not without its price.*"

Prex and Dea stood motionless, their eyes locked together for a moment, a silent communication passing between them. They had been through so much—trials that had tested their very limits, battles that had left them scarred but unbroken. And now, before them, lay a choice that could alter the course of their lives forever.

"*What cost?*" Prex's voice broke the silence, low and filled with a mixture of curiosity and unease.

The figure's light dimmed even further, casting long shadows over the stone floor as it lowered its hand slightly.

"*To heal is to forget,*" it said softly, the words lingering in the air like a haunting melody.

"*To restore what was lost, you must surrender a part of yourself. To seek the truth is to face it in its entirety, to know it in all its painful, unrelenting clarity. Whatever path you choose, it will change you. The question is—are you prepared for that?*"

The weight of the words hung heavy between them, and Dea felt a shiver run down her spine. She knew the cost of healing all too well—the sacrifices made, the memories erased, and the things left behind. But she had never been one to shy away from the difficult choices. She had faced her fears, her regrets, and her deepest wounds. She had endured, and she would continue to endure.

"*We've come this far,*" Dea said, her voice firm, but tinged with the rawness of their shared journey. "*We've faced everything together. Whatever this choice brings, we will face it together too.*"

Prex stood beside her, his expression resolute, his hand still clasped firmly in hers. The weight of the moment settled in his chest, but the bond they shared, forged through trials and triumphs alike, gave him the strength to face whatever lay ahead. He nodded once, a silent affirmation that they would move forward, side by side.

With a shared breath, they stepped closer to the pedestal, their feet moving almost in unison as they reached for the Heart of All Things. The moment their hands touched the cool surface of the sphere, a surge of energy shot through them. The light within the crystal flared to life, expanding outward in a brilliant explosion of color that engulfed them entirely.

The power of the sphere coursed through their veins, a torrent of energy that filled every corner of their being, igniting their very souls with a warmth that was both exhilarating and terrifying. The light grew brighter, blinding them momentarily, and in the depths of that brightness, memories began to flood their minds—visions of their journey, both the highs and the lows. They saw the faces of friends and enemies, the battles fought and the tears shed. They saw moments of laughter, fleeting joys, and the quiet, intimate moments they had shared. They saw their sacrifices, the things they had lost along the way, the pieces of themselves that they had given up in their pursuit of this moment.

The memories twisted and turned within the light, swirling together, as though they were all part of a greater tapestry—a web of fate that had woven their lives together. And yet, beneath the surface of it all, they could feel the weight of the choices they had made, the cost of their actions, and the knowledge that nothing could ever truly be the same again.

The light intensified, and Dea felt herself being pulled deeper into it, the very essence of her being merging with the brilliance around her. She grasped onto Prex's hand, grounding herself in the only thing that remained constant—him, their shared love and trust. She could feel him beside her, his presence a steady anchor in the maelstrom of emotions and memories swirling around them.

As the light began to fade, they found themselves standing together, still holding the sphere, but now surrounded by an overwhelming sense of stillness. The world around them had transformed. The air was thick with a sense of completion, of something having been irrevocably altered. And yet, they could not yet comprehend the full extent of the change.

Dea's voice broke the silence, soft yet filled with determination. *"We are ready. Whatever the outcome, we will face it. Together."*

Prex's gaze met hers, and in that moment, they both understood. The choice they had made was not just about what they stood to gain or lose—it was about the journey they had shared, the trust they had built, and the love that had carried them through it all. And as the last remnants of light faded into the distance, they knew that whatever came next, they would face it as one.

When the blinding light finally receded, they found themselves standing in a realm that felt like a dream—an ethereal transformation of the world they once knew. The city of light, which had once seemed desolate and cold, now stood bathed in a brilliant warmth, its towering spires gleaming with vitality. The once barren streets were alive with color, adorned with flowers that swayed in the breeze, their petals shimmering with a soft, iridescent glow. Trees of silver and gold stretched their limbs toward the sky, and the air, heavy with the scent of blooming blossoms, seemed to hum with an energy of its own.

The void, that vast and endless chasm they had traversed, was now but a distant memory, replaced by a lush landscape that seemed to stretch into infinity—an expanse of limitless possibilities, an untouched world that awaited the mark of their footsteps. The horizon, once a blur of desolation, now brimmed with a promise of renewal.

Prex, his chest heaving with exhaustion, turned to Dea, his face pale but his eyes glistening with an emotion too vast to be contained. Tears welled up in his eyes, each drop carrying the weight of their journey, the struggles, the sacrifices, and the triumphs they had shared.

"We made it," he whispered, his voice thick with the realization

of their accomplishment, as if he had to say it out loud to make it real.

Dea, her own eyes brimming with unshed tears, reached for him, her fingers trembling as they touched his cheek. The joy that bloomed in her chest was matched only by the sorrow of all they had left behind. She had never known love could be so all-consuming, so fiercely beautiful, and yet so fragile. *"We did,"* she echoed, her voice a soft murmur, like a prayer or a vow.

They embraced, their bodies pressing together in a quiet moment of shared relief. The weight of their journey, the fears and uncertainties that had once threatened to tear them apart, melted away in that simple, sacred union. Here, in this moment, there was no past, no future—only the now, and the undeniable truth that their love had guided them through every trial.

From the shadows of the golden garden, the figure that had been their guide spoke once more, its voice as harmonious as a lullaby. The words seemed to resonate within their very beings, a deep and unspoken understanding threading through them.

"You have chosen wisely," the figure intoned, its voice like a melody that swirled around them.

"The path you have walked was not one of ease, but you have prevailed. May your love guide you in all things."

As the golden figure's form began to dissolve into the light, leaving behind nothing but the faintest trace of its existence, Prex and Dea stood there, hand in hand. The world around them shimmered, the air thick with the promise of new beginnings, of adventures yet to be written. But one thing remained clear: the bond they shared was unshakable. Whatever lay ahead, no matter how difficult, they would face it side by side. They had built this world, not with the power of the void, but with the strength of their hearts, their unity, and their unwavering commitment to each other.

The golden garden, now quiet and serene, stretched out before them, its beauty beyond words. Yet, it was not the garden that captured their hearts, but the knowledge that they had forged their destiny with their own hands. The light that enveloped them was not just a reflection of the world they had helped create—it was a testament to their love, a love that had defied all odds and triumphed over every darkness.

As they gazed into the future, the weight of their decision settled upon them like a cloak of wisdom. They had chosen together, not out of fear or desperation, but because their hearts had known the truth all along. The journey was never about finding the right answer, but about trusting each other, about facing the unknown with courage, and about allowing love to lead the way.

And so, hand in hand, they stepped forward into the next chapter of their lives—a chapter not written by fate, nor by any external force, but by the choices they had made, and by the love that would continue to guide them through whatever trials lay ahead. They were no longer just two souls in a world of uncertainty; they were creators of their own fate, the architects of their own destiny. And with each step they took, they knew that no matter what came next, their hearts would remain unbroken, their bond eternal.

The final echoes of the golden figure's voice faded into the distance, and the garden, now their new home, stretched endlessly before them—a canvas upon which they would write the rest of their story. The story of love, courage, and the undying light that shone from within.

Epilogue

The city was quieter than usual, wrapped in a thick fog that clung to the streets like the last whisper of a dream. The glow of streetlamps barely pierced through the mist, casting only fractured halos of light onto the cobblestone roads. Somewhere in the distance, a saxophone played, its melancholic notes drifting through the air like echoes of something long forgotten.

Prex Donovan stood at the edge of Pier 17, his hands buried deep in the pockets of his coat. The wind tugged at the fabric, but he didn't move. His eyes, sharp as ever, were fixed on the water, watching as the waves swallowed the last remnants of a torn photograph. He had memorized every detail before letting it slip from his fingers—the face that wasn't his, but should have been. A version of himself that had existed in another time, or perhaps another reality.

The case was closed—at least, that was what the papers would say. The painting, The Veil of Elysium, had been lost to fire, or so the museum claimed. The gallery's director had issued a statement condemning the *"tragic accident,"* though Prex knew better. It hadn't been an accident. Some things were never meant to be found, and those who sought them often paid the price.

Beside him, Dea Turner exhaled slowly, her breath visible in the

cold air. She had a thousand questions, but she knew better than to ask them now. Some truths were too heavy to speak aloud. Instead, she settled for the one thing she could say with certainty.
"It's not over, is it?"
Prex smirked, though there was little humor in it. *"It never is."*
She sighed, wrapping her arms around herself as she turned to face him. *"What now?"*
He tilted his head slightly, considering the weight of that question. The answer lay in the letter tucked inside his coat—a cryptic message delivered without a return address, its contents a riddle only someone like him could decipher. Another trail to follow, another set of shadows to chase.
"We keep moving," he said at last. *"There's always another mystery."*
Dea studied him for a moment before nodding. *"And Mercer?"*
Prex's expression darkened. Mercer had disappeared, slipping into the night like a ghost with unfinished business. His warning still echoed in Prex's mind—words laced with something dangerously close to regret.
"You've stumbled onto something far beyond your depth."
"I don't think we've seen the last of him," Prex admitted. *"But when he comes back, we'll be ready."*
A distant foghorn sounded, low and mournful. Dea turned toward the city, her silhouette barely visible against the mist.
"I suppose we should get going," she murmured. *"Before the next ghost finds us first."*
Prex lingered for a moment longer, his gaze returning to the water. Secrets, like the tide, always had a way of returning. It was only a matter of time before the past came calling once more.
With a final glance at the river, he turned and followed Dea into the city, vanishing into the fog like a whisper lost to the wind.

To Maaya, My Muse

Dear Maya,

As I sit here, pen in hand, heart heavier than I'd like to admit, I find myself writing to you—my muse, my ache, my impossible dream. Perhaps this letter will never reach you, or perhaps it will find its way to your hands one day, when time has softened the sharp edges of everything I feel for you. But for now, let these words exist as they are—an unfiltered confession of love, longing, and acceptance.

Loving you has never been a choice; it's been a force, as natural as the air I breathe, as relentless as the tide. From the moment you stepped into my world, something in me knew—knew that you were different, knew that you would matter in ways no one else ever had. And you do. You always will.

I know you cannot love me the way I love you, and I have made peace with that truth, even if it shatters me in quiet moments. Love, after all, is not a contract, not something to be negotiated. It simply is. And mine for you has always been unconditional. I do not love you because I expect something in return. I love you because you are you—because your laughter is the most beautiful sound I have ever heard, because your presence makes the world feel a little less chaotic, because when I look at you, I see poetry, even in silence.

I have often wondered what it would be like if things were different. If the universe had been kinder, if our hearts had been aligned in the same way. But that is not our story, is it? Our *story is one of stolen moments, of words unspoken, of a love that exists in the spaces between what could have been and what is. And that's okay. Because even in this unrequited form, my love for you has been the most real, the most profound thing I have ever known.*

So, I will carry this love, not as a burden, but as a gift. A reminder that my heart is capable of feeling something so vast, so pure. And though I will never be the one you look at with the same longing that fills my eyes when I look at you, I am grateful—grateful to have known you, to have loved you, to have been touched, however briefly, by the magic of your existence.

With all the love my heart holds,
Yours, always.
Stephen Shubrai

About the Author

Stephen Shubrai is a writer deeply fascinated by the intersection of mysticism, ancient knowledge, and the unknown. Drawing inspiration from lost civilizations, esoteric manuscripts, and the enigmatic nature of reality, their works weave intricate narratives that blur the line between history, myth, and dark fantasy.

With a passion for occult symbolism, alchemical traditions, and forgotten lore, the author crafts stories that immerse readers in shadowy realms where secrets whisper from the past, and knowledge comes at a cost. The Hermetic Inscription is a testament to this vision—a novel rich in hidden meanings, celestial mysteries, and haunting beauty.

When not writing, Stephen Shubrai can be found deciphering obscure texts, exploring arcane philosophies, or losing themselves in the aesthetics of Art Nouveau and cosmic horror. Their work is for those who seek stories that don't just entertain, but invite readers to uncover something deeper—something that lingers long after the final page is turned.

Follow Stephen Shubrai on:

*Instagram:Stxphxn_0901_*

www.ingramcontent.com/pod-product-compliance
Lightning Source LLC
LaVergne TN
LVHW041917070526
838199LV00051BA/2641